Mandy's Story: Courage

Finding Herself Series
Book 1

Erica J Whelton

Publisher: Sunseri Design Publishing
ISBN: 978-1-956069-07-5

Printed in the United States of America

To my parents. Thanks for the support on
this journey to fulfill my dream.

Table of Contents

Inside every strong woman is
a broken little girl
who had to learn
how to get back up and
not to depend on anyone
Unknown

Chapter One

It had been a long workday, and I was dragging my feet heading home. Mama was probably going to be in her usual rotten mood and would have done nothing all day except drink herself into a stupor. What a welcome home.

This week, I'd been working extra hours to help my neighbor, Ms. Graham. She'd twisted her ankle, so in addition to the other clients I cleaned for, I was helping around her house more than usual. It was the reason I was running late tonight.

Reaching the door, I took a deep breath, mentally preparing to face whatever hell was waiting beyond it. Don't get me wrong, I loved my little brother and sister; they were the best thing in my life, but Mama was too much. Abusive one moment, neglectful the next.

"Hello. I'm home," I called out.

"Mandy! Mandy! I'm so happy you're home." Missy came running to me, giving me a huge hug. Then she lowered her voice. "She's been so mean today."

"Well, I'm here now." I kissed her head, then scanned the messy living room. It would be a long night of cleaning for me. Between home and work, I was constantly cleaning. "Go play, and I'll start dinner."

She smiled as she skipped off to her room. She and our baby brother, Davy, mostly stayed in there away from Mama, only coming out when I was home.

No sign of Mama; she must be in her room. Hurrying to the kitchen to start dinner, I wasn't at all surprised by the mess that awaited me there as well.

The trash can overflowed onto the floor. A sticky substance had originated on the counter and dripped down the front of the cabinets. And then the dishes, piles of them. But I bet she hadn't even fed the kids.

Missy had probably fed them both. She didn't know yet how to clean up after herself, and who could blame her? She was only four. That's what a mother is supposed to be for: to teach and guide, nurture and love. Not our mother, but other mothers.

I muttered under my breath as I got to work.

Finally, with the kitchen cleaned, I could start cooking. That's when I heard the telltale sound of glass breaking from the living room, immediately followed by Mama cursing and Little Davy crying.

"Now what?" I whispered to myself as I rushed out of the kitchen. I rounded the corner to see that Davy had knocked over Mama's glass.

Her drink of choice was the indicator of her mood. Beer was the safest; anything else was bad, oh so unbelievably bad. A glass meant it wasn't beer because, for her, beer came in a can.

The sight that met me as I came around the corner caused something in me to snap like raw animal instinct. Mama was holding Davy up to her face and screaming at him. My tiny, two year old baby brother looked like a rag doll in her hands.

Pure rage boiled from my soul. I charged at her as a growl escaped my throat. I grabbed Davy and handed him to Missy, who was peeking from the safety of the hallway, and in the same motion pushed Mama back. She fell in a lump to the floor.

"Missy, you and Davy go back to your room and lock the door! Do not open it until I come to get you!"

Missy nodded and led a crying Davy down the hallway.

Mama tried getting up, but I pushed her back down. I didn't know and didn't care what her intentions were right now, but I had a few things to say to her first.

I crouched down so I was eye to eye with her, my body shaking with adrenaline.

"Don't you EVER touch him again! Either of them! Do you hear me? He didn't ask to be born." My voice trembled as I barked out the words. "You did that! You brought us all here. Don't you touch him or her or me ever again!"

She spat in my face and slurred out, "You little bitch!"

I straightened, standing above her with arms crossed to deter her from going after the kids. I'd stand here as long as it took to protect my brother and sister.

But after only a few minutes, she crawled down the hall to her room, I assumed to sleep it off. I stepped into the hallway to watch her, ensuring she made it into her room without further incident. When I was confident she wouldn't pursue them, I started cleaning up the broken glass and liquor, silently cursing her as I did.

While cleaning up yet another of her messes, I marveled at myself for standing up to my mom. She'd been my abuser and torturer, and I'd brazenly confronted her, defending my sweet brother.

"I'm a badass." I grinned.

I'd never defended myself against her, just always taking it, thinking I'd deserved it for some odd reason. Of course, it didn't make logical sense to feel that way, but perhaps it was all the belittlement I had received my entire life.

However, when it came to my siblings, I would not let anyone hurt them. To date, I'd kept them out of her way or put myself in the path when I couldn't. Today had been a bad day. The first we'd had in a long time. Months.

Heading down the hall with the skeleton key, I unlocked the door to their room to find Missy with a crying Davy on her lap, murmuring to him. She was trying to comfort him through her own tears.

"It's okay, Little Davy, it's okay. Mandy will take care of us," she said through her own sobs.

That's when she saw me. Her face was red, streaked with tears, and I could see fear and sadness in her eyes. At four years old, she was so mature, too mature for her age. I sometimes forgot how young she was by the way she acted. It broke my heart. She deserved to enjoy her childhood. Moments like this weren't helping.

I sat on the floor, gathering them into my lap.

"Yeah, it's okay now. Mama went to bed and should sleep until tomorrow." I hugged them a little closer, kissing their heads. "I love you both and will keep you safe."

After a few minutes of cuddles, I said, "I'm going to finish getting dinner ready. You both stay here and play quietly. Everything will be okay."

Honestly, I wasn't sure if it would be, but I had to believe I could keep them safe, or at least try. I wanted something different for their lives. Unlike my own childhood, which had mostly been about survival and hiding from Mama and her friends, I wanted them to laugh and play, be carefree. They didn't need to know about what I'd been through. No, I wanted them to be little kids, to the best of my ability, despite Mama still living in the house with us.

My siblings' father, Jimmy, hadn't been around in over a year. He and Mama had broken up before Davy was born, and while he used to visit the kids, those visits had become few and far between. I didn't entirely blame him for staying away. Whenever he came over, Mama would yell at him, then beg him for another chance, then curse at him when he refused. It was exhausting to witness, so I could only imagine how exhausting it was to experience.

Still, I couldn't help feeling a little resentful. He had somewhere else to go. I didn't. These kids were innocent in all of this, and someone had to look out for them. Since their birth, that someone had been me.

I sighed. I couldn't dwell on all of this now. First, I had to feed Missy and Davy, then follow our nightly routine and just try to keep things as normal as possible.

Dinner was ready, so I walked back down the hall to the kids' room to find them absently playing with their toys. Mostly just pushing them around but not making sounds. It was heartbreaking to see. I wanted to pack them both up right now and run away from here and her and this sad, angry life.

Instead, I put on a brave face and got them both seated at the table. They kept looking toward the hallway, listening for Mama. I tried to keep the dinner conversation light.

"How was fishing with Grandpa Dixon?"

He wasn't our grandpa, simply a friendly neighbor. His wife had passed a few years ago, which gave him extra time in his day to help us.

"It was good," Missy whispered and looked toward the doorway.

"Did you catch anything?"

"Grandpa Dixon did, but we didn't," she added.

Davy nodded his agreement. He often let Missy speak for him.

"It was nice of him to take you both fishing. We'll have to bake him some cookies or something as a thank you."

They looked at me but didn't reply. My distraction attempts weren't working, so next I tried asking about their favorite cartoons, which they usually talked about all the time. Nothing. Missy had always been my little chatterbox, but not tonight.

At least they still ate all their dinner. If I had to choose one over the other, eating was more important.

That night, I slept in their room to ensure Mama didn't try anything.

"Won't it be fun? It's like we're having a sleepover party," I said, as upbeat as possible.

I had hoped they would feel safer with me in there, but Missy kept eyeing the door. We hadn't had a rough night like this with Mama in months. It always set the little kids on edge.

Mama was always grumpy with us. Snapping when she was hungover, or verbally lashing out when she was drunk. But it was rare now that she hit us, and the times it came to that, I always put myself in the way so it wasn't directed at my siblings. Most of the time, we all just stayed out of her way. We had learned her cues. Unfortunately, today had just been a bad day.

"It's okay, Missy girl. I'm here."

She nodded in reply, giving one last look at the door, but finally settled enough to sleep. I listened to their breathing as they drifted off.

Sadly, for me, sleep didn't come as easily. Instead, I lay awake thinking about Mama and all she had put us through.

It would be my eighteenth birthday soon. My plan had always been to leave when I turned eighteen, though I'm sure I could have left sooner without Mama trying to find me. However, things changed once the kids were born. I had to think about them now, not just myself.

How would I be able to look myself in the face knowing I'd left them to be abused by the one person who was supposed to love them the most?

I stared at the ceiling in the darkness, listening to their soft breathing beside me. I didn't know what the future held, but I knew one thing for certain: I was going to do everything in my power to give them what I didn't have, just as I'd done since their birth.

Chapter Two

The next day, Mama was quiet. Too quiet. She didn't drink or have her friends over, as she usually did. For most of my life, she'd been predictable: drinking too much, partying too hard, taking out her life's problems on me. The silence scared me more than her wrath.

Each day I was nervous about leaving the kids, but I had to work so we could eat. None of my neighbors were available to babysit, not even Ms. Graham, who was always willing to help. She was still nursing that bad ankle, which made it near impossible for her to run after two young children, even ones as well behaved as Missy and Little Davy.

I tried to finish all my houses quickly, and since most of the homes were within walking distance, I could easily stop by between clients to check on things.

After a week of paranoia, I let my guard down a bit and stopped checking on them as often as I should have. Mama hadn't done anything in a week, and things had started to feel more normal. I was beginning to think things were going to be okay.

I should have known better. That's how life worked. When you let your guard down, or when too much good was happening, something awful followed. Or maybe that was just my life.

One afternoon, I arrived home to find the little kids on the living room floor, crying hysterically. Missy was trying to comfort Little Davy but not doing a good job, as she was crying herself. When I walked into the house, they both ran to me, throwing themselves into my arms.

"Mama's gone, Mandy. Mama's gone," Missy sniffed.

"What?" I asked, thinking I hadn't heard her correctly.

I wouldn't have expected them to be upset about her being gone. Maybe they were simply scared of the unknown, like I suddenly was. This was both frightening and a dream come true.

"Mama's gone. She packed some things and left." Missy choked out the words between sobs.

"Gone? Did she say where she was going? Did she say anything?" I tried to keep my voice calm, but in my shocked state, I don't think I pulled it off.

"She said... she said she was going away and never comin' back. She left this." Missy handed me a crumpled, soggy piece of paper.

I read it, then reread it to make sure I understood it correctly.

Mandy,

I'm done. I can't do this anymore. Since you think you know so much, you can have the kids. Here's your chance to prove that you're better than me. Don't fuck it up as I did!

Love,

Mama

She was really gone. My wish had come true, but the timing was awful. I wasn't prepared, and I wanted this on my terms, not hers.

I felt the room spin, so I sat down without saying a word. I didn't know what to say or what to think. The note crumpled further in my fist as I tried to process what was happening.

Part of me wanted to laugh. Part of me wanted to scream. And some small, traitorous part of me felt the sting of abandonment, even though I knew better than to want her here.

Immediately my brain started hopping from thought to thought. What was I going to do? I had almost raised myself to this point and was already raising two children, but this was different. There was no adult over the age of eighteen in the house. Not yet. Soon I would be, but soon wasn't now.

How was I going to pay the bills? I had money from working, sure, but was it enough to cover the electric bill, water bill, cable, and phone bills each and every month? Maybe for a few months, but then what? And when were they due? Had Mama paid them for this month?

I made enough to easily handle our food and clothes, plus I saved as much as possible. I shopped with coupons, planned meals carefully, and watched every penny. Without Mama around, and more specifically her partying friends, the food should last us longer. That part should be doable.

Then there was the house. I knew there wasn't a mortgage on it, but I thought I'd heard about property taxes and insurance. I might be able to handle the monthly bills with what I had saved, at least for a little while, but I had no idea about the bigger expenses. I would have to research those.

When my grandmother died, she'd left Mama the house, her car, and a large cash inheritance. I didn't know if any of it remained or if I had any right to access it. I doubted it. Mama's drinking and partying had started after grandmother passed, and she'd probably drunk it all away. I would have to investigate that later, too.

Too many questions and not enough answers. I realized the little kids were watching me, waiting for my reaction. Looking down at their red, tear-streaked faces, I shook myself out of my own shock and panic, putting on a happy facade for their benefit.

"Do y'all want a snack? How about some TV?"

"Yay, yeah." They cheered, but the joy was muted.

I sliced up an apple and an orange, then got them settled in front of the TV. One of their favorite Disney movies was on. It would be a good distraction while I tried to figure out what to do.

While they were busy with the movie, I took the opportunity to sift through the piles of bills on Mama's desk. I found all the ones I knew of: electric, gas, water, and cable combined with our home phone line. We were probably one of the few households left with a landline.

"Good. One less bill," I muttered to myself.

Nothing about the inheritance from grandmother. I found a few of Mama's bank statements, but my name wasn't on the account, so I had no right to any of that money.

As I skimmed the statement, I saw she had quite a bit in her account.

"Wow. No wonder she doesn't work." I rolled my eyes.

She hadn't spent any of this on us. The household bills, I supposed, but nothing beyond the bare minimum. All those years I'd worked and scraped and saved, and she'd been sitting on money the whole time.

It looked like all the bills had recently been paid, so that was at least one positive. It meant I had some time to figure out how much I had stashed away in all the jars and cans I'd hidden in the yard over the years.

For now, my priority was to feed the kids and act like everything was normal. I had been faking it for most of their lives. What was one more day or two until I had a solid plan?

I organized and stacked the bills to go through in more detail later, thankful that Mama hadn't switched to paperless billing and that she'd at least kept up with paying what was due.

For all her flaws, we'd always had a roof over our heads, power, and running water. We'd never slept on the street. Some people couldn't say that. I'd learned not to take those things for granted, even if I resented everything else.

I pushed away from the desk and headed to the living room to check on the kids. They were happily munching their fruit and watching the movie. Missy caught me looking and smiled brightly before turning her attention back to the screen.

Their eyes were still red and puffy from crying, but they looked calmer. The hiccupping sobs had stopped.

I sat down with them to watch the end of the movie. Little Davy climbed into my lap, and I wrapped my arms around him. It was the little things like this that I treasured.

When the movie ended, I took them outside to play. Anything to keep their minds and bodies busy so they wouldn't dwell on the change. Plus, I often took them out after work. I liked to keep us as close to a routine as possible.

After a few games of tag, I went inside to start dinner and let them continue playing. I would make their favorite: spaghetti with meatballs. Funny how I'd already planned to make it today, before any of this happened.

As I cooked, I watched them from the window. They ran, laughed, and played without a care in the world. I was glad to see them acting like regular little kids, that the drama of Mama leaving hadn't affected them too deeply. Time would tell if there would be any lasting effects.

I had worked hard to shield them from her so they could grow and develop as children should. Compared to some others their age, they seemed a bit more reserved, a bit more watchful. But they still knew how to play. They still knew how to laugh. That had to count for something.

Once dinner was ready, I got them inside and washed up. They were good eaters, which made my job easier. I remembered all too well what it was like to go hungry. I was thankful for all those who had helped me along the way, especially in those early years.

Missy was back to her old self at dinner, chatting away about their games.

"... and then Davy jumped over the bucket, and I missed him. I almost tripped, but I didn't. I'm too quick to fall." I stifled a laugh because I knew she believed that with her whole heart. "I finally caught him when he went around the tree, but I went around the other way."

Davy giggled and nodded along with her story.

"Wow. That sounds like fun."

"It was." She giggled.

After dinner, I cleaned up while the kids played in the backyard some more. Missy would invent various games and adventures, then direct Davy in his role. I'd overheard them go on an African safari once. Another time, they were fish underwater: she was a clownfish, and he was a swordfish. I loved her imagination and that she was helping to build his.

Tonight's adventure was pirates looking for buried treasure.

"Arr, Pirate Davy, we need to find the treasure. Arr, let's look at the map," Missy commanded.

"Arr... Arrr..." Davy seemed to like the pirate word.

Once I was satisfied with the kitchen, I joined them outside. It was a perfect evening. We got out here as much as possible. The house itself was sad and run down, despite my efforts to keep it clean.

When it started to get dark, I got them inside for baths, story time, and bed. Our nightly routine. I always read to them before they fell asleep.

Reading had given me an escape when life got too heavy, and I wanted to pass that love on to my brother and sister. We were currently working through Charlotte's Web. I'd recently taught Missy to read, and she loved to practice. She would ask to read small sections aloud, and though some parts were above her level, we would work together to sound out the harder words. She tried so hard, and she was getting better every day.

After story time, I tucked them in and kissed them goodnight. It was only then, with them safely asleep, that I could let myself fall apart.

I wandered into the living room and sank into the old couch, letting out a sound that was half moan, half sigh. For so long, I'd daydreamed about being free of Mama. But on my terms. Not like this.

It all came down to money. I needed money to leave and to live. That was one of the reasons I'd started my cleaning business in the first place.

I'd been about ten years old when Ms. Graham found me hiding in her garden shed. I'd been crying, though I wouldn't tell her why. She didn't push. Instead, she asked if I'd like to earn a few dollars helping her with some chores around the house. I think she knew I needed an escape more than I needed the money, at least at first. Over time, I asked other neighbors if they needed cleaning or yard work, and soon I had a small business going.

It gave me purpose each day and income that enabled me to care for my brother and sister. While it began as an escape from Mama, her friends, and her parties, it became much more. I had independence. I could provide things Mama wasn't willing to, like food that wasn't scraps and clothes that actually fit.

From the beginning, I'd tried to save more than I spent, hiding cash in various jars and containers buried in the backyard. I made myself a rule: what went in stayed in. If I needed to spend something extra, the next deposit would just be smaller.

I had no idea how much I'd accumulated out there. I really needed to dig it all up and see just how fruitful all that work had been.

I allowed myself another moment to wallow before I jumped up. Now was a good time to dig. It had gotten dark enough to conceal what I was doing. I didn't need to give the neighbors any more gossip.

Not that Ms. Graham would talk, but Mrs. Maxwell on the other side of us was the worst gossip in Glenn Lake. Once she heard Mama had left, she would spread it all over town.

I tried not to think about that as I went out to gather my money. It took a while in the dark to find all my hiding spots. When I was done, I hoped I'd found them all.

I had started out at thirty dollars a week helping one neighbor. It slowly grew to a few more people, and now I was working for ten clients who paid me anywhere from fifty to seventy-five dollars a week, sometimes more with tips or holiday bonuses.

In the first couple of years, I'd saved almost every dollar, taking out only small amounts for necessities. But in the last few years, I'd become the sole provider for two children. Mama allowed her friends to eat our food, the food I bought, so I had to purchase more than we needed and hide the non-perishables where they couldn't find them.

I didn't mind providing for my brother and sister. I minded providing for Mama and her freeloading friends. And now, knowing she had money in the bank the whole time? It felt like a slap in the face.

It didn't matter now. The trash had taken itself out, so to speak. My hope was that she stayed gone.

I brought my nest egg into the house. It took several trips. Nearly six years of saving, all of it here on the floor in front of me. I knelt down and started counting.

When I finished, I couldn't believe it. Nearly thirty thousand dollars. I counted it again. Then again. It was correct.

I sat back on my heels and stared at my small fortune.

"Not bad for a kid doing yard work and housecleaning for neighbors," I said aloud, fighting the urge to roll around in it like some cartoon character.

This was a huge success. Almost unbelievable. But that was my life: unbelievable in all the wrong ways, and now maybe, just maybe, in the right ones too.

I might actually be able to make this work without Mama. It would take careful budgeting and planning, but I made enough to support us. If I could pick up a part-time job somewhere, that would help even more.

Tomorrow I would open an actual bank account. That was probably a better option than hiding cash in the backyard. But for tonight, I split the money into three piles and hid them in three different places in the house.

To say I was paranoid would be an understatement. With this much cash and after the childhood I'd had, who could blame me?

I checked every window and door twice to make sure they were locked. Then a third time, just for my own peace of mind.

I made my way down the hallway to peek at the children. They were sleeping peacefully, their faces soft and untroubled.

I wandered through the house, picking up stray toys, a random sock, and a shoe. The place was beat up and neglected, but I did my best to keep up with what I could.

Once I was done, I grabbed my pillow and blanket and settled on the couch for the night.

Sleep came in fits and starts. The slightest sound woke me. What if she came back drunk? What if she tried to take the kids?

I could call the Sheriff, but I doubted a seventeen-year-old half-sister had as much legal standing as their mother. I didn't think I had a leg to stand on if she tried to take them.

Mother. She didn't even know what the word meant. Nearly everyone in Glenn Lake would side with me, but that wouldn't matter if she took them somewhere else. We were strangers outside this town. Houston was only thirty minutes away. She could disappear with them, and no one there would know us.

If that happened, there was a good chance I would never see them again.

I stared at the ceiling in the darkness, listening for sounds that never came. That thought, losing them, was too painful to hold for long. I pushed it away and waited for morning.

Chapter Three

The kids woke up happy and bouncy, less stressed than most days.

"Good morning, Mandy!" Missy said, hopping into her seat at the table.

I set a bowl of cereal in front of her and kissed her head, then helped Davy into his chair and gave him his breakfast. I kissed his head, too.

"Good morning, sweeties. Did you sleep well?"

"I did. I had the bestest dream ever. It was about kitties. I love kitties." She chatted away while Davy ate his cereal and nodded along with her.

Today was the first day of our new life. I had to open a bank account, find a regular babysitter, and look into getting a part time job to supplement my housecleaning work. I also had two houses scheduled, so it was going to be busier than usual.

After breakfast, I got them dressed, packed a bag, and headed next door to Ms. Graham's house. I hated to ask, but I needed them somewhere safe while I ran my errands.

"Good morning, Ms. Graham," I said when she opened the door.

Ms. Graham was a special person in our lives. She had built not one but two successful businesses from the ground up, during a time when that was rare for women. She'd never married or had children, though I didn't know the reason. She was beautiful, kind, and thoughtful. Even now, at eight in the morning, she wore pearls, and her white hair was styled in a perfect French twist.

The kids ran to her. "Grammy!"

She'd come up with this nickname for them to call her, a play on her last name and her role as a grandmother figure in their lives.

"Oh, good morning, dears. Are you scheduled to do work for me today? I thought..." She trailed off as she hugged the little kids.

"Oh no, not today. I wanted to ask if you'd watch them for me this morning. I'm sorry it's last minute."

"Mama left us," Missy added flatly. Little Davy nodded.

"Oh, my." Ms. Graham glanced at me. "Yes, yes. Of course I can watch them for you. For as long as you need." She gestured for us to come in.

"Thank you. I just need to walk into town to handle a few things." Downtown Glenn Lake was close enough to walk from where we lived, which worked well since I didn't drive. "I need to open a bank account. I also want to apply for some jobs."

"Oh? You're not going to clean any longer?"

"I'll still clean houses, but I feel like I need a little more income."

She nodded. "Do you want me to drive you? I know you can walk, but it would be easier in the car."

"No, I'll be okay. It'll be good for me to clear my head. Plus, it's a nice day."

"It is lovely today." She looked at the kids and then back at me. "Well, take your time. And if you need me to watch them this afternoon so you can do your houses, I'd be happy to keep them longer."

"I don't want to impose."

"No imposition at all." She smiled at the kids. "We'll have so much fun. Maybe we can go to the park and then make cookies."

"Oh, yay! I want to go to the park," Missy said, jumping up and down.

"Cookie, cookie!" Davy chanted.

They each had their own agenda. Ms. Graham and I shared a laugh.

"I really appreciate it. Thank you."

As I was leaving, I realized I needed a cell phone. I was probably one of the few seventeen-year-olds without one. I would have to stop by the hardware store to see if it was doable on my budget. An odd place for cell phones, but that's where they were sold in our small town.

When I stepped into the bank, Mr. Mulroney greeted me immediately. He owned and managed the bank, which his family had started when Glenn Lake was founded back in the late 1800s. It had passed from his grandfather to his father to him. He had three daughters, so I supposed one of them would take over when he retired.

"Good morning, Ms. Mandy. How are you today?" He had a big, booming, friendly voice that matched his warm smile.

"I'm well, Mr. Mulroney. How are you?"

"Good, good. What can I do for you today?"

"I'd like to open a bank account with some money I've saved."

"Great. Step into my office, and we can get started."

I followed him down a short hallway. He offered me water or coffee on the way; I declined and took a seat across from him. His office was neat and organized but filled with personal touches: family pictures, a small plant, a pencil holder shaped like a golf bag, and a slinky on the corner of his desk.

"Alrighty," he said, settling into his chair. "We can open a new account, or I can add it to your current account. You know about that, right?"

I sat up straight. "What current account?"

"Didn't your mother ever tell you...?" He paused and shook his head slightly, as if stopping himself from saying what he really thought. "No, I suppose she wouldn't."

I was used to people's reactions to Mama. I had emotionally disconnected from her years ago, so when people commented, it didn't hurt my feelings anymore. But I had a feeling what he was about to say was going to shock me.

He clicked through some screens on his computer, moving too quickly for me to follow.

"When your grandmother passed, she left money for both you and your mother. Yours is in your name only. Your grandmother was insistent on that." He turned from the computer to look at me. "Your mother tried many times to get it, but your grandmother had given me strict orders not to allow it. I would never cross her. Even from the grave, that woman scares me." He winked.

"Really?" I exhaled and sat back in the chair, stunned. "I didn't even think she knew I existed. Or at least, that she didn't care that I did."

"Oh no, Mandy. She was disappointed in your mother's choices, certainly. But she loved you. She bragged about you whenever I saw her. She thought you were so smart, always talking about your good grades and how quick witted you were."

I twisted a piece of hair around my finger, trying to process his words. "Wow. I didn't know. I always thought she hated me. I never really got a chance to know her."

I sat with that for a moment. All those years living in her house, and I'd believed she wanted nothing to do with me. I remembered how she would look at me sometimes, her expression unreadable. I'd assumed it was disapproval, or worse, disgust. Maybe I'd been wrong. Maybe she'd been looking at me the way a grandmother looks at a grandchild she loves but cannot reach.

The thought settled in my chest like a stone. A lost opportunity. A relationship that might have been, if things had been different. If Mama had been different.

I mentally shook it off. I couldn't change the past, and I had more pressing concerns.

"So, um, how much is in the account?"

"About thirty-two thousand dollars." He turned the monitor so I could see the total. I nearly fell out of the chair. "She left most of her money to Becca, but she wanted to make sure you had money for college. I suppose she didn't know you'd be raising two siblings at seventeen."

I let that sink in. With this money plus what I had saved, I might be able to make it last for quite a while. A year or more, if I was careful. And I was good at stretching a dollar.

We split my savings between a checking account and a savings account, with more going into savings. Then he gave me a quick lesson on online banking and how to manage the accounts.

My only experience with money management to this point had been burying jars in the backyard and cutting coupons.

"This has all been very helpful, Mr. Mulroney," I said. "Thank you for your time."

"Of course. Always happy to help one of my favorite residents."

I stepped outside and stood on the sidewalk, letting the news settle over me. I now had sixty-two thousand dollars. Yesterday, I hadn't even known I had a bank account. Not bad for a kid doing odd jobs for neighbors.

My whole life was strange and unbelievable. I couldn't decide if I wanted to laugh or cry, dance in the street or sit down on the curb and have a good scream. My life was either really good or really awful. There was almost never anything in between.

Now I had to decide: get a job to make that money last longer, or keep doing what I was doing with the housecleaning and try to expand it into a real business?

Either way, I needed to figure out childcare. The kids couldn't be home alone. Even when Mama had been there, it had barely counted as supervision, but at least it was something.

Ms. Graham would help, but I hated to take advantage of her kindness. It was too much to ask her to watch them every day. I could also ask Mr. Dixon and maybe Mrs. Dailey, but I needed a more reliable solution.

Perhaps I should look into one of the two local daycares. The Little Village Learning Center had a good reputation and a preschool program for Missy. But I didn't know how much it would cost or whether it was even the right thing to do.

It was hard being a parent to children who weren't mine. But I loved them and wanted to make sure I did right by them.

In the end, I decided to apply for a few jobs as a backup plan. If something worked out, it would supplement my cleaning income. If not, I still had my regular clients. It couldn't hurt to try.

I stopped in at a few retail shops and the thrift store. They had me fill out applications, but they weren't hiring at the moment.

"We'll call you if something comes up," was the standard answer.

I also applied at the grocery store. The owners, the Donavons, had known my grandparents and were always kind to me. I'd done yard work and cleaning for them a few times, and they liked my work ethic. Others had mentioned how dependable I was.

Unfortunately, they weren't hiring either, but like the others, they said they'd call if something opened up.

Word had spread about Mama. I'd known it would, this being a small town, but I wasn't sure how everyone had found out so quickly. I hadn't told anyone except Ms. Graham, and she wasn't a gossip. Maybe Mama had told her friends, and they'd told others. I might never know.

Small towns were like that. Gossip traveled fast. I could feel people watching me as I went in and out of stores. Some whispered. Others smiled at me with pity in their eyes.

Ms. Butler, the librarian, was heading into the hardware store as I approached.

"Oh, Mandy, hi." She touched my arm lightly. "I'm sorry to hear about your mother leaving."

"Thanks, Ms. Butler."

"She didn't take care of you kids anyway. You do such a fine job. You're all better off."

I nodded and managed a smile.

"Well, if you need anything, you know where to find me." Her eyes were watery.

I had to get away before she cried, because if she did, I would too. And I hated crying. It was a weakness that had never gotten me anywhere except more beatings from Mama or whoever she was with at the time.

"Thanks. I do." I continued quickly down the sidewalk.

This seemed to be the theme with everyone I ran into. Those who didn't just stare would stop me to offer condolences, always followed by some version of "you're better off." It was true, probably. But it still stung to hear so many people say it out loud.

Why couldn't I have a normal life? A mother and father who worked and took care of their kids without causing drama all over town? I didn't even have a father. Or at least, not one I knew.

I pushed those thoughts aside and kept moving.

I applied at Mr. Burger and then Big Ron's Diner. Both were hiring and had a few applicants to consider. They said they would let me know within the week.

After that, I headed to the hardware store to pick out a cell phone. I was relieved to see Ms. Butler had already left. She meant well, but I'd had enough sad looks for one day.

The cell phone was easy enough, and the plan fit my budget. I was finally a modern girl. The only thing missing was a driver's license, but that would have to wait. At least I had a picture ID.

With my errands complete, it was time to start my regular work. I headed to the Wilsons to get started on my first job of the day.

The Wilson triplets were five now, in kindergarten, and all three were in after school activities. Grace did soccer and Girl Scouts; Blake and Steven played T-ball and were in Boy Scouts. Mrs. Wilson had been put on bed rest while pregnant with them, and that was when they first hired me. It helped ease the burden while she finished her pregnancy, and I'd been working for them ever since.

I loved working for them. With both parents working full time and three busy kids, I knew I made a real difference.

Today I got a load of laundry started. There were always piles of laundry with three kids. Then I vacuumed the downstairs and emptied the dishwasher. I put together a chicken casserole, attached the cooking directions, and left it in the fridge. Last, I moved the laundry from the washer to the dryer, folded what had already been dried, and headed out.

Mr. Dixon's house was a few blocks over. It was a pleasant day, and the sunshine felt warm on my face as I walked. I tried not to think too hard about the future. One day at a time.

"Hey, Mandy girl, how you doing today?" He greeted me from the porch when I walked up.

"I'm good. How are you?"

"Doing well." He paused and lightly squeezed my arm. "I heard about your mother. Please let me know if you need any help with the kids. I love spending time with them."

"Thank you. I'll keep that in mind. They sure love their Grandpa Dixon." I smiled. "So, besides the yard, what did you need done today? Deviled eggs for tonight?"

"That would be wonderful. I also bought stuff for sandwiches, but I couldn't put them together. My hands are bothering me today." He rubbed his thumb into his palm as he spoke.

"I don't mind at all. Happy to help."

I headed inside to start the eggs, set a timer, and took it with me to the yard. I was back in the kitchen before the timer went off. While the eggs cooled, I put together sandwiches for his poker night: ham and cheese, roast beef, and turkey with Swiss.

As a final touch, I made a batch of cookies. I knew Mr. Donavon would be there tonight, and he had a legendary sweet tooth.

Once I was done, I said goodbye to Mr. Dixon and headed back to Ms. Graham's to pick up the kids.

I could hear them in the yard as I got closer. I paused for a moment to listen, their laughter floating over the fence. They were just being children. Playing without fear, without worry.

It made me happy to know I could give them that, even if I couldn't give them much else.

Chapter Four

A week later, Mr. Burger called to say I got the job and asked if I could start the following week. Of course, I said yes. Having extra income would relieve some of the financial pressure I was feeling.

Ms. Graham and another neighbor, Mrs. Dailey, agreed to take turns watching the kids while I worked. With a bit of creative scheduling, I figured out how to keep my cleaning and yard work clients as well.

My first day at the new job was a little over two weeks from the day Mama left. It felt like a lifetime ago, but the kids and I had adjusted quickly to life without her.

My only real struggle was at night. I found myself listening for every little sound, unable to fully relax. I didn't trust Mama. What if she came back? What would she want? What would I do? The worry made for long nights and little sleep, which made the days feel even longer as I fought through the exhaustion.

But the house was cleaner now. The food I bought was ours to eat. There were no strangers coming and going at all hours. It was just the three of us, and we were happy.

On the morning of my first day, Mrs. Dailey came over to watch the children. She was best friends with Ms. Graham; they'd moved to Glenn Lake around the same time. Unfortunately, her husband was currently fighting cancer, so she hadn't been able to help us as much as she used to when he was well. I appreciated her being here even more because of that.

The kids were excited for me. Well, Missy was excited, and Davy was excited because Missy was.

"I want a full report of what you do when you get home. I love their French fries! I hope you get to make French fries." Missy gave me these instructions while I was getting her and Davy dressed for the day.

I kissed them both goodbye and headed into town. The walk was easy, and the morning was beautiful.

Glenn Lake was a lovely little town, located south of Houston with a population of roughly twenty thousand and growing. There was a traditional town square lined with small businesses, charming cafes, and not a chain store in sight. Tree-lined sidewalks led to Glenn Lake

Park and the lake that had inspired the town's name. It was quaint and peaceful, the kind of place where neighbors looked out for each other.

Our neighborhood was one of the original ones, developed in the early 1980s. Mama had been born and raised here. I'd moved here when I was about five, after my grandparents were in the car accident that killed my grandfather and left my grandmother unable to live alone.

While I hadn't enjoyed my childhood, I loved Glenn Lake. I walked to my new job with a sense of pride, waving to people I knew and smiling at the few I didn't.

The first hour was spent filling out paperwork and watching training videos. Then I was introduced to Cindy, who would be training me. I followed her around all day, mostly watching, but she let me take orders and run the register for the last two hours of my shift.

Sadly, for Missy, I didn't get to make French fries. I saw them being made, though. To a four-year-old, that probably sounded exciting, but it wasn't much of a spectacle. Someone opened a bag of frozen fries, dumped them into a basket, and lowered them into the oil for a few minutes. They came out golden and crispy, filled with fatty goodness, which was all that mattered in the end.

The day flew by, and before I knew it, my shift was over. I practically floated home. I couldn't wait to tell the kids about my day and give them the treat I'd brought: burgers and fries for dinner. We rarely got fast food of any kind. They were going to be thrilled.

I hadn't scheduled any cleaning jobs today so I could focus on my first shift. I wasn't sure yet how I would handle six hours at the restaurant followed by cleaning houses, but I'd figure that out tomorrow.

Instead of the warm, excited welcome I expected when I got home, I found Mrs. Dailey and Ms. Graham sitting on the porch. Mrs. Dailey was sobbing. When they saw me, they both stood.

"CPS came." Ms. Graham's voice was flat, businesslike. "They took the kids."

The words didn't make sense at first. They hung in the air like something spoken in a foreign language.

"What?" My heart slammed against my ribs. I rushed up the porch steps. "What did they say? Why?"

"They said there was a tip called in about your mother leaving, and that you weren't old enough or capable of taking care of them." Ms. Graham's jaw was tight. "I tried to tell them you were the one who had always cared for those children. We both did." She gestured to Mrs. Dailey, who was whimpering quietly, her face half buried in Ms. Graham's shoulder. "I told them you were more capable than your own mother. More capable than most mothers. But they wouldn't listen."

"Did they leave a number? Someone I can contact?"

My mind had shifted into a strange, cold clarity. Fact finding. That was all I could do right now.

"Yes, dear. Here." She handed me a business card. "He said to call once you got home, and he would explain."

I took the card and ran inside, calling thank you over my shoulder. Both women followed me into the house. Mrs. Dailey still couldn't pull herself together, and Ms. Graham kept one arm around her while watching me. My hands shook as I dialed the number.

"This is Scott Meeks."

"Hi, Mr. Meeks. My name is Mandy Walker. I believe you took my brother and sister today."

"Oh, yes, Ms. Walker. I'm so sorry I couldn't speak to you directly, but we did have to remove your siblings from your care today. I'm sure it will be a relief to you—"

"I'm sorry?" I cut him off. "A relief? Why would having my baby brother and sister stolen from me be a relief?"

I felt my face flush with anger. Did he really just use the word relief?

"I understand it must be a burden at your age, and with your busy social life." His tone was condescending, almost smug. It sent a chill down my spine.

"My busy social life? I have no social life. I take care of this house, my siblings, and until a few weeks ago, my mother. I have more responsibilities than most adults twice my age."

"That's not what we were told. But it doesn't matter. You're not the parent. While you are old enough for us not to need to take custody of you, you're not old enough for us to grant you custody of Melissa and David."

"I am nearly eighteen. My own mother had me when she was fifteen. She was far from fit to raise a child, but I was left in her care." I fought the lump rising in my throat. I was not going to cry. I would not give him that satisfaction. "I just don't understand."

"Why don't you come down tomorrow, and we can discuss this in person. We'll need to interview you anyway. Eight a.m. The address is on the card."

"Will I be able to see them?"

"No, not at this time. They're in the process of being placed in a foster home. Be here at eight, and we can discuss it further. Now, if you'll excuse me, I have other cases that require my attention. Thank you."

"But—"

He had already hung up.

I stood there, the phone still pressed to my ear, listening to dead air. Slowly, I turned to face my neighbors. Was this really happening?

CPS had taken them on some anonymous tip. No proof. No real investigation. Right now, I couldn't process it. It was too much. I could almost feel my heart cracking down the middle.

"I'll drive you in the morning," Ms. Graham said quietly. "We can leave at seven."

I nodded, not trusting myself to speak.

The ladies stayed with me a little longer. I made us hot tea while they attempted small talk and tried to comfort me. Mrs. Dailey eventually stopped crying, which helped me hold myself together. She was the first to leave, needing to get home to her husband. Ms. Graham stayed a bit longer, making sure I was okay. I told her I was, but we both knew it wasn't true.

After she left, I wandered through the house. It felt all wrong. Too empty. Too silent.

I walked down the hall to the kids' room and stopped in the doorway. My throat tightened.

Their toys were scattered across the floor, as if they'd been in the middle of playing when everything was interrupted. A few dresser drawers hung open. Had they been allowed to pack some of their own clothes? I hoped so. At least they would have something familiar.

I kept picturing them scared and crying in some strange place, surrounded by strange people. They had always depended on me to protect them. And now I wasn't there.

"I should have been here," I whispered to the empty room. "I could have stopped them."

The tears started then, sliding down my cheeks faster than I could wipe them away.

I forced myself to move, walking back down the hall to the kitchen. The paper sack of burgers and fries sat on the table where I'd dropped it. I stared at it, and a fresh wave of grief rolled through me.

They would never hear about my first day. They would never get their treat.

I looked inside the bag. The fries were cold and limp, well past saving. Without another thought, I threw the whole thing in the trash and turned away. I couldn't stand to look at it. I couldn't stand to think about what should have been.

I walked back to the living room and climbed into the old, worn armchair, pulling a blanket around myself. And then I let go.

I cried the loneliest tears of my life. I hadn't cried like this in years. I'd grown numb to pain after so much abuse and neglect. But Missy and Davy were different. They were my heart. My purpose. My reason for getting up every morning.

The house was painfully quiet. No chattering from Missy. No sweet giggles from Davy. Just silence, pressing in from every corner.

My emotions swung between rage and sorrow. I cried until I had nothing left, pleading with the empty room to bring them back.

I was so lost in my grief that I couldn't even think about tomorrow, beyond the trip to CPS. I needed to hear what they had to say before I could figure out what to do next.

But I knew one thing for certain. I was going to fight for them. Whatever it took.

Chapter Five

At some point, I fell asleep. I slept fitfully, waking with a start just before six in the morning. Panic shot through my body first, then the stab of heartbreak, then the emptiness creeping back into my chest like something that had taken up permanent residence.

I showered and dressed quickly, taking extra care with my appearance. I wanted to make a good impression on CPS. Most of my clothes were casual, meant for cleaning houses and doing yard work, but I managed to find a pale pink blouse and navy slacks among Mama's abandoned belongings. Paired with brown flats, I looked presentable. Responsible. Like someone who could be trusted with two children.

My only goal for the day was talking to Mr. Scott Meeks and getting my brother and sister back. I was convinced that once he met me in person, he would see I wasn't some partying teenager. He would realize I was more than capable of raising them. He had only taken them because he hadn't met me yet. Once he did, everything would be fine.

I had to believe that.

I checked my appearance one more time, grabbed my purse and keys from the foyer table, and headed to Ms. Graham's house.

She was ready as promised, waiting on her porch. Without a word, we climbed into her car and drove north. Once we were out of Glenn Lake and on the highway toward Houston, she started giving me advice.

"Now, dear, don't let them bully you. You're far more fit to raise those children than your mother ever was."

"But I don't think I have any legal right to them. I'm not their mother, and I'm not eighteen yet. At least, that's what he said on the phone."

"I did a little research last night, and the age of majority here is actually seventeen, from what I could tell." She squared her shoulders like she was preparing for battle. "We'll have to see what he says first. And if necessary, we hire a lawyer."

"I don't know if I can afford a lawyer. I have some money, but aren't lawyers expensive? I don't want to lose them, but I definitely won't have a chance at getting them back if I spend everything and can't support them." I shook my head and sighed. "I'm just so heartbroken right now. I don't even know what to think."

"I will help you."

"Oh no, Ms. Graham, I can't let you do that. I can't—"

"Nonsense." Her voice was firm. "You are like a granddaughter to me, and those children are special. I can't stand by and watch this happen to good people." She paused, her eyes still on the road. "I made a promise to your grandmother to look out for you. I intend to keep it."

I sat back in my seat, stunned. Another piece of the puzzle falling into place.

"You made a promise to my grandmother?"

"I did. Before she passed."

I stared out the window at the passing scenery, trying to absorb this. First, I'd learned that my grandmother had left me money. Now I was learning she had asked our neighbors to watch over me. It explained why Ms. Graham had never called CPS herself, despite knowing what went on in our house. She had been protecting me in her own way, honoring a promise made to a dying woman.

All those years, my grandmother had seemed so cold to me. Snapping in anger, always seeming sad and distant. I had stayed out of her way, assuming she resented my presence. But now, looking back, I could understand her better. She had survived the car accident that killed her husband but was left with chronic pain and limited mobility. She had watched her daughter spiral into addiction and abuse. She had been powerless to stop it.

Maybe the coldness I'd felt from her wasn't resentment at all. Maybe it was grief. Maybe it was helplessness.

Learning these things about her made me feel cheated. I wished I'd had a chance to know her before she died. When things settled down, I would ask Ms. Graham and some of the other neighbors about her. I wanted to hear their stories, even if it was secondhand. I wanted to know who she really was.

"Is that why you never called CPS to have me removed?" The question came out before I could stop it. I put my hand over my mouth. "I'm sorry. That was rude."

"Not at all, dear." She glanced at me briefly. "Honestly, the thought crossed my mind more than once. But your grandmother asked me to let you stay together, to keep an eye on things without interfering unless it became truly dangerous. She believed you were strong enough to survive it, and she was right." She paused. "Would you have wanted to be removed?"

I thought about it. "Honestly, I don't know. There might have been times I fantasized about having different parents, a different life. But now, with the kids, I can't imagine being anywhere else."

She nodded and focused on the traffic, which was growing heavier as we approached the city. I rarely left Glenn Lake, so I often forgot how large and crowded the outside world could be.

"I think I need to call Jimmy," I said after a while. "They're his kids. He has a right to know."

"He hasn't seen them in over a year. I'd be surprised if he were interested in helping." Her lips pressed into a thin line.

"He isn't around because of Mama. You know what she's like." I sighed. "I know he loves those kids. You can see it in his eyes when he talks about them. Or at least, you used to be able to." I let my voice trail off.

"I'm sure he does. But he has an odd way of showing it." She was never one to mince words. "I suppose we'll play it by ear and see what this Mr. Meeks has to say."

I knew her well enough to understand what that meant. She was letting me think the conversation was over, that I had won some small point. But she wouldn't drop it easily.

We arrived at the CPS office a few minutes early. I gave my name to the receptionist and told her I was there to meet with Mr. Meeks. She told us to have a seat.

After nearly twenty minutes, a man in his mid-thirties emerged from a side door. He was heavyset, and his suit looked like he had slept in it. There were dark circles under his eyes, and his face was flushed, as if he had been rushing around.

"Ms. Walker?" He addressed me. I nodded and stood. "I'm Scott Meeks. Why don't you come back?" His eyes moved to Ms. Graham with obvious suspicion.

"This is Ms. Graham, my neighbor and friend. May she join us?"

"We met yesterday." His tone made it clear the experience had not been pleasant. "I don't think that would be appropriate."

I wasn't surprised. Ms. Graham was a tough woman. A tough old bird, as she liked to say.

"But—" I looked at her, uncertain.

"That's okay, dear." She patted my arm. "I don't mind waiting here. You go find out about your brother and sister." She gave Mr. Meeks a pointed look before settling back into her chair and pulling a book from her purse. Always prepared.

I followed him through a maze of hallways and offices. I barely registered what any of it looked like. I was too busy trying to memorize the path in case panic overtook me and I needed to flee. My heart pounded in my chest, but I kept my head high, projecting a confidence I didn't feel.

His office matched his appearance. Papers were scattered everywhere, drawers hung open, and there were no personal photographs or decorations that might help me understand him as a person rather than a bureaucrat. My impression was chaos and disorganization. I forced myself to keep a pleasant expression. The fate of my family was in this man's hands.

"So, Ms. Walker." He settled into his chair. "I just have a few questions for you, and then we'll send you down for a drug test."

"A drug test?"

"Yes. The tip we received indicated you're a heavy drug user. We need to verify that before we can even consider letting you visit the children."

"So I will get to visit them today?" I asked, latching onto the only positive thing he'd said.

"No, not today. We won't have the results back for a few days, possibly up to a week, depending on how fast the lab can process them. Until we get those results, we can't schedule a visit." He picked up a pen, ready to take notes. "Now, let's get started with some basic questions."

He went through the preliminaries: my name, age, my relationship to the children in custody. I kept my voice calm and my face neutral, even though I was screaming inside.

Then he moved to the investigation questions.

"Do you use drugs?"

"No."

"Ms. Walker, don't you think we should be honest with each other?"

"I'm not lying. I've never used drugs. When I was young, I watched my mother use them. She hasn't in several years, but I swore I never would." I struggled to remain calm. For Missy and Davy's sake, I had to hold it together.

"Well." He smirked. "We'll find out soon enough, won't we?"

I wanted to reach across the desk and slap him. Instead, I kept my hands folded in my lap.

"Next question. The tip indicated that you have many people in the house at all hours, including men. How many men are you bringing around the children?"

"Wait. What?" I couldn't hide my reaction to this one. "Are you asking if I—" I stopped, my face flushing hot. "I have never... I'm still a virgin." The last part came out in a whisper.

"I'm not suggesting anything." His tone said otherwise. "We just want to ensure the children aren't being exposed to certain behaviors. But the tip mentioned multiple men, so I have to ask."

"It's just the kids and me. Sometimes a few neighbors come by to help, like Ms. Graham and Mrs. Dailey, who you also met yesterday. I would never put them in harm's way."

I reminded myself that he was just doing his job. Social workers were overworked and underpaid. That was probably why his office looked like a disaster zone. But if he would just listen to me, really listen, this could be one less case on his desk.

"I think that's enough questions." He set down his pen with more force than necessary. He seemed as frustrated with me as I was with him. "Let me walk you to the lab so you can submit a sample for the drug test. They'll also do a breathalyzer."

I didn't bother to respond. I knew I wouldn't be able to find civil words. He had already made up his mind about me, and nothing I said was going to change it. The drug test results would speak for themselves.

We walked through the maze of hallways again. By now, I was completely turned around. We finally arrived at a small lab area. He handed a form to the woman at the desk and told me to take a seat.

"I'll call you in a few days when we get the results to discuss next steps." He gave me a dismissive once over before leaving.

A few minutes later, I was called back to a small office with an attached bathroom. Once the samples were collected, I was shown out. The whole thing had taken less than an hour, but it felt much longer. I was emotionally drained, and I still had to work at Mr. Burger and clean houses afterward.

Ms. Graham and I drove home mostly in silence.

"Do you think it could have been Mama?" I asked as we neared Glenn Lake. "I can't imagine she would do something like this. What would be the point?"

"I wouldn't put much past her at this point. She's changed so much over the years." Ms. Graham kept her eyes on the road. "But if I had to guess, I'd say it was one of the more gossipy neighbors. Someone like Mrs. Maxwell."

"Maybe. I don't think she likes children."

"She's always been grumpy, but I can't imagine her being deliberately cruel. She probably thought she was helping."

I had my doubts. I'd had more than a few run ins with Mrs. Maxwell over the years. She had yelled at us, waved a broom over her head, chased the kids and me away from the fence line. Though looking back, maybe she had been yelling at Mama's party guests, not us. We had always tried to stay out of sight during those parties, playing in the far corner of the yard behind the shed. Mrs. Maxwell would have seen us through the broken fence boards. Maybe she had drawn her own conclusions.

Once home, I thanked Ms. Graham and promised to keep her updated. Then I changed clothes and headed to my shift at Mr. Burger.

Unlike my first day, today dragged. Every minute felt heavy. There was no joy in it, nothing to look forward to when I got home.

After my shift, I went to Mr. Dixon's house. He wanted his yard looking nice for his grandchildren's visit this weekend. His lawn was his pride and joy, and I was grateful for the distraction.

After that, I dropped in on a few of my other clients to see if anyone needed extra work done. I knew I was stalling. I didn't want to go back to that empty house.

By the time I finally went home, I was exhausted. I showered, ate some leftovers standing at the kitchen counter, and collapsed into bed.

Sleep came in fragments. I kept hearing Little Davy crying and Missy calling for me. Each time, I startled awake, heart pounding, only to remember they weren't there. Then I would lie in the darkness, waiting for sleep to take me again.

I missed them so much. I prayed they were okay.

Chapter Six

The days blurred together. Each one looked the same: cleaning houses in the morning, working at Mr. Burger in the afternoon, then cleaning more houses until I was too tired to think. At the end of each night, I collapsed into bed exhausted, only to lie awake missing Missy and Davy, tears soaking my pillow until sleep finally took me.

This was my cycle for three days. Work, wait, cry. Work, wait, cry.

Then I finally got the call I had been waiting for.

"Hello?" I answered, not recognizing the number.

"Ms. Walker?" A male voice.

"Yes?"

"This is Scott Meeks from CPS. I'm calling with the results of your drug test."

My heart stuttered. "Yes?"

"No drugs were found in your sample. You're clean."

Relief flooded through me, even though I had known the results would come back negative. There had been a small, paranoid part of me that worried something would go wrong, that they would find a way to use even this against me.

"Well, I'm glad that's cleared up," I said. "When can I see Missy and Davy?"

"I'm sorry, but I can't schedule a visit at this time. They're still settling into their foster home, and we don't want to disrupt their new routine. Soon, though."

I gripped the phone tighter. I didn't want them settled into their foster home. They should be home with me. But I bit my tongue. I would wait for the next steps. I would play by their rules.

"I'd also like to work on bringing them home," I said, keeping my voice steady. "What will that take?"

"First, there will need to be a full investigation before I can allow that. A home inspection, verification of your employment, and proof that you can financially provide for them."

"Okay. Yes. I can do all of those things. I'll do anything to get them back. They're my responsibility, and I'm sure they're scared without me."

"Well, okay then. I'll have someone in my office call you to schedule the home inspection."

"And you'll let me know when I can visit them?"

"As soon as we're able to get something scheduled, I'll call you. Thank you."

He hung up before I could respond. I was starting to get used to his abrupt phone manner.

I was scheduled to clean for Ms. Graham that day, so I went over to tell her about the call and scrub her bathrooms before my shift at the restaurant.

"They can't do this." She gave a soft stomp of her foot. "They're just stringing you along."

"Do you think so?" I looked up at her from my spot on the floor, where I was scrubbing the tub. She leaned against the counter, arms crossed, watching me work.

I had never dealt with anything like this before and was completely naive about the process. My world had been small, both in terms of the people I interacted with and the experiences I'd had outside of Glenn Lake. Ms. Graham knew far more about these things than I did.

"Yes, I do. And I think it's time we find a lawyer. I'm sure you have rights. I did more research last night. I believe we can fight this."

"I do have the money grandmother left me," I said, scrubbing at a stubborn spot while I gathered my thoughts. "But I don't want to spend it all right away. I want to give them a chance to make this right." I paused. "And I'd hate to antagonize them and then never get the kids back."

"I have no family and more money than I need. I can pay for the lawyer, and I'm willing to do it. But I can't force you to hire one." She sighed. "I'll try to be patient. Though I think you're being too trusting of CPS. I know they're probably trying to do what they think is right, but this whole situation is frustrating."

She was probably right. I was being naive. But I didn't know what else to do. This was all new territory for me. Yes, I could hire a lawyer and come out swinging, but part of me wanted to believe the system would work. That if I just followed their rules and proved myself, they would see the truth.

The fighting spirit that had helped me survive my childhood was growing stronger with every day Mama stayed gone. I wasn't going to let them walk all over me forever. But for now, I had to play their game.

I finished cleaning Ms. Graham's house, changed into my work clothes, and headed to Mr. Burger. Then I continued with my new routine: working myself into exhaustion so I wouldn't have to feel the emptiness of that house.

It was another week before I heard from CPS again. They wanted to schedule a home inspection and another interview. I had a day off coming up, so we set the appointment for then.

Four days. I had four days to get ready.

I threw myself into preparing. Decluttering, mostly. Mama had left behind years worth of accumulated junk, and I packed it all into boxes, storing what might be useful in the shed and attic, throwing out the rest. Then I gave the house a thorough scrubbing. I kept things clean as a matter of habit, but after all the decluttering, the place needed a deep clean.

It felt good to have something to do. Something I could control.

The house was old and hadn't been well maintained. I couldn't fix the worn flooring or patch the cracks in the walls. Those things would have to wait. But I could make it clean. I could make it presentable.

I stood in the living room when I was finished, looking around at my work. The surfaces gleamed. The windows sparkled. The air smelled like lemon cleaner instead of stale beer and cigarette smoke.

It wasn't perfect. But it was the best I could do.

I just hoped it would be enough.

Chapter Seven

The appointment was at ten, and I was as ready as I could be. The beds were made. Every counter had been wiped twice. Still, I walked through the house double and triple checking everything.

If time didn't hurry up, I was going to wear a hole in the already worn out floors.

At a quarter to ten, there was a knock on the door.

Good, I thought. They're early.

I hurried to the door and pulled it open. But it wasn't CPS.

It was Jimmy.

It took my brain a moment to process that he was actually standing there. I couldn't even react until after he spoke.

"Hi, Mandy. I'm sorry to just drop by..."

"Oh, Jimmy." A mix of emotions surged through me. Guilt, relief, hope. It was all so overwhelming that I burst into tears. "I'm so sorry."

"What's wrong?" He stepped forward instinctively, putting his arms around me.

"They took the kids." The words tumbled out between sobs. "I've been trying to get them back. Mama left, and I think someone is out to get me, and..." I couldn't stop crying.

These past few weeks had brought more tears than I'd cried since I was eight years old, when Mama's abuse had started and my life turned upside down.

He put his hands on my shoulders and looked me in the eyes. "Wait, what? Back up. Who took the kids?"

"Child Protective Services. They took them. I got a job, and while they were here with the babysitter, CPS came and took them. Someone called in a tip that Mama had left and that I was unfit. They said I was drinking, doing drugs, sleeping around." I was trying to control my crying and get the whole story out. Weeks of stress and exhaustion had left me nearly hysterical. "That's crazy, right? I keep thinking maybe Mama called them, but that doesn't make sense. Do you think she would do that?"

"Whoa, Mandy, slow down. Start with where your mom is." He looked over my shoulder into the house, as if he didn't quite believe my story and needed to see for himself that no one else was there.

"I don't know where she is. She hit Little Davy, so I pushed her and told her never to touch us again. By the end of the week, she was gone." I took a breath. "That was about a month ago. I haven't heard a word from her since."

"And you think she might have called CPS on you? That seems like it would cause her more problems than it solves." He paused, considering. "Then again, after the last year we were together, I don't think I know her at all. Anything is possible." He refocused on me. "So, the kids are in CPS custody. Tell me about that."

"I haven't gotten many answers. But I have a home inspection scheduled for ten, so in just a few minutes." I glanced at the clock. "I don't know if it will get me the kids back. Even though my drug test came back clean, they seem hesitant to give me custody. I've done research, so I know I'm old enough. But I guess in their line of work, they see a lot of bad situations and have to be careful." I shook my head. "Honestly, I'm starting to think they're giving me the runaround. That's what Ms. Graham says too."

I was rambling, which I never did. But I was trying to fill him in on everything, and I was still shocked to see him standing in my doorway.

"Well, I'm their father. I can get them back." His voice was calm, certain. "I assume you're okay with me staying for the home inspection."

"I don't mind. And it's too late to change anything now anyway. They're here."

I gestured toward the driveway, where Mr. Meeks and a mousy looking woman were walking up the sidewalk.

By the looks on their faces, this wasn't going to go well. But they didn't know I had Jimmy on my side now. I had never been one to believe in princes coming to rescue princesses. I didn't see myself as a damsel in distress. I had always believed I could save myself. But this situation might have been beyond my abilities. I needed backup.

"Hello, Mr. Meeks," I said as they stepped onto the porch.

"Hello, Ms. Walker. This is Ms. Jenson. She's here to assist with the home inspection and take photographs." He wore another crumpled suit, this one with a stained tie. He seemed to work constantly but at least managed to change clothes.

Both of them eyed Jimmy with curious, suspicious looks. They were about to get a surprise.

"Let me introduce you to James Palmer," I said. "He's Missy and Davy's father."

Their expressions shifted to shock, though they recovered quickly.

"Mr. Meeks. Ms. Jenson." Jimmy's voice was steady and authoritative. "I understand that my children were removed from Ms. Walker's care without my permission."

"Were you aware that her mother left?" Mr. Meeks asked.

"No. I didn't know until ten minutes ago, when I arrived to visit my children and discovered they were gone. But I'm not surprised. Becca was unfit to be a mother. It's remarkable how well Mandy has turned out despite that."

I felt my cheeks warm at his words.

"So you were aware that Ms. Walker was caring for the children?" Mr. Meeks pressed.

"Yes, I was. She has been caring for my children since they were born." He emphasized the words my children. It was brilliant. "I trust her completely. If I didn't work offshore, I would have custody of them myself. But I left them with Mandy knowing they were in excellent hands. Now I want them returned to her immediately."

I looked at him as if seeing him for the first time. I hadn't known he thought that about me. Was that really why he'd left them here? Because he trusted me that much? Or was this just an act for CPS? I might never know, but if I got the chance, I would ask him.

"We'll need some proof of identity," Ms. Jenson said. "A driver's license, and do you have any paperwork like an AOP? An Acknowledgement of Paternity? You may have signed one when the children were born."

"I do have that. I live about fifteen minutes away. I can run home and get it while you do the inspection, then meet you back here."

They both nodded. I invited them inside, shooting a slightly panicked look at Jimmy.

"You'll do great," he whispered so only I could hear. "I'll be right back."

I nodded and followed Mr. Meeks and Ms. Jenson into the house.

"Where would you like to start?"

"May we see the children's bedroom?" Ms. Jenson asked softly.

"Yes. Currently, they share a room."

I walked them through the living room to the hallway that led to the bedrooms.

"At this end is my room. That end was Mama's, when she was here. And here, between my room and the bathroom, is the kids' room."

I pushed the door open. Seeing their room unused for nearly two weeks sent a fresh wave of tears to my eyes. I blinked to keep them from spilling over.

"As you can see, they have beds, toys, clothes."

Ms. Jenson pulled out a small camera and began taking pictures. Mr. Meeks made notes in his notebook.

"Is there a plan for them to have separate rooms as they get older?" he asked, pen ready.

"If Mama stays gone, I'll move to her room, and one of the children will take mine."

Neither of them responded. They just nodded.

"What would you like to see next?"

"The bathroom," Mr. Meeks said.

After the bathroom, I showed them the rest of the house and the backyard. Ms. Jenson took pictures while Mr. Meeks made notes and asked questions. It felt like a lifetime before Jimmy returned, but finally he did.

"Well, Mr. Palmer, this does prove paternity as far as we're concerned." Mr. Meeks handed back the driver's license and AOP. "And obviously, this is you. Are you both able to come to our office? The inspection here looks fine, but we need our supervisor to sign off. With this new information, it will take some time to get everything in order."

"Does that mean I can have the kids back?" The question burst out before I could stop it.

"I can't say yes for certain, but yes, it's looking very likely."

Relief flooded my body. I wanted to dance. I never danced.

We climbed into Jimmy's truck and followed them to the CPS office in Houston.

The wait at the office was excruciating. We sat in hard plastic chairs while Mr. Meeks disappeared into the maze of hallways. Nearly an hour passed before Ms. Jenson came to get us.

"We can take you to see the children now," she said. "They've been brought over from their foster placement."

My heart leaped into my throat. I was going to see them. Finally.

She led us to a small visiting room with a table and chairs. And there they were. Missy and Little Davy, sitting at the table with coloring books in front of them.

"Mandy!" Missy shrieked and launched herself at me.

I caught her and held on tight, tears streaming down my face. I didn't even try to stop them. Davy toddled over and wrapped his little arms around my legs.

"I missed you so much," I whispered into Missy's hair. "I'm so sorry. I'm so, so sorry."

"It's okay, Mandy. I knew you'd come."

I pulled back and looked at her face, then at Davy's. They looked okay. Healthy. Maybe a little tired, but okay.

"I hope I can take you home today," I said, "but we have to wait until these people say yes." I gestured toward Ms. Jenson, who stood nearby keeping a close eye on us. She shifted her weight and wouldn't meet my gaze. I hoped I'd made my point that this wasn't my fault. I didn't want the kids to resent me. "Look who else is here. Your Daddy came with me."

I needed Missy to remember him, especially with Ms. Jenson watching. The last time she'd seen Jimmy had been so long ago, but I had to hope her memory would help us now.

Missy looked at him. For a moment, nothing. Then her eyes widened with recognition.

"Daddy! Daddy, I missed you!" She threw herself into his arms.

Davy hung back, uncertain. He hadn't seen Jimmy since he was nine months old. He looked at me, then at Jimmy and Missy.

Finally, he gave in to Missy's enthusiasm and toddled over for a hug too. Davy trusted Missy and me to protect him, but he was always cautious with new people.

"Scott is still talking with our supervisor," Ms. Jenson said. "I can take you all to a conference room to wait. It will be more private."

Once in the conference room, she brought us drinks and snacks and put cartoons on the TV for the kids.

"Is there anything else you need?"

"No, thank you, Ms. Jenson," Jimmy said with a warm smile. "Just ready to take the kids home."

She nodded and left us.

We got as comfortable as possible. Little Davy sat with Jimmy, fascinated by this man he'd been told was his Daddy.

Missy told me all about the foster home. How she got to make cookies with the foster mom, Ms. Tia. How they had a little poodle named Buttercup who slept in bed with her.

"Ms. Tia was nice to us. Buttercup is so cute. I'll miss her the most." At four years old, Missy was remarkably articulate and understood her own feelings well. "But I'm ready to go home. Maybe we can get a dog?"

"Maybe," I said, though the last thing I needed was one more creature to care for.

About two hours later, Mr. Meeks finally came into the conference room. We were all anxious to leave, and the kids were getting tired and cranky.

"Good news. My supervisor has approved the release. You can take the children home today."

"Thank you," Jimmy said.

I grinned. "Let's go home, kids!"

Mr. Meeks gave us the children's clothing and car seats and showed us out. He tried to apologize for all the trouble, but I kept my head high and Missy's hand in mine as I walked out of that office.

I knew I was being petty. The past two weeks had been some of the hardest of my life, and in my mind, he bore responsibility for that. If I were honest with myself, I knew he had just been doing his job. But I also knew that if Jimmy hadn't shown up when he did, I might not have gotten the children back this quickly.

Once we were in the truck and headed home, I finally felt my body relax. I sat in the front seat, listening to Missy chatter in the back, watching Little Davy's sweet face break into random smiles and giggles. He kicked his little legs with joy.

It made my heart whole again.

When we pulled up at home, Ms. Graham came hurrying out of her house.

"Oh, look at that! Look at that!" She walked to the edge of her yard, and I went to meet her there. "I'm so happy to see those two beautiful children. How? What happened?"

"Jimmy." I nodded toward him. "He showed up right before the home inspection and saved the day."

"Oh, I'm so happy for you all. What a wonderful day."

"Thank you for all the support. It means so much."

"Of course, of course." We hugged. "Well, I'll let you get those two settled in. Let me know if you need anything."

I helped Jimmy carry the kids' things inside, and we got everyone into the house.

"So, I was thinking," he said once the kids were settled and their belongings put away. "Would you mind if I stayed here a few nights? Maybe until I head back offshore? I could help out with the kids, and I'd love to spend more time with them."

I didn't hesitate. "Sure. You can sleep in Mama's room."

There were three bedrooms in the house, roughly seventeen hundred square feet. I had my own room. Missy and Davy shared. That left Mama's room or the couch.

"That's okay," he said quickly. "I can take the couch."

"Are you sure?" I eyed the couch skeptically. It wasn't comfortable. I should know; I'd been sleeping on it for most of the past week. Threadbare in spots, the support long gone, it sagged badly in the middle.

"It'll be fine. Just a few days."

With that settled, I left to clean a few houses. I had considered canceling, but I knew Jimmy could handle things here, and I needed the normalcy. I gave him my cell phone number in case he needed me.

I hurried through most of my cleaning but kept my weekly tea appointment with Mrs. Lewis. We had a standing date, and no, I didn't get paid for it, though she was one of my regular clients. Today was strictly social.

She was a recent widow, and her children all lived in other states. She had the best stories, and I enjoyed listening to them. I never knew if they were true or embellished. It didn't matter. Telling them brought her joy, so I listened with enthusiasm, even to the ones I'd heard a hundred times.

When I got home that evening, the aroma of cooking hit me the moment I walked through the door. My stomach growled. It was the first time I'd felt genuinely hungry since the kids were taken.

I headed straight to the kitchen.

"Surprise," Jimmy said with a smile when he saw me. "I know dinner is usually your thing, but I figured I could help. You've had a big day and a few stressful weeks."

"That's so nice. I don't mind at all."

He had made pork chops, twice baked potatoes, and green beans. It was wonderful to have someone else cook for a change. I remembered the few times Jimmy had cooked for us when he was dating Mama. It was always delicious.

During dinner, Missy told me all about their afternoon adventures. Jimmy had played along with every one of her imaginary games. Today, apparently, she had been a princess captured by an evil troll. Jimmy and Davy were the brave knights who rescued her.

A bit of reality woven into fantasy. It made me sad to think about, but I supposed this was how she was processing what had happened.

I cleaned up after dinner while Jimmy played Candyland with the kids. I had found the game at a garage sale a few months ago, in near perfect condition.

After a few rounds, he helped with the nighttime routine, supervising their bath while I started some laundry. Once they were clean and dressed in their favorite pajamas, they climbed into Missy's bed for story time. We were still working through Charlotte's Web.

Jimmy listened as I read, and when Missy took over for a few pages, his eyebrows rose. He looked at me and mouthed, "Wow."

I smiled. I was proud of what I'd accomplished with the kids, especially teaching her to read.

Once they were tucked in for the night, I got Jimmy a pillow, blanket, and sheets for the couch.

"Are you sure you want to sleep out here?" I nodded toward the sagging cushions. "Mama's bed is a lot more comfortable."

"I'm sure. I know she's gone, and the room looks spotless. But it still has some memories I can't deal with right now."

"Okay. I understand." I hesitated, then said, "Well, I'm going to turn in early. I've had a lot of sleepless nights lately. Good night."

"Good night, Mandy. Sleep well."

I started down the hallway, then turned back. "Jimmy? Thank you again for showing up when you did. Your timing was perfect."

"You're welcome. I just wish I'd come sooner. I'll never be able to apologize enough for staying away so long." He paused. "Thank you for taking such good care of the kids. You'll never know how much that means to me."

I smiled, feeling heat rise to my cheeks. I had never been good at accepting compliments. I was grateful for the shadows of the hallway.

"Good night," I said again, and headed to my room.

For the first time in weeks, I slept through the night.

Chapter Eight

Jimmy was already awake when I got up. I was used to being the first one moving around in the morning.

"Good morning," he greeted me with a bright smile, then gestured with his coffee mug. "There's coffee."

"Good morning. Thanks so much." I headed for a mug and the pot. "Did you sleep okay?"

"Not awful. You?"

"Better." I took a sip. "Is this new?"

"Yeah, I was up early, so I ran back to my apartment for a change of clothes and a few other things. Including the coffee. You like it?"

"I do." I usually bought the cheapest brand our local grocery store carried. I could get used to this.

"So, I wanted to talk to you before the kids get up." He sat down at the table, and I took a seat across from him. "I plan to file for sole custody. I wanted to ask, not assume, if you'd still want to have guardianship. It would mostly be when I'm offshore, and then when I'm off rotation, I'd have them either here or at my place."

I wasn't completely surprised. We had tabled this conversation the day before. Not having the kids for those few weeks had shown me how hard it would be to lose them. If he took them away entirely, I didn't know what I would do. But this arrangement made sense. With him gone every other month, I would still have them most of the time.

"Yes. That's probably the right thing to do." I wrapped my hands around my mug. "And of course I'd want them here with me, at least as much as it makes sense for everyone."

"Great. I'll start looking for a lawyer who can work with us. We'll figure out all the details after we meet with someone."

The kids woke up shortly after, so I got them cereal while Jimmy ate and then started researching lawyers on his laptop. I could hear him tapping and clicking while I cleaned up the kitchen and got the kids dressed for the day.

"Hey, I think I found one," he called out. I went to join him in the living room. "She's got fifteen years of family law experience and good reviews online. I'll give her a call."

"Sounds good." I knew nothing about lawyers, but I trusted his judgment.

While he was on the phone, I took the kids outside to run around. I didn't want them disturbing his call. Missy immediately organized them into a game of pretend. Her imagination never ceased to amaze me.

Having had to nearly raise myself, I had never gotten to indulge my own imagination. Growing up in survival mode didn't leave much room for make believe. I used to daydream about being free from Mama, but this wasn't exactly what I had pictured back then.

After about thirty minutes, I heard the back door creak and looked up to see Jimmy coming outside to join us.

"She doesn't have any openings until after I'm supposed to be back at work, but after I explained the situation, she's squeezing us in."

"Wow." I was impressed. Most professionals wouldn't rearrange their schedule for a stranger. "So you liked her?"

"Yeah. She seems sympathetic and knowledgeable."

"Well, that's good."

"She wants us to write out statements about everything that happened. Mostly from your point of view." He looked at me. "Are you okay with that?"

"Yes. I'm fine with it. It might even be therapeutic to tell my story."

"Great. So, what's the plan for the day?" He smiled at the kids, who were now chasing each other around the yard.

"Well, we finished our book last night, so we need to return it to the library. They have story time today, which the kids always love."

"Sounds fun. Let's go."

The story time featured Green Eggs and Ham. Both children thought it was hilarious and asked if we could borrow more Dr. Seuss books. I agreed but also picked out Charlie and the Chocolate Factory as our next chapter book. I had read it before but thought the kids would enjoy it.

After the library, we headed to FunStuff Pizza. It was a school day, so the place wasn't crowded. We pretty much had the run of it.

We ordered a pizza and found a table near the play area so we could watch them climb and jump around. The food counter and kitchen ran along one side of the building, with tables and booths positioned around the play equipment. The play area was full of slides, tunnels, climbing ropes, and ladders. In the center was a massive ball pit. Everything was brightly colored and cheerful. I could easily imagine the place packed on weekends.

"I've never been here before," I said, scanning the room.

"No? Your mom...?" He stopped himself and shook his head. "Never mind. I brought Missy here once, before Davy was born. I think she might have been too young to fully enjoy it at the time."

"They seem to like it now." I nodded toward where Missy and Davy were laughing in the ball pit.

Davy's head was sticking up above the balls, and Missy was trying to help him stand, but they were both laughing too hard to make any progress. Finally, they managed it and climbed up into the tunnels above the pit, giggling the whole way. We watched them in comfortable silence for a few minutes, sipping our drinks.

Jimmy glanced at me. His mouth twitched like he was about to say something, then thought better of it. He looked back toward the kids. I suddenly felt awkward. I shifted in my seat and brushed a stray hair from my face.

He turned back to me. "I'm sorry you didn't get much of a childhood. Or a normal high school experience. You had to take on all this responsibility when the two adults who should have been responsible let you down."

The words caught me off guard. No one had ever put it quite like that before.

"Oh, it's okay. For me, this is normal." I shrugged. "I know it probably seems bad from the outside, but I did the best I could. At least I graduated. That's something, right?"

"Definitely. It's a great accomplishment. Finishing early while raising two kids is remarkable."

"I had a few excellent teachers who helped guide me."

"Well, it really is amazing. You've done incredibly well for yourself, including finding ways to support yourself." He leaned forward. "You know, you're quite an entrepreneur. You could probably turn what you're doing into a real business. Get more clients, hire employees. The whole thing."

Something fluttered in my chest at his words. No one had ever talked about my future like it held real possibilities.

"I've actually been thinking about that," I admitted. "I just don't know if I could fit it all in right now with my job at Mr. Burger and my current clients, plus taking care of Missy and Davy."

"Quit Mr. Burger." He said it simply, like it was obvious. "I worry about you spreading yourself too thin. You're going to wear yourself out." He studied me for a moment. "I can help pay for things. Kind of like child support. I've been paying your mom, but hopefully the lawyer can help us get that redirected. I want you to be able to focus on yourself and the kids instead of working yourself into the ground. Life's too short, and you're too young to burn out."

I sat with that for a moment. It felt strange, someone offering to take care of me. I had been the one taking care of everyone else for as long as I could remember.

"I don't know. I mean, I like the people I work with." I paused to process what he was really offering. "Though it would be easier to not be away from the kids so much. I'm already doing the cleaning work."

I looked over at the play area and watched Missy and Davy emerge from a tunnel, their faces flushed with joy. They were my world.

"I don't want to pressure you at all. I'm just looking out for you." He reached over and gave my hand a light squeeze. I felt heat rise to my cheeks at the simple touch. "I'll support you no matter what you decide."

He was right. I had only taken the Mr. Burger job because I thought it was the responsible thing to do. A moment of panic, really. Fear that there was no safety net, as unreliable as that safety net had always been.

Mama was an adult, a legal guardian. She had fifteen years of experience that I didn't have. And after the CPS situation, I knew people might not take me as seriously as they would a parent.

But the truth was, my cleaning work was already a full-time job. It paid the bills. It gave me flexibility, since I could set my own hours. Some of my clients didn't even mind if I brought the kids along in an emergency.

It really was a near perfect situation. I had just been too scared to trust it.

"You're right. I'll quit." The decision felt lighter than I expected. "It'll be easier for everyone, and it's what we're already used to."

"That's great." He smiled warmly. "I think you'll be happier focusing on your business. And I'm glad to do whatever it takes to lighten your load."

Our pizza arrived, and Jimmy rounded up the kids while I put a slice on each plate and cut it into pieces. They bounced over to the table, all smiles and giggles.

"Nandy, did ya see me? Did ya see me?" Davy asked as Jimmy helped him into the booth.

"I did. You were way up there." I pointed to the tunnels and slides.

He looked back at the play area with the biggest grin. His chubby little face was rosy from all the excitement.

"After we eat, you have to play with us," Missy announced. "You will have the mostest fun ever in your whole life. Like, ever!"

"As soon as we all eat lunch," I told her. "Now eat up so we can go play."

We ate while the kids cast anxious glances at the play equipment every few seconds. They were bursting with excitement, and I couldn't blame them. It did look like fun.

Once we finished, we all headed to the ball pit and played for the next hour. We climbed and slid and jumped around together. It was wonderful to let go of worry for a little while and just enjoy the moment with my two favorite people.

Oh, and Jimmy.

I had to work at Mr. Burger that evening for my first closing shift. I decided I would give my two weeks' notice tonight. As I got dressed in my uniform, I rehearsed what I would say. I hated to quit after only a few weeks, but I really did need to focus on Missy and Davy and my clients.

Jimmy was right. Quitting made sense. I wasn't sure what I had been thinking when I took the job in the first place. Panic, probably. The terror of knowing there was no safety net beneath me, however unstable that net had always been.

I thought about starting an official business out of my cleaning work. I was already doing it, really. I just needed to figure out how to make it official. A real, legitimate company. Another step forward that made sense for the kids and for me.

Once I was ready, I went to say goodbye to Jimmy and the kids. They were playing some kind of card game that I was pretty sure Missy had invented. Jimmy looked completely lost, but he was smiling and enjoying their laughter.

"You're still getting off at nine, right?" He laid down a card. "Got ya, Missy."

She giggled. "You didn't get me. That's a two of diamonds. You can't play it on a nine of clubs."

"I'll be there just before nine," he said, then scratched the side of his head as he studied his cards. "Do you know how to play this game?"

"No, she doesn't," Missy spoke for me. "I always beat her too."

"She's right. She wins every time." I kissed her head, then kissed Davy's. "Well, I'm off."

They all waved goodbye. I was walking to work, but Jimmy had offered to pick me up afterward. I appreciated that. I had never walked home that late before, and I didn't like being out after dark if I could help it. Glenn Lake was safe, but better cautious than sorry.

The afternoon was beautiful, and the walk was easy. I passed people walking their dogs, neighbors pushing strollers, folks sitting on porches with iced tea. I waved to the ones I knew, which was most of them. Once I reached the town center, a few shop owners were sweeping their sidewalks or washing windows.

I loved Glenn Lake. It had the perfect balance of small town coziness and diversity, with just enough artistic flair to keep things interesting.

I arrived at Mr. Burger a few minutes early, which gave me time to talk to Marvin, the shift manager. He led me back to the small office.

"Thanks for talking to me." I took a deep breath. "I've never done this before, but I need to give my two weeks notice."

"You just started." Marvin crossed his arms over his chest. He looked upset, and that was the last thing I wanted.

I felt anxiety bubbling up, self-doubt creeping in. Maybe I shouldn't quit. Then I pictured two sweet faces and knew it was the right thing. I squared my shoulders and tried to give a relaxed smile.

"I know. I'm sorry. My brother and sister were taken by CPS. We just got them back, and I feel like I need to focus on caring for them. I really am sorry."

He studied me for a moment. The silence made me nervous. I had never done this before and didn't know what to expect.

Finally, he dropped his arms and relaxed. "That's fine. If you can finish out the current schedule, I'll leave you off after that."

I nodded. "Okay."

"Get clocked in and work the front register."

The evening wasn't too busy, but there was enough of a steady flow that time passed quickly. Before I knew it, my shift was over. I clocked out and handed my register to Marvin to count.

"Looks good," he said after counting it out. "By the way, I found someone to cover the rest of your scheduled shifts, so you don't need to come back."

"Oh. Are you sure? I don't mind finishing out the schedule."

"No, it's okay. Here's your check. You can keep the shirt and name badge."

"Okay. Thanks."

I felt oddly sad as I walked out, but it saved me from having to come back, I supposed.

Jimmy was waiting in the parking lot. I climbed into the truck.

"How was work? You okay?" He must have read something in my expression.

"He gave me my check and said he wouldn't need me anymore. Is that weird?"

"Yes and no. Texas is an at will state, which means they can let you go whenever. And you did give notice, right?"

"Yes."

"So, it worked out." His friendly tone put me at ease. "And you probably won't need a reference from them for future jobs. Not with your business going strong." He winked. "Right?"

He made it sound so simple. Maybe I was overthinking things. That was one of my flaws. But the way he smiled at me made me feel like I could do anything.

"I guess you're right. I've never had a job like that before. I'll miss it a little, but I'd rather be with the kids." I glanced back at them in their car seats. Their eyes were heavy as they fought sleep. "I guess it's another one of those odd, good things that have happened to me."

On the short drive home, he told me about their evening, and I told him about mine. I could hear the kids' slow, steady breathing from the back seat. They had finally given in to sleep. I looked back at their peaceful faces and smiled. It was so good to have them home.

When we got there, we carried the kids inside and settled them into bed. Jimmy was on his laptop in the living room when I came out of my bedroom after showering and changing. We still needed to finish our statements for the lawyer.

"I'm done with mine," he said without looking up from the screen. "Just rereading it one more time. Then you can work on yours."

"Thanks." I sat on the couch and turned on HGTV while I waited.

"Okay, I think mine is good. Your turn."

I sat at the laptop and started typing out my story. It took about thirty minutes to get it all down. Then I proofread it, added a few things, deleted others. In total, it took about an hour.

"I'm finished," I said, turning toward him. "Do you want to send it, or should I?"

"I'll send it. I have already drafted an email. Just need to attach the statements and hit send."

"Okay. Well, I'm going to head to bed. Thanks for everything, Jimmy."

"No, thank you. I can have peace of mind leaving the kids with you." He smiled. "Let's hope everything works out with the lawyer tomorrow."

"Good night."

"Good night, Mandy."

I walked down the hallway to my room, feeling something I hadn't felt in a long time. Not just relief, though there was that.

Something more like hope. Like maybe, for once, things were going to work out.

<h1 style="text-align:center">Chapter Nine</h1>

The next day, Ms. Graham came over to watch the kids. She brought doughnuts and bottles of chocolate milk for them. They loved it. We rarely got doughnuts, and they were getting quite spoiled lately, but after everything they had been through, they deserved it.

We told her what time we expected to be home and headed to the appointment. I was nervous and hadn't slept well the night before. I had tossed and turned, running through various scenarios in my mind. The good, the bad, the ugly. I glanced over at Jimmy. Had his night been as rough as mine? Was he as nervous as I was?

"One thing we need to think about," he said as we merged onto the highway, "is getting you driving. If something happens while I'm away, you need to be able to drive."

My heartbeat kicked up at the suggestion.

Me, drive? The thought was intimidating. But I knew he was right. He had a way of pushing me out of my comfort zone, and maybe that was exactly what I needed.

Driving had been on my mental list of things to eventually learn, but I had never been in a hurry. I had no reason to leave Glenn Lake at the moment. But as the kids got older, they might want to see the beach, or go to a baseball game, or have school field trips that required transportation.

"I know. You're right. But I've never driven before. I've never even turned a car on."

"I can teach you, or we can get you into a driver's ed class. Your choice."

"Maybe. Do you think the class is expensive?"

"Don't worry about money so much. I'm here to help you now." He paused. "I mean, I get it. Money is important. But you aren't alone anymore." He smiled at me, that same smile that made me feel like I could do anything. "Besides, being able to drive is part of taking care of the kids. And if we get you set up as a real business, you'll need transportation. Can't have the boss without a car, right?" He winked.

"Yeah. Can't have that." I felt my cheeks warm, so I turned to look out the window. I hoped he didn't notice the blush. I was used to my older neighbors being kind to me, but I rarely had a man my own age treat me with such respect and encouragement.

We pulled up to the lawyer's office, located in a ten-story blue glass building just outside of downtown Houston. We parked in the attached garage and took the elevator to the seventh floor.

"Hello, welcome to Barker Family Law. Are you Jimmy Palmer?" The receptionist greeted us warmly.

"Yes, I am."

"Great. Please have a seat, and I'll let her know you're here."

A few minutes later, a woman emerged from a side door. My first thought was that she didn't look old enough to have fifteen years of experience, unless she had started practicing law at my age, which I knew wasn't possible.

"Hi, Jimmy. Laura Barker. Nice to meet you." She shook his hand, then turned to me with a smile. "And you must be Mandy."

I nodded.

"Nice to meet you too," Jimmy said. "Thank you for seeing us on such short notice. I know it must have been inconvenient to rearrange your schedule."

"Not a problem at all. It sounded urgent. Why don't y'all follow me back."

She led us to her office and gestured for us to sit. I glanced around. It looked like how I had always imagined a lawyer's office would look. Dark wood furniture, leather chairs, and shelves of law books lining one wall. A few framed photographs sat on her desk, showing two young girls who looked like smaller versions of her with darker complexions and long dark hair.

"I reviewed the statements you both sent, along with the letter Becca left." She folded her hands on the desk. "This is a fairly straightforward case, especially with Mandy turning eighteen in a few weeks. What can CPS say then? We can request that you have custody of your children, Jimmy, and then give Mandy written power of attorney to care for them. We can also request a restraining order so Becca can't contact them, or we can include language about supervised visits. It's up to you. Once a judge approves it, there's nothing she or CPS can do without taking you to court."

"That's exactly what we want." Jimmy leaned forward. "As you know, I'm out of town a lot for work. Mandy has been the primary caregiver since the children were born, and I want that to continue." He glanced at me for confirmation. I nodded. "Also, I forgot to mention on the phone, I currently pay Becca child support. Since she doesn't have the children, is there something we can do to redirect that to Mandy instead?"

"We can definitely add that. We won't be able to change it officially until we go to court, since a judge will have to rule on it." She picked up a stack of papers from her desk and handed them to Jimmy. "Here is the custody agreement and power of attorney for your review. Before I add the child support language, why don't you both look these over to make sure everything else is correct. That way I can make all the changes at once."

We reviewed the documents. Everything looked good. Jimmy told her the amount he paid Mama for the children, and she typed it into the document along with some additional wording. She printed out the revised forms, and we signed everywhere she indicated.

"Okay, now I just need your driver's license or a picture ID to include with the filing, and then we'll request a court date." She smiled. "After I make copies, we can talk about the living arrangements, because that might be a little trickier. There isn't always a clear-cut answer."

I was thankful I had recently gotten a picture ID. I seemed to need it constantly these days. We handed over our IDs and waited while she excused herself to make copies.

"This sounds positive," I said, turning to Jimmy.

"It does. But I'll feel a lot better when it's settled."

I nodded. Nothing was final until a judge signed off on it, but having the wheels in motion was a relief.

Laura returned and handed us a stack of papers, still warm from the printer. That warmth felt like security to me. This stack of documents represented protection for the kids and for me.

"Thank you so much," Jimmy said. "This will give us all some peace of mind."

"You're welcome. This is my favorite part of the job. Helping families stay together." She smiled. "Do you have any final questions?"

"No. But just to confirm, you'll call us when you have a court date, and we'll go from there?"

"Yes. As soon as I get a date, I'll let you know." She turned to me. "And Mandy, I know Jimmy is leaving again soon. If you have any trouble while he's gone, call me immediately. I'm on your side in this."

"Thanks so much." I smiled, feeling a little lighter than I had in weeks.

"It was nice to meet you both. Let me walk you out."

Back in the truck, we headed south toward Glenn Lake. We made small talk but didn't discuss the lawyer or the pending court case any further. As we got close to home, Jimmy suddenly pulled into the empty parking lot of a large, abandoned business.

"Okay. Time for your first driving lesson." He put the truck in park and unfastened his seatbelt.

"Oh, no no no no." I waved my hands in front of me. "I'm not ready. I can't."

"Sure you can. You have to learn sometime, and what better time than now? Come on." He hopped out and jogged around to my side, opening the door. "Don't be scared."

"But don't I need a learner's permit?"

"Technically, yes. But it's fine for a few minutes in a parking lot. We can get you the permit later." He grinned, dismissing my last excuse.

Reluctantly, I got out and walked around to the driver's side. Jimmy showed me how to adjust the seat and mirrors, then explained the basics.

"You move this to D to go forward. The pedal on the left is the brake. The one on the right is the accelerator, or gas pedal." He pointed to each one. "Now put your foot on the brake and move the shifter to drive. Then push the gas, just a little bit."

"I'm not sure about this. But okay."

I put my foot on the brake and slowly shifted into drive. Then I moved my foot to the gas and pushed a little too hard. In my panic, I slammed on the brake, which caused the truck to lurch forward with a sharp jerk.

Jimmy chuckled as he held onto the dashboard. "Try it again, but with a little less oomph. You can do it."

He flashed me one of his warm smiles, and I felt like the little engine that could.

I tried again, this time with less gas, and the truck inched forward. It might have been a snail's pace, but I was moving without giving us whiplash.

"Okay, good. Put a little more pressure on the gas. Just a little. Get a feel for how much to apply." He coached me patiently. "Good. That's it."

We moved across the parking lot, and he instructed me to turn the wheel. Soon I was driving slow but steady circles around the lot. He encouraged me to go a little faster each time until we were moving at a decent speed.

"Now try pulling into a parking spot. Use the lines as a guide."

"Okay." I felt more confident than when we started, though I was still nervous.

I eyed a spot a few yards away and drove down the row until I reached it. I turned the wheel and pulled in, but I didn't land between the lines on the first try. Jimmy had me circle around and try again. It took three more attempts before I got it. Not perfect, but the truck was inside the lines on both sides.

Success.

"Great job! Now drive to the exit and we'll switch. I think it's time to relieve poor Ms. Graham. Missy has probably talked her ears off by now."

I drove to the exit and we switched places. He high fived me as we passed in front of the truck. I was smiling and laughing as I climbed back into the passenger seat.

"Thank you for the driving lesson. That was actually a lot more fun than I expected."

"No problem. We can practice a few more times before I leave. We probably won't be able to get your license until after my next rotation. There's a one-day course for adults you can take once you're eighteen. Then you don't have to do a full driver's ed program."

"Good to know. I'll look it up when we get home."

When we arrived, Little Davy was coloring at the table with Ms. Graham.

"Hello, dears. How did it go with the lawyer?" she asked.

"It went well," Jimmy said, taking a seat next to Davy. "She's going to submit a request for a court date, and hopefully this will all be behind us soon." He looked at Davy's paper. "Great picture, kiddo. Can I color with you?"

"Yeah." Davy handed him a blue crayon.

"Thank you for watching them, Ms. Graham." I hugged her. "As always, we appreciate it."

"My pleasure. I love these children. They're the grandchildren I never had." She smiled at Davy.

He looked up at her and grinned. His little dimples appeared on his chubby cheeks. I dropped a kiss on his head and went to let Missy know we were home.

I found her in their bedroom, sitting on the floor and quietly crying, clutching one of her favorite dolls.

"Oh, sweet girl, what's wrong?" I dropped down beside her and pulled her into my lap.

"I don't want to leave you and Daddy." Her voice broke. "I wanna stay here."

"Oh, baby. You don't have to leave us. We're here for you."

"But..." She hiccupped through her tears. "You went to talk to a lady today about what happened to us. They're going to come take us again."

Fresh sobs shook her little body. My heart ached.

"No, sweetheart. We talked to a lady who wants to make sure that never happens again. She's going to help us. You don't have to worry." I gently wiped the tears from her cheeks with my thumb.

"Really?" She sniffed.

"Really."

She threw her arms around my neck. "I love you, Mandy."

"I love you too, baby girl." I held her tight. "Now let's go thank Grammy for watching you."

She scrambled to her feet and skipped into the kitchen. She gave Ms. Graham a huge hug.

"Thank you for watching us today, Grammy. And Mandy said I never have to leave her again. Those mean people won't come back."

"That's right, little girl. That won't happen again." Ms. Graham gave her an extra squeeze.

Jimmy looked at me with a questioning expression. I mouthed that I would tell him later.

We visited with Ms. Graham a little longer before she excused herself to have dinner with the Daileys. Jimmy took the kids into the backyard to play catch, so I used the quiet time to research getting my driver's license.

I looked up the requirements for Texas. There was a lot of information, but Jimmy was right. I would need to pass the written test, which would give me a learner's permit, then take a one-day adult class, and finally pass the driving test. Simple enough. I could study while he was gone and practice driving when he came back. We still had nearly two weeks before he had to leave.

I printed out the handbook so I could study. I had always been good at school, so this should be manageable. While it was printing, I headed to the kitchen to start lunch. The kids had requested grilled cheese and tomato soup.

They came inside just as I was getting the last sandwich onto the plate. The tomato soup was already in bowls, steaming hot.

"Thanks for lunch, Mandy. This looks good." Jimmy smiled at me.

The kids echoed his appreciation. Little Davy declared it was his favorite, though to be fair, everything was his favorite.

Missy launched into a complete play by play of everything that had happened outside. My heart could have burst with the love I felt for them. I was so grateful to have them home. I would never forget how I had felt when they were gone. That lonely, empty ache was burned into my soul. I would never take them for granted.

Jimmy watched the kids with an expression of love and contentment. Our eyes met across the table, and we shared a smile.

It almost felt like a real family. In some strange, unexpected way, maybe it was.

Chapter Ten

The following two weeks passed in a blur of working and getting things in place for Jimmy's absence. Even though he still had to pay Mama the child support until we went to court, he set up a small direct deposit into my bank account to help me with the children.

I sat down and figured out exactly how much the bills were, then created a budget and payment schedule to keep everything organized. Routine and organization were my mantras for life. They had gotten me this far, and I didn't see any reason to change now.

We also got Missy signed up for preschool at Little Village Learning Center. It turned out to be less expensive than I had expected. A week of tuition was equal to what I earned from cleaning for one client, and I cleaned for at least two or three clients a day. On busy days, I did four. I had thought it would cost a lot more. Ms. Graham promised to help get her there until I could drive, since the school was across town and not easy to walk to with the little ones in tow.

I didn't think Davy was ready for school yet. He still seemed so young and small to me. Jimmy didn't argue. He trusted my judgment. Ms. Graham and Mr. Dixon said they would take turns watching him when I worked. For some jobs, I could bring him along like I always had. He was well behaved.

Missy would be starting a few weeks behind the other children, but I had been working with her for nearly her whole life. She could read, write simple sentences and most common words, and she knew her colors, shapes, and how to count to one hundred. She could even do some basic adding and subtraction.

I figured she would catch up quickly. She had a natural ability to learn. But perhaps I was biased because she was my sister.

When the day came to say goodbye to Jimmy, the mood was somber. The kids sobbed quietly and clung to him.

"I promise I will check in with you as much as I can," he told them. "Phone service and internet can be sketchy out there, but I'll call or email whenever it's possible."

He had left me a number to call if there was an emergency. It went to the company's main office, and they could get in touch with him if there was a problem.

He crouched down to hug the kids one more time, murmuring words of encouragement. Then he straightened and hugged me.

"I'll be back before y'all even have a chance to miss me." His eyes looked a bit teary. When he saw that I noticed, he blinked hard and flashed a quick smile. "And call Laura immediately if you have any trouble. Like she told us."

He turned and headed to his truck. When he reached it, he turned and waved once more. Then he was gone.

I felt instantly alone. It was a strange feeling, because obviously I wasn't alone with both kids standing right beside me. But there was an emptiness I couldn't quite explain. Something I had never felt before.

It was a holiday for the preschool, and knowing Jimmy was leaving, I hadn't scheduled any clients. I wanted to focus on the kids.

"Well, now it's just the three of us. What do you want to do first?"

"Cartoons!" they both yelled.

I chuckled at their enthusiasm and turned the TV to their favorite show. I sat with them for a few minutes, but my mind kept drifting elsewhere.

I was sure the time until Jimmy came home would fly by. But I was nervous. What if Mama came back and caused problems? What if CPS decided they had made a mistake and tried to take the kids again? Several scenarios ran through my head, and none of them were good.

But at least I didn't feel entirely alone anymore. I had a growing number of people on my side, and Jimmy was the most powerful ally when it came to the kids.

For once, I had backup. That counted for something.

Chapter Eleven

Finally, my eighteenth birthday arrived. The relief I felt at reaching this milestone was indescribable. It meant freedom. I was free to make my own choices. Free to leave and never look back. There was nothing Mama could do now, if she ever came back.

For my siblings, it was a different story. If things didn't work out with Jimmy getting custody and Mama returned, they would be stuck with her. And if that happened, I wouldn't leave them. I would never leave them behind. Ever.

Hopefully, the judge would rule in our favor once they heard our case, and none of us would have to worry about the what ifs. But today, I wouldn't think about that. Today, I would focus on celebrating.

Several of our neighbors came over to help. Mrs. Dailey baked her famous strawberry cake with cream cheese frosting. She decorated it simply with soft, looping waves in the icing and placed bright pink candles on top.

Ms. Graham brought vanilla ice cream. Mr. Dixon brought eighteen bright helium balloons.

"One for every year," he declared as he thrust them at me. His broad smile and the crinkles around his eyes were warm and genuine. I loved having him in my life.

His granddaughter, Claire, was visiting for the weekend, so she came along. We had known each other for years. She was the closest to my age of anyone I spent time with, and it was nice to have her there.

She was probably the most stunning person I had ever seen. Her heritage was a beautiful mix of cultures. Her grandfather was Jamaican, her grandmother English, and her father Vietnamese. She had long, thick, toffee brown hair with honey-colored highlights. Her almond shaped eyes were set in a heart shaped face, and her skin was a flawless olive complexion.

When I first met her, her beauty had been intimidating, especially to someone who felt so plain in her own skin. But she was just as sweet and friendly as her grandfather, and her grandmother had been too before she passed.

We had a lovely celebration. Missy and Davy especially loved having everyone over. They ran around laughing, dancing, and hugging each person. The adults played a few card games and visited.

It felt like our own little family. Once again, I was reminded that I wasn't alone in life, even though I often felt that way. I was blessed with these wonderful people who supported me, cheered me on, and loved me like family.

After everyone left, Davy was napping and Missy was coloring at the kitchen table. The phone rang. I thought it would be Jimmy.

"Hello?" I answered with excitement. I felt a blush form across my cheeks.

"Mandy? Hello, it's Mom."

I stared at the phone for a second, blinking in disbelief.

"Hello? Mandy?" she repeated.

"Um, hi, Mama." My voice caught in my throat as the reality set in. It was Mama, not Jimmy. What did she want? Why was she calling?

"Happy birthday, baby girl." She sounded cheerful, almost gushing. "You didn't think I'd forget your birthday, did you? October third. It changed my life forever."

"Thank you, Mama." I managed to choke out the words.

"How are the kids? How are you doing? I'm sure you have everything under control. I swear you were born grown." I couldn't tell if she was being sincere or sarcastic.

"We're all doing well." I wanted to add, like you care, but I kept my mouth shut.

"Aren't you going to ask how I am?"

I wanted to say no. Instead, I asked. No sense upsetting her. I was upset enough for both of us. I didn't trust her. Not after knowing her for eighteen years.

"Well, I'm in Florida right now. Doing well. Living with a man named Mike. I'm sober. Trying to clean up my act, you know." She went on, but I stopped listening.

She always said what she thought I wanted to hear when she thought I wanted to hear it. I had heard it all before. Her words had become meaningless. I needed actions, not words. Love, not abuse.

"That's nice, Mama," I said when she finally finished her update. "I'm glad you're happy and doing well." I tried to sound supportive, but I wasn't. I just wanted this call to end.

"Thank you." There was a male voice in the background that I couldn't quite make out. "Oh well, I better go. Mike is grilling us some fish, and he just said it's ready. I have a little cake here too, so I can celebrate my baby girl's birthday."

"Oh. Well, have a good evening. Thanks, Mama."

I was left shaken by the call. So much for my feeling of freedom, when a simple phone call could send me spiraling. She was acting as if nothing had happened. As if everything was fine.

For her, life was dandy. She was in Florida with some man, having grilled fish and cake. Meanwhile, we had spent years suffering under her abuse and neglect. You don't get over something like that overnight. Did she think we had simply forgotten? Or was it that she had forgotten?

The phone rang again. I almost didn't answer it. But I took a deep breath. I had to have courage if I was going to protect my brother and sister.

"Hello?"

"Happy birthday!" It was Jimmy.

I burst into tears.

"Mandy, what's wrong?"

"Mama called." I said it through my sobs. "I just hung up with her. Why did she call? Why does she even care?"

"Oh, Mandy, I'm sorry. It'll be okay." His voice was calm and steady, and it helped settle my nerves.

"But what if she tries to come back?"

"We have our hearing soon, and with that paperwork filed, I'm sure everything will be fine. You can also call Laura Barker like she told you."

His voice was reasonable and reassuring. Exactly what I needed. Someone saying out loud what my own internal voice was trying to tell me over the other voice in my head. That other voice was my mother's.

You ruined my life, it would say.

"I hope you're right," I said. "She told me she's living with someone in Florida. Said she had a cake to celebrate my birthday." I laughed bitterly. "What a joke. She never celebrated before. She would just drink herself into a stupor and then yell at me about ruining her life. Happy birthday to Mandy, the life ruiner."

"She thinks that's what love should be. She doesn't understand that it isn't love, that it's not how you treat people." His tone stayed light and encouraging. "Don't let her get you down. It's your birthday, Mandy the lifesaver. At least that's what you are to me and Missy and Little Davy." He paused. "Did Mrs. Dailey make you a cake? I love her cakes."

I smiled despite myself. "Yes. Strawberry with cream cheese frosting. It was so good."

We caught up for a few more minutes. I told him how the kids were doing, and he confirmed his travel plans for the following week. We had planned for him to move in with us full time when he got back.

The plan was to switch bedrooms around so he wouldn't have to sleep on the couch. I would move into Mama's room, and he would take mine. It would be strange, but we thought it could work.

"Well, I better let you go. I'll see you Thursday. Enjoy the rest of your day."

"Thanks, Jimmy. See you Thursday."

After we hung up, I sat for a moment, letting the two phone calls settle in my mind. One had shaken me. The other had steadied me.

Maybe that was what having people in your corner really meant. Not that the bad things stopped happening, but that you didn't have to face them alone.

Chapter Twelve

The next day was my driving class. I had taken my written test a week earlier and received a perfect score. Still, I was nervous about the actual driving.

Ms. Graham dropped me off and took the kids to the zoo. They had never been before, and I hoped they would love it. I had gone once on a school field trip. Mama hadn't had the money for the admission fee, but Ms. Graham had paid my way.

I owed that woman so much. She had always taken care of me.

The driving class was interesting. I learned a few things I hadn't known before and reinforced what I had studied. A bit more practice, and I would be ready to get my license.

Ms. Graham and the kids were waiting for me when the class ended. Missy immediately launched into a detailed recap of their day at the zoo. Little Davy was out like a light in his car seat, clutching a stuffed tiger that Ms. Graham had bought for him. Missy had an elephant.

"And they were giving them a bath when we got there. You go to the elephant barn, and they have this big window. The zookeepers talk about the elephants while another one gives them a bath. They had the cutest little baby elephant. She was only a few months old. Then we saw the bears and the lions and the zebras. Oh, and they had a petting zoo!" She barely paused for breath.

I smiled and made encouraging sounds. "Oh yeah? Wow, that sounds amazing."

When we got home, I thanked Ms. Graham as I scooped Davy out of his car seat. He snuggled against my shoulder with a soft sigh. My heart warmed as I looked down at his peaceful face. I would never tire of this feeling.

Inside, I got Davy settled on the couch, still asleep. Missy grabbed a book and curled up under a blanket on the other end.

With them occupied, I logged into the computer to check my email. Nothing new from Jimmy. Just some bills and inquiries from potential new clients.

My disappointment at not seeing his name in my inbox surprised me. But it shouldn't have. His emails always had something encouraging in them, something that made me smile. I was really looking forward to seeing him in a few days.

I clicked through the messages, responded to a few, and starred the bills so I could find them easily when it was time to pay. Then I reviewed my schedule for the next day. Three houses. Not a bad day. Mr. Dixon was going to watch Davy.

I tried to distract my mind, but my thoughts kept drifting back to Jimmy. I had never had a crush on anyone before. Was that what this was?

No. It couldn't be. First of all, he was Mama's ex. The father of my half siblings. That was too strange. He was just one of those kind, helpful people who had come into my life at the right moment. He was a friend. A really handsome friend.

I shook the thought away and pushed back from the computer.

Missy had moved to their room, so I went to join her. We played together for about thirty minutes before Davy woke up and wandered in, still groggy. He climbed into my lap and watched us, giggling occasionally.

I asked him about the zoo between rounds of playing with Missy. He said he liked the tigers best and that the lions were big. He also told me about eating cotton candy.

"It was sooooo nummy in my tummy, Nandy." He rubbed his stomach with a look of pure bliss. "Have you haded cotton candy, Nandy?"

"I have. And I agree, it is very yummy in the tummy." I tickled him.

He giggled and squirmed.

"I'm so glad you had fun. You'll both have to thank Ms. Graham. Maybe draw her a nice picture."

"Yes! I want to draw a picture for her right now." Missy jumped up, put her dolls away, and ran out of the room.

"Me tooo," Davy said, scrambling after her.

I looked down at the doll still in my hand. "I guess we're done for today, dolly. Back you go."

I placed it in the bucket and followed the kids to the kitchen. I helped them get colored paper from the drawer and set out the crayons.

These were things I had bought with my cleaning money. Thanks to back-to-school sales the previous summer, I had stocked up on paper, crayons, markers, and scissors. I used them to teach Missy, and they helped Davy with his fine motor skills. He couldn't really draw last year, but with practice, he was getting better every day.

They each made a picture for Ms. Graham. When they finished, they were so excited that they wanted to deliver them immediately. I agreed, and we walked next door.

"Well, hello. What do I owe this pleasure?" She opened the door with a warm smile.

"We drew you these to say thank you for taking us to the zoo!" Missy announced. Davy nodded enthusiastically.

"Oh my, aren't these lovely." She studied them carefully. "Let me guess. This is the baby elephant getting a bath." She looked at Missy, then turned to Davy's picture. "And this must be the tiger. I would recognize him anywhere."

They were both proud of themselves and thrilled that she knew what the pictures were. In fairness, Missy's did look like an elephant. Davy couldn't quite draw yet, but at least he had gotten the colors right. Orange and black.

She hugged them both.

"I just made some cookies. Would you like to come in for one or two?"

They were inside before I could even answer.

"I guess that's a yes," she said with a chuckle.

The kids climbed onto the stools around her kitchen island. She heated water for tea and set a juice box in front of each child along with a warm cookie fresh from the oven.

"I made them for our church potluck tomorrow. As always, I made some extra for these two." She nodded toward the children.

They happily munched their cookies and continued talking about the zoo. I could tell they had really loved it.

Then Missy changed the subject to school. They were learning about circles, and she announced that she was the best at drawing them. Then she jumped topics again, talking about how Daddy was coming home on Thursday.

Davy perked up. "Daddy? Morrow?"

"No, on Thursday." Missy said it slowly and with great emphasis, as if speaking more clearly would help him understand.

"Oh," he said with a dazed expression. He had no concept of days of the week yet.

"He's still too little to understand how the days work," I explained. "But don't worry. He'll get it."

"I not little. I big. Look at my muscles!" Davy bent his arms to show off.

"Oh my, those are big muscles," Ms. Graham exclaimed, giving his arm a gentle squeeze. "You're getting so big, Davy. We'll have to stop calling you Little Davy."

"Yes. I big Davy now."

He stood up in his chair and pushed out his chest, hands on his hips, head held high like the superheroes he had seen in cartoons. He was adorable.

I drank in the moment. How could Mama have walked out on this? They weren't even my children, just my siblings, and I loved them more than I could explain.

"I can't tell you how much it means to have your help and support," I said to Ms. Graham, pulling her into a hug. "I couldn't have made it this far without you."

"You're welcome, dear. I'm more than happy to help. Like I've said many times, you're like a granddaughter to me. I think I get as much out of helping you as you do."

She sent us home with a small bag of cookies, adding that they could only have them if they ate all their dinner.

"We will," Missy said, speaking for both of them.

Davy nodded without taking his eyes off the bag.

We headed home so I could start dinner. The evening unfolded like usual. Playtime, dinner, bath, story time, then bed for the kids.

After they were asleep and I had finished my nightly cleaning, I got myself ready for bed. It was nice not having to hide at night anymore. No more sneaking in, hoping not to get caught. No more cleaning up beer cans, broken bottles, and cigarette butts. The house no longer smelled like vomit and smoke.

It smelled like home cooking and clean laundry. It sounded like the laughter of little children. Hand drawn pictures hung on the fridge. There were no random strangers wandering in and out at all hours. No worries about waking up next to someone I didn't know.

And soon, Jimmy would be back.

The thought half surprised me and half didn't. I had never believed in knights in shining armor or Prince Charming. I believed in working hard and protecting myself. But I let him be my last thought before drifting off to sleep.

I guess Missy wasn't the only one with a vivid imagination.

Chapter Thirteen

The following week flew by as we went about our normal routine. Work and school, home and family time. Before we knew it, Thursday had arrived.

Missy didn't want to go to school that morning. I promised her that Daddy would be there when she got home, or soon after. He had said he should arrive just after lunch if nothing went wrong.

But that was my life. A series of things going wrong. Things had been going well for a while now, and part of me was waiting for the other shoe to drop.

After dropping Missy off at school, Ms. Graham kept Davy while I headed to the Wilsons. In addition to my regular cleaning, I had agreed to cook some meals for them to keep in the freezer. They provided the ingredients, and I put everything together. It seemed to be working well so far.

When I arrived, I let myself in and got straight to work. I washed dishes, started a load of laundry, then moved on to cooking, labeling containers, and loading their freezer. I included grilled chicken and salad for their dinner that night, which I left in the fridge.

By the time I finished, I had created a week's worth of meals, done all the dishes, and completed two loads of laundry. It took most of the morning, but I always felt good about my work.

After that, I headed to Mr. Dixon's to mow his yard and weed the front landscaping. Claire was visiting, so we chatted for a few minutes while I pulled out the mower.

"I'm heading to the store if you need anything," she offered.

"Can you grab me a gallon of milk?" I tried to hand her a five.

"My treat. You're so wonderful to Granddad. I think I can spend a couple bucks on you."

"Thanks, Claire!"

She drove off, and I got to work. Forty-five minutes later, the front and back were mowed and edged, and the landscaping was weeded. I was putting the equipment in the garage when Claire came home.

"Good timing," she said as she got out of the car. "It looks great. I know Granddad loves having your help, and I appreciate not having to worry about him so much."

"I enjoy it, especially helping him out. He's done a lot for us."

"Has he been out to see you? I don't think he's feeling well." She pursed her lips with worry.

"Yes, he came out with some ice water for me, and we chatted for a minute. But I think you're right. He said his back was bothering him again. Said we must be getting a storm soon."

She chuckled. "He's almost always right about that."

I helped her carry the groceries inside and said goodbye before heading home with my milk.

When I got to the house, my stomach did a little flip at the sight of Jimmy's truck in the driveway. I heard him playing with Davy in Ms. Graham's backyard, so I went into our house first to put the milk away, then headed over.

"Nandy!" Davy exclaimed when he saw me.

"Hey, kiddo." I scooped him up into my arms, then smiled at Jimmy. "Hi. Welcome back."

"Thanks. Good to be back." He walked over and gave me a quick hello hug.

It was a brief embrace, but it felt like security and protection. And something else I couldn't quite name.

Ms. Graham was sitting on her porch. I waved as I walked over to sit beside her. She asked about my day, and I asked how Davy had been for her, though I already knew the answer. He was always well behaved. We watched Jimmy and Davy kick a ball around for a few minutes before it was time to pick up Missy.

"She's going to be so excited that you made it in time," I told Jimmy. "She didn't want to go to school today because she was afraid she'd miss seeing you."

"I can't wait to see her either. I couldn't get here fast enough." He held out his keys to me.

"You want me to drive?" I asked, surprised but excited. I wanted to show him how much I had improved.

"Yep. Ms. Graham said she's been letting you practice. She thinks you're ready."

"Well, yeah. I think I am." I walked confidently to the driver's side and slid in.

We drove to Missy's school. I parked, and Jimmy gave me a high five.

"You're definitely ready for that driving test," he said.

When we got to Missy's classroom, she came running.

"Daddy! I missed you!"

She started introducing him to her teacher and friends. He had met the teacher before, but they both pretended for Missy's sake that they hadn't.

Then we all loaded up to head home. Missy talked the entire trip, filling her Daddy in on everything he had missed.

"And Joey was mean to me today. He said girls are gross and boys are the best. Then he tried to push me, but I was too fast. So Ms. Christy put him in timeout and made him say sorry. He's always mean. My friend Lily brought a picture of her dog for show and tell. It's a black and white dog, the kind the mean lady in the cartoon wants to make into a coat. I'm supposed to bring my show and tell tomorrow. I'm bringing the doll with brown hair that you gave me, Daddy. That's my second favorite. My other favorite is the blonde one with curly hair that Mandy gave me. I took that one last time."

She could certainly talk, and she remembered everything. I wasn't sure she even paused to breathe between sentences.

"I missed this," Jimmy whispered to me. "I missed all of this." Then he sat back with a contented smile.

When we got home, the kids pulled him inside to show him all the pictures they had drawn. Missy showed him her schoolwork. Davy started showing him random things around the house, most of which weren't new. He had missed the point of what Missy was trying to do, but it was so cute that neither Jimmy nor I corrected him.

Jimmy acted excited about each and every thing. He smiled over at me. Watching them made me happy, and my heart skipped a beat. Then I felt that strange feeling again when I looked at him. The one I couldn't quite explain. I told myself it was just the kids' excitement rubbing off on me.

I left them and went to start dinner.

As I cooked, I heard footsteps coming down the hall. I looked up as Jimmy walked into the kitchen. He had been playing with the kids in the bedroom.

My breath caught a little when I saw him.

He had taken off his jacket and was wearing a plain black t shirt. His arm muscles strained against the sleeves, and the barbed wire tattoos on each arm were visible. His dark hair was getting longer than he usually kept it, almost a messy, out of bed look. His dark gray eyes had a spark to them. He looked happy and relaxed.

Had he always been this handsome? It was like I was seeing him in a new light. I had to mentally shake myself to stop thinking like that.

Okay. Maybe I did need to admit this was a crush. But not today. I wasn't ready.

"Smells good in here. What's on the menu tonight?" he asked.

"Sausage and peppers with pasta, salad, and garlic bread."

"Sounds great. I missed your cooking almost as much as I missed the kids." He smiled and got a glass of water. "The food on the rig isn't bad, but it's not home cooked good. Especially when you're the cook."

"Thank you. I made this at the Wilsons today, and it sounded good." I blushed at the compliment. I was never good with them, even simple ones. Thankfully, my back was turned, so he didn't notice.

We were silent for a minute. The only sounds were the kids' voices from down the hall and the tick of the kitchen clock.

"Did your mom call again, or just that one time?" he asked.

"Just that one time. I'm glad. I don't really want her back in my life or the kids' lives. We're so much better off without her."

"Yeah. You're all better off without her." He looked down at his feet.

More silence. Why were we suddenly so awkward around each other? Well, I knew why I was. I couldn't stop thinking about his arms and that smile. I felt my cheeks flush and turned to stir the sausage that didn't need stirring. At least it gave me an excuse to look away.

"Do you need help with anything?" he asked, glancing around.

"No, I've got it handled. If you want to play with the kids or watch TV, that's fine." I turned and smiled at him, trying to sound casual. I hoped it came across that way and not as self-conscious as I suddenly felt.

"Okay. Holler if you need anything." He nodded and started down the hall, then paused at the doorway. He glanced back at me, and for just a second, something flickered in his expression that I couldn't read. Then he continued on to the kids' room.

I sighed. Why were we being so awkward? Was it just me? A crush? Or just getting used to each other again after he had been gone?

"It's just the time apart," I whispered to myself. "I don't have crushes. I have kids to raise. Sort of."

I looked over my shoulder to make sure Jimmy hadn't come back. I was alone, so I focused on cooking.

Once dinner was ready, I called everyone to the table. Missy filled the conversation, and Jimmy asked her lots of questions. Davy contributed mostly nods and giggles. At least there was no awkward silence.

After dinner came the regular evening routine. Bath, story time, bed for the kids. Before long, it was just Jimmy and me.

We sat in silence for a few minutes until I decided to share what I had been working on.

"So, I've been thinking about what you said. About starting my business as a real company. I did some research. Want to see what I found?"

"Of course," Jimmy said, brightening.

I turned on the computer and showed him the websites I had bookmarked, then went over my notes. This conversation was much easier than the awkward one before dinner.

"I'm just not sure where to start. I guess I need a company name and then register for a tax ID?"

"Yeah, that's where I'd start." He looked from the computer to me. "I can help while I'm home. I think you need to set up guidelines for what services you offer and any other policies you can think of."

"That's a good idea." I wrote it in my notes. "I do a little of everything right now. Mostly house cleaning and yard work, but I also cook."

We were both quiet for a moment. Not the awkward silence from before, just both of us thinking. We chatted about it for a few more minutes before saying goodnight.

The next day, we rearranged the house to fit Jimmy into it. I moved my things into Mama's old room, and Jimmy took over mine.

It was a task I couldn't have done alone. I had needed to wait for him to help move the larger furniture. I had taken care of the smaller things while he was gone.

Moving the bedrooms around solved several problems. It got Jimmy off the uncomfortable couch, gave him some privacy, and helped me clear away more remnants of Mama.

I was thankful to have him so close in case something happened again with the kids. And he was extremely helpful. I actually had more free time with him here.

I usually took weekends off, but since my driving test was scheduled for Monday, I took advantage of Jimmy being there to watch the kids and moved my Monday clients to the weekend. I didn't want them to miss out.

Overall, it was a good weekend. It was nice to have Jimmy back. The house felt complete now. Like a home, not just a house.

Chapter Fourteen

On the morning of my road test, we made arrangements for Davy to stay at the daycare for the day. Jimmy thought it would be good for him to start going part time, and this could be a trial run. I had been hesitant at first because he was still a baby in my eyes, but Missy had been there for almost two months now, and I thought Davy might enjoy it too.

I was nervous when we pulled up, but he was grinning from ear to ear.

"I a big boy now, Nandy," he assured me.

His confidence helped me relax. Maybe we were doing the right thing.

"Yes, you are. You're going to have so much fun today."

We walked him to the classroom for his age group and were greeted by his teacher. She showed us around, pointed out where to put his bag, and introduced him to the other children. He smiled at them. The teacher directed the kids to a table with puzzles, and Davy glanced at us once before joining in.

I almost cried watching him. He was growing up so fast.

"He'll be fine," Jimmy whispered in my ear.

I smiled at him and looked once more before we walked out and took Missy to her class. She ran in, greeting her friends and teachers with enthusiasm.

"Bye, Mandy! Bye, Daddy!" She waved as she joined her classmates.

My brother and sister were growing up, and there was nothing I could do to slow it down. I might as well embrace it. Honestly, I was proud of them and happy they were getting these experiences. Time to just be little.

We had to drive to another town for my road test. Even though Glenn Lake had a DMV office, it was a small operation that only handled renewals, IDs, and written tests. Not the driving portion.

When we arrived, I already had all the necessary paperwork, so I drove the truck into the driving test line to wait. There were two cars ahead of me. Jimmy stayed to keep me company.

"Nervous?" he asked.

"A little. What if I fail?"

"You won't. You've been practicing for weeks. You parallel parked perfectly last time."

"That was in an empty parking lot. This is different."

"It's the same skill. You've got this." He smiled at me. "And if you don't pass, we just come back. No big deal."

Somehow that made me feel better. The pressure lifted a little.

I watched the car ahead of us pull forward. "This time last year, I never would have imagined being here."

"Waiting in a DMV line?"

"Any of it. Having my own business. Getting a license. Having help." I glanced at him. "Things are really different now."

"Good different, I hope."

"Yeah. Good different."

He smiled, and I felt the last of my nervousness ease.

Finally, it was my turn. Jimmy hopped out, and the officer climbed into the passenger seat. He introduced himself, and I handed him my paperwork. He reviewed it quickly, nodded that everything was in order, then directed me to parallel park.

I mentally crossed my fingers and said a quick prayer before following his instructions. When I finished, he got out and checked my position. He gave me a thumbs up before climbing back in.

I gave myself a mental high five.

We drove around for the next fifteen minutes as he directed me this way and that. Forward, park, backward, then back to the DMV. Finally, he told me to pull into an empty parking spot near the entrance. I sat there while he reviewed my score.

He handed me a paper.

"Congrats. Take this to line two."

That was it. I had passed. I could legally drive now. In my mind, I was officially a grown-up.

Jimmy met me at the door. I gave him a double thumbs up and a cheesy grin.

"So that means you passed? Congrats!" He gave me a quick hug.

"Yes! He said I need to go to line two."

"Want me to wait with you or sit?"

I glanced at the line. It didn't look too long.

"You can sit. It shouldn't take long."

He found a seat while I went to stand in line. After a few minutes, it was my turn. I handed the woman behind the desk my paperwork. She typed some information into the computer, asked me to step back for my picture, clicked a few more buttons, and printed out my temporary license.

"The actual license should arrive in seven to ten days. Next!"

A lot of buildup for a piece of paper, and the DMV staff seemed thoroughly unimpressed. But I was licensed and happy to have reached another milestone. Jimmy seemed more excited than I was.

"This is great! Now we need to work on getting you a car. Want to go look?"

"Not yet. I want to save up a little more first. Soon, though."

"I can help. You do so much, and nobody looks out for Mandy."

After thinking for a moment, I said, "Okay. Let's at least look."

He let me drive and gave me directions to a nearby dealership. It was where he had gotten his truck, and he had known the salesman since kindergarten.

We pulled in, and he asked for Ty. A few moments later, a lanky cowboy with red hair cut into a flat top came striding over with a big grin.

"Hey, bro, what's up?" The cowboy said when he reached us.

He and Jimmy did one of those bro hug handshake things that guys do. I fought the urge to roll my eyes, but seeing Jimmy with his friend was funny and a little endearing.

"Not much, man. This is Mandy. Mandy, this is my buddy Ty."

"Hi, Mandy. Nice to meet ya. Heard a lot about you. So, whatcha looking for?"

"I'm not really sure. I never thought I'd own a car." I paused to consider. "Something used and not too expensive. Enough room for at least two car seats in the back. And air conditioning, of course."

"I think we can find you something. Let's walk over here."

I noticed him and Jimmy exchange a look. Had they planned this? No, couldn't be. It must have been more guy stuff I didn't understand.

We looked at a few cars. They were fine, but nothing caught my eye or felt like me.

"Well, we just got a car in that might fit the bill," Ty said. "It's in the back getting detailed right now. Let me see how close they are to finishing."

He jogged off. Jimmy and I browsed the cars nearby.

"If you want," he said, "I could cover the monthly payments, and you pay the down payment. That way you could get something a little newer, and it might open up your options. Just a thought."

"I appreciate it. Maybe. But I don't want to owe you or anyone."

"I promise this isn't something I expect you to pay back. It's a gift. It'll give me peace of mind while I'm away, knowing you have reliable transportation. I care about you, and I want you to have things you've never had."

I smiled at him. His offer was sweet, and I knew he was sincere. But I would have to think about it. Chances were good I would give in. I really could use a reliable car.

"Okay, okay. Let's see what this car is. If we don't like it, I'll take you up on your offer."

Ty came back driving a blue Chevy Malibu. It was in good condition. At first glance, I couldn't see anything major wrong with it. Just a few slight door dings that were barely noticeable. My pulse quickened as I looked it over.

Could this be my car?

He held the door open and gestured for me to look inside. The interior was immaculate. Spacious for a small to midsize car. Standard radio. The AC seemed to work, which was critical for Texas heat. My excitement grew.

"So, this is a Chevy Malibu," Ty said. "Priced at eighty-five hundred, and we can do that with tax, title, and license. All in. What do you think? Test drive?"

"Yes. I'd like that."

Right price, right style. I tried not to let my emotions show, but the moment he drove up, I had felt it in my bones. This was my car. I wanted to squeal with joy.

Don't get ahead of yourself, I thought. Test drive first.

"Of course. Take it out, and when you get back, we can talk more. Just look around or ask for me. I'll probably be inside."

Jimmy climbed into the passenger seat as I adjusted the driver's seat and mirrors. We pulled out of the lot, and I knew within less than a mile that I was driving my new car.

After a few blocks, I pulled into a parking lot so Jimmy could test it and give me his opinion. He had more experience than I did.

"This is nice. Drives smooth," he said as he drove. "What do you think?"

"I like it. It feels like a good fit. But do you think I could offer less? Maybe seventy-five hundred?"

"I think that's fair. He can say no and counter, or he can accept. What do you have to lose?" He smiled. "And my previous offer still stands if this doesn't work out."

"Thanks. I think I'm going to buy it, even if he doesn't take my lower offer. But obviously, don't tell him that."

The excitement bubbled up and escaped as a giggle. Jimmy looked over and smiled.

"Exciting, huh?"

"I never thought I'd be able to get a car. At least not at this point in my life. I knew it would happen someday, but that day is today." I could barely sit still.

"I'm happy you're able to take these steps for yourself now instead of waiting."

We got back to the dealership, parked, and headed inside to find Ty. He met us at the door and led us to his office. I made my offer. They accepted. After all the paperwork was signed, that was it.

I had a car.

I was giddy as I followed Jimmy back to Glenn Lake. I couldn't believe I had a car and my license. This was the best day.

We dropped Jimmy's truck off at the house, moved the kids' car seats into my car, and headed to pick them up. We were both anxious to hear how Davy had done.

When we arrived, the director, Brenda, came out of her office to greet us and give us an update.

"He did great. He really fit in well. Made friends quickly and joined right in with every activity."

"That's wonderful," Jimmy said. He hesitated, glancing at me. "I think we'd like to have him come full time."

That caught me off guard. We had only talked about part time. But it would definitely help me work more without worrying about overburdening Ms. Graham or Mr. Dixon. My sense of relief surprised me.

"Wonderful! We'd love to have him. Since you already filled out the paperwork for today, we don't need anything new. Just bring diapers, extra clothes, and so on. Like you did today."

I couldn't believe how easy that had been. Why hadn't I looked into this sooner?

I thought about how I probably would have gotten here eventually on my own. But having Jimmy's support and encouragement helped me move forward faster. He gave me the push I needed to build my confidence and get my life going. Most of what I had done before had been about survival, not actually living. That was changing now.

We thanked her and headed to the toddler room. Davy was playing with another little boy, stacking blocks and chattering in a mix of baby talk and real words. My heart melted. He was adorable.

When he saw us, he announced to his new friend that his Nandy and Daddy were there.

"Nandy! Daddy! This is my friend Wyan."

"Hi, Ryan," I said.

The boy grinned but didn't reply.

"Are you ready to go home, Davy?"

"No go home yet, Nandy. I playin'."

"You can come back and play again tomorrow," Jimmy told him.

Davy shook his head and kept building his tower.

"I got a new car. Do you want to see it?"

His face lit up. He told Ryan he would be back later, then said goodbye to the other children and his teacher. We grabbed his bag and headed to Missy's room. She was thrilled to hear that Davy would be coming to the same school.

"I saw him on the playground today and waved. He was playing with some other kids. My bestest friend Olive and I talked to him. He looked happy." She paused just long enough to notice the car.

"Oh! This is a pretty car. I like blue. Blue is my favorite color. But I also like pink. Pink might be my favorite. Do they sell pink cars? When I grow up, I'm getting a pink car."

I think she'd had a good day.

For the next week, we fell into a routine. I worked. The kids went to school. Jimmy tackled projects around the house.

I had done the best I could with the old house, but mostly that meant keeping it clean and cooking meals. I didn't have much knowledge of carpentry, flooring, or plumbing.

Jimmy fixed the bathroom faucet that had leaked since I moved into this house thirteen years ago. He patched the holes in the walls from Mama's parties and painted every room. He replaced the kitchen flooring that had worn down to the subfloor in spots from years of neglect. He had plans for more projects too. Screen doors on the front and back. Repainting the exterior.

Since I was sleeping in Mama's old room now, Jimmy decided to surprise me by painting it. Unfortunately, I came home while he was in the middle of it.

"Oh, wow. This looks great."

He jumped slightly. "Mandy! You're home. I was hoping to be further along."

"No, this is going to be amazing. I love this color."

"I knew you wanted blue. Hope you don't mind that I picked this one." He looked at me hopefully.

"I was struggling to choose. I love it. It makes it feel a lot less like Mama's room."

"The only problem is I'm not sure it'll dry in time for bed. Or that the smell will fade enough for you to sleep in here."

"That's okay. I'll sleep on the couch."

"Or you can take my bed, and I'll take the couch."

"We'll figure it out later. I really appreciate all the help. It's almost like a new house."

After the paint dried, I added curtains I had found at one of the thrift shops in town. I had driven to a few stores in surrounding cities before finding what I wanted right here in Glenn Lake.

With the paint and curtains, plus some artwork I found, and my own belongings in the room, it didn't feel like Mama's space anymore. It felt like mine. I had never had a room like this before. It felt good to make something my own.

Jimmy also traded our old, stained couch for his cleaner one. His wasn't brand new, but it didn't smell like stale cigarette smoke or have mystery stains. The fabric on our couch had been thinning and tearing in places. It was soft and fresh and still had cushion support.

I took on a few new clients and stayed busy. Most days I cleaned four or five houses, sometimes more, sometimes less. For the first time, I bought a planner to keep track of appointments. With so many clients now, I needed a system.

My new company was called Helping Hands by Mandy. Maybe not the most creative name, but I liked it. Once I had the name, I applied for a tax ID and figured out how to pay my share of taxes. What had started as something a child was doing had become a real business almost overnight.

I couldn't have been prouder of myself.

Things in my life had finally started to look up.

Chapter Fifteen

Missy received her first invitation to a birthday party. That was something I had never experienced. I had gotten one invitation when I was young, and Mama refused to let me go. No reason. She just wouldn't take me.

After that, no one invited me again. Most of the kids thought I was weird anyway.

I would make sure Missy got to attend every party she was invited to.

This one was for her friend Olive, or as Missy called her, her bestest friend in the whole world. The party was at Glenn Lake Park on Saturday.

Jimmy and Davy were going fishing with Mr. Dixon while I took Missy to the party. Davy was thrilled to spend the day with his two favorite guys. It was all he could talk about for days beforehand, and I wasn't sure I would get him to sleep the night before.

These were the little moments I loved witnessing. My brother and sister were getting to enjoy being children, making fun memories, not having to worry about anything. It was why I worked so hard.

When we arrived at the park, we saw an inflatable bounce house, a petting zoo, and the pavilion covered in pink and green streamers and balloons. Kids were running everywhere. Some yelled out to Missy, and she waved, but her eyes were scanning for one specific person.

"Missy!" Olive broke free from the woman she was talking with and ran toward us. The girls hugged, then ran off hand in hand to play.

"Hi, you must be Mandy. I'm Olive's mother, Kate. Nice to meet you."

She looked a few years older than me, though I was a poor judge of age. Her dark hair was cut in a neat bob with hints of purple in it. I had seen others with vivid hair colors, and it looked fun. Maybe I should consider doing something like that.

"Hi, nice to meet you too. The decorations are pretty." I gestured toward the pavilion.

"Thanks. Olive's favorite colors." She glanced over her shoulder. "Well, help yourself to a drink. We have sodas and bottled water in the cooler over there, and iced tea on that table. Hot dogs will be served shortly." She gestured around as she spoke. "Oh, excuse me. A host's job is never done." She laughed lightly and headed off to greet another guest.

I grabbed a soda from the cooler and wandered around, smiling at the other guests. Everyone was friendly. I recognized a few people from town, but I didn't know many of them. I assumed they were Kate and Olive's family or lived in the newer section of Glenn Lake.

The town had different groupings depending on which neighborhood you lived in. I mostly stayed in my area, which was where the older folks lived. It was one of the first neighborhoods built during the housing boom of the late seventies and early eighties.

Olive and her mom lived on the west side, where everything was new and much of it still under construction. I knew the town was growing and had heard it would double in size over the next few years. It had already doubled since I was Missy's age. I just hoped it wouldn't lose that small town feel as it expanded.

I found a seat at one of the picnic tables facing the bounce house. I could see Missy and Olive bouncing and laughing together. I was so glad she was having fun.

My phone chirped with a text from Jimmy, checking in and telling me they were having a good time. I replied, then got up to take some pictures of Missy and her friends. They all made silly faces for the camera, laughing at each other. It warmed my heart to see her enjoying herself with friends.

A small pang of jealousy shot through me. This was something I had never gotten to do as a child. But the feeling passed quickly. More than anything, I was happy that Missy was getting these experiences.

More guests arrived, and the kids played for a while longer before Kate announced that lunch was being served. Parents rounded up their children and helped them get food. I got Missy settled next to Olive, as the birthday girl had requested.

After lunch, a clown arrived. He did magic tricks and made balloon animals for all the children. His assistant did face painting. Missy and Olive both got matching butterflies painted on their faces.

Then came the cake, followed by presents. Olive made a big deal about each gift, thanking every giver with enthusiasm and a hug. She squealed with joy when she got to Missy's.

"I love puzzles! I love puzzles with kittens! Missy, how did you know?"

"You're my best friend, Olive. I know everything."

They both laughed like it was the funniest joke in the world.

Kate looked over at me and smiled, mouthing, "How cute."

Once the gifts were unwrapped, parents started gathering their children to leave. Kate asked if we minded staying a little longer so Olive would be entertained while she cleaned up. I didn't mind at all and offered to help.

We had the park back to normal in no time, then Kate and I watched the girls play for a few minutes. We got to chat during the cleanup and while the girls ran around.

Kate was a single mom with just Olive. She suggested we try to arrange some playdates. We exchanged phone numbers and promised to get the girls together soon.

It was nice. For the first time, I felt like I might be making a friend my own age.

Chapter Sixteen

Jimmy and Davy were home from fishing when we arrived. Davy was bursting with excitement.

"Grandpa Dixon caught the biggest fish! It was like a whale almost. It ate up my little fishy." He said it with a full pout.

Jimmy smiled but shook his head no at me. I figured the story wasn't quite accurate, but I played along with Davy's imagination. It was naptime for him, and I always had Missy play quietly or read during his nap, so I got them both settled.

The house was in good order with Jimmy being home, so I took advantage of the quiet time to read. I didn't get much time for my favorite hobby, but I tried whenever I could.

Jimmy was in the backyard making repairs to the shed. It was one of his last projects before he had to go back to work the following week.

A family of opossums had moved in recently, and he'd had to evict them. Now he was repairing the holes in the floor, walls, and roof to discourage them from coming back. I thought of how that shed had helped me hide part of my savings over the years, and sometimes myself.

I tried to read, but my mind kept drifting. Finally, I set the book aside and went outside to see if Jimmy needed help.

My breath caught when I saw him shirtless. He wasn't one of those heavily muscled guys, but he had just enough definition to make you stare. I should have kept reading, but it was too late. He had already seen me. No retreating now. I managed a weak smile.

"Hey, Mandy." He looked up from the sawhorse where he was cutting planks of wood.

"Hey," I choked out. "I wanted to see if you needed some help."

"Sure. That'd be great."

I helped him measure out planks, cut the wood, and hold pieces in place while he nailed them. We worked for a solid hour before the floor and walls were repaired.

"Looks great. I appreciate the help. Would have taken me twice as long on my own."

"You're welcome. It looks much better."

Davy was awake by then, so we cleaned everything up. Jimmy went to shower while I started dinner, and the kids played in the yard.

Except for my distracted thoughts about the man living in our house, it was just another ordinary day.

Once again, the time came for Jimmy to go back to work. It always felt like time flew by too fast when he was home.

There were more tears this time than the last. The kids were really getting used to having him around. He had started talking about finding an office job, one where he could be home every night. I liked that idea.

He promised to call and email when he could. We all hoped the time would pass quickly. We would have our court date when he got back. I wasn't sure if that was something to look forward to or dread, but I still wanted the days to fly by so our family could be back together.

While he was gone, we would have Thanksgiving. But he would be home in time for Christmas. We had already started shopping for the kids. It was exciting because, for me, this was a first. We had never really celebrated Christmas before.

"You promise to wait to put up a tree until I get back?" he asked the kids.

"We promise, Daddy," Missy confirmed. Davy nodded.

We had never gotten to have a tree. I had tried a few times when I was younger, but Mama's friends would destroy it before Christmas morning. This would be the first year I could really enjoy decorating. I hoped I could wait until Jimmy got back.

I wanted to make some of the ornaments with the kids. They loved crafts, so I thought it would be fun. I had found ideas online and had already started gathering supplies. It would keep us busy for the month and maybe help contain our excitement until Jimmy came home again.

Kate and I had plans to take the girls to the zoo on Saturday. We would have a picnic at Hermann Park afterward. I was looking forward to it. I hadn't been to the zoo since fourth grade, when I went on a school field trip.

But more than the zoo itself, I was looking forward to spending time with someone closer to my age. Possibly making a real friend.

Until then, we went about our usual routine. Work, school, home. Cleaning, cooking, playing.

The days passed, and I found myself thinking about Jimmy more than I probably should have.

Chapter Seventeen

The morning finally came to meet Kate and Olive at the zoo. While I drove, Missy and Davy talked nonstop about the time they had gone with Grammy. All the animals they had seen, all the snacks they had eaten. Davy wasn't usually much of a talker, but when he got excited about something, he could outpace even Missy. He was definitely an animal guy.

When we arrived, the parking lot was still relatively empty. Kate had warned me that we needed to get there early because it would be packed by ten.

I found a spot near the entrance and saw Kate pull in behind us. Missy started waving immediately and ran to Olive the moment we got out. They hugged like they hadn't seen each other in a year, even though it had only been yesterday. Davy was so giggly and bouncy that I wasn't sure I could get him to sit in the stroller, but he finally settled in.

I headed to the membership window to purchase a pass. Once that was done, we went inside. The girls walked hand in hand, chattering away. They were both talking at the same time, and I couldn't figure out how either of them could follow the conversation, but they seemed to have no trouble.

We started at the Galápagos Islands exhibit near the entrance. The kids were mesmerized by the penguins waddling around and diving into the water. Davy pressed his face against the glass, watching the sea lions glide past. We saw the giant tortoises moving slowly through their habitat, ancient and unhurried.

"They're so big!" Missy said, eyes wide.

From there, we wandered through South America's Pantanal, where we spotted the giant anteaters and capybaras. Davy wanted out of the stroller when he saw the giant river otters playing in the water. He ran from viewing window to viewing window, trying to keep up with them. It was fun to watch him like this.

We made our way through the African Forest to see the gorillas and giraffes, then headed to the Children's Zoo. The kids wanted to ride the Wildlife Carousel, so we bought tickets. The girls picked animals next to each other, and Kate stood with them. Davy chose an elephant a few rows ahead, so I stood beside him. I took pictures of him and the girls to share with Jimmy.

Kate and I had a lot in common. We liked the same types of books, music, and movies. She wasn't much older than me, just twenty-four.

She had met her ex-husband in college and gotten pregnant with Olive almost right away. They married quickly and divorced almost as fast. She had moved to Glenn Lake to be near her parents and to escape bad memories.

We spent about two hours walking around. By then, it was getting crowded and nearing lunchtime. The kids were hungry and getting whiny, so we decided to head to the park to eat.

Back at the car, I was surprised to see the parking lot jam packed. People were circling, searching for spots. I had to apologize to a few who thought we were leaving when I was just grabbing our lunch.

We found a shaded picnic table near the duck pond, not far from the path where the train ran. I took more pictures while we ate, saving them to send to Jimmy.

When the kids finished eating, they ran off to play a game nearby while Kate and I talked.

"This might seem rude," she said, "but how is it that you're raising your brother and sister?"

"It's a long story. The short version is that our mother is a drunk who ran out on us one day. She'd been drinking and tried to hit Davy. We got into a fight, and a week later, she was just gone."

"Oh my. I'm sorry. That has to be rough. Basically, being a single mom without actually being *the* mom."

"Yeah. But I enjoy taking care of them. It might seem unfair, but I wouldn't have it any other way."

"So... she was abusive?" Kate sounded uncomfortable asking, but curious.

"Yes. Mostly just to me. I was able to protect them." I nodded toward the kids. "That one night was the only time it almost got out of hand with them. I was able to stop it. I'm thankful I was there." I couldn't imagine what might have happened if I hadn't been home.

"I'm sorry to hear that." Kate paused. "My ex-husband was too. It was kind of the same story. He tried to hit Olive, so I fought back and left him. I'm glad she was so young at the time. Hopefully she doesn't remember." She thought for a moment. "She never mentions it. It's been almost three years, and I've worked hard to get us to this point. I'm so thankful my parents were able to help."

"That's awful. But I'm glad you're both okay."

We looked over at the kids for a moment, watching them in silence.

"I'm glad we did this today," Kate said with a smile. "I need a friend, and Olive loves Missy."

"I hate to admit this, but I've never really had friends. Not ones my own age, anyway." I thought of Ms. Graham, the Daileys, and Mr. Dixon.

"Never?"

"Not really. I have a few neighbors who look out for me. Claire, Mr. Dixon's granddaughter, is the closest to my age, but she doesn't live here, so I only see her sometimes. I'm not sure I'd call us friends exactly."

"Well, you can't say that anymore." Kate reached over and squeezed my hand.

We looked at each other and smiled. It was nice to have a friend. We agreed to get together often.

Davy fell asleep almost as soon as we got in the car to head home. Missy looked tired too, and when the backseat went quiet, I knew she had dozed off as well. I drove home in near silence, just the slow, steady breathing from the backseat and the radio playing softly.

Missy woke when we pulled into the driveway, but Davy stayed asleep even while I carried him to bed. While he napped, Missy and I worked on some Christmas ornaments. I had bought white pipe cleaners and red pony beads from the craft store. We strung the beads onto the pipe cleaners, leaving a little space for the white to show through, then bent them into the shape of candy canes. We each made about a dozen before Davy woke up.

Once he was awake, I got them both painting plastic ornaments that were like sun catchers. They were proud of their work. We left everything to dry and went outside to play.

When Jimmy got back at the beginning of December, I hoped we would have a nice collection of handmade ornaments to put on the tree. We were off to an excellent start. I had more ideas too. Next time I was near the craft store, I would pick up additional supplies.

The weekend before Thanksgiving, Kate and Olive came over. We had planned to make salt dough ornaments with the kids, but somehow Kate and I ended up doing all the work while the children played in the other room.

"How did it end up being just the two of us doing this?" She laughed.

"I don't know. They seemed so excited this morning."

"Olive has been talking about it for days. She kept telling me how she and Missy had all these plans. I guess it wasn't what they expected."

"Is it ever?"

We both laughed.

"So, nosy me," Kate said, "you live here with their father? Your mom's ex-boyfriend?"

"Yeah. I know it must seem weird. It was just me and the kids at first, but then the whole CPS thing happened, Jimmy showed up, and it evolved into this. He's kind of like a stepdad, I guess." Though in my mind, I had never thought of him that way. I didn't really know how I thought of him. He was just Jimmy.

"I don't think it's weird. Actually, it's interesting. There's no right way to be a family." She said it so matter of factly that I knew she was sincere.

We continued shaping ornaments while switching topics.

"How is Missy's reading? Olive tells me she can read really well."

"Yeah, she actually does."

"Olive can't, and she's not interested in trying. I know she's still young, but I can't figure out how to get her engaged. I read to her every night, and sometimes she just shuts me down."

"I don't know what to say other than Missy has always been interested. I think some people like it and others don't."

"Maybe so. But as someone who really loves reading, it's almost heartbreaking not to have a reader." She sighed.

"I understand." I paused. "Oh, did you download the new book?"

Our favorite author had a new release out. Kate had a Kindle, but I didn't. I would have to wait for the library to get it in stock or find it at a store. Maybe I should buy myself a Kindle now that I had a little money.

"I did, but I haven't started it yet." She grinned. "You should really get a Kindle. It will change your life. Well, your reading life anyway."

We finished the ornaments and put them in the oven to bake. Kate helped me clean up, and then we moved to the living room with iced tea and chatted until the ornaments were ready. The kids wandered out a little later, so I fixed them a snack. Once the ornaments had cooled, Kate and Olive headed home.

"That was the most fun day," Missy said after they left. "I liked having Olive come over. I hope we can play again soon."

"I enjoyed it too."

It was nice to have a friend.

Chapter Eighteen

Thanksgiving morning, Ms. Graham would be joining us for lunch. I had bought a small turkey, and we were having stuffing, mashed potatoes, green bean casserole, and cranberries. Ms. Graham was bringing dessert and rolls.

With just the four of us, we kept it small, but somehow it still ended up being a lot of food. We would have leftovers for days. That was something I had never experienced before. I liked it.

Missy was telling me all about Pilgrims and Indians while I prepped.

"And they came over on three ships. The Nina, the Pinta, and the Santa Maria. Did you know that, Mandy?"

I said I didn't and encouraged her to keep going, even though I did know.

The parade was on television, and Davy squealed with delight every few minutes when a new float or balloon appeared. He recognized some cartoon characters and not others. He loved the marching bands and tried to copy their moves.

"Look! Nandy, Nandy! Big Bird! Oh, Cookie Monster! ELMO! Nandy, come see!"

I peeked in and tried to match his excitement with my responses. It was fun to see him so happy.

When Missy finished her pilgrim facts, she went to watch with him. I could hear her singing along with some of the performances. I didn't even know she recognized those artists.

They watched until the end, and when Santa Claus appeared in the final float, they both got extremely excited.

"Mandy, I hope Santa knows what I really want most of all for Christmas."

"What's that, sweetie?" I already knew. Jimmy had already bought it. It was sitting in our attic right now, waiting for Christmas morning. But I loved hearing her talk about it. She got so animated.

"A pink and green dollhouse with lots of furniture and a doll family to go in it. Remember the one we saw at Target that time? That's the one I want. Do you think Santa can make that?"

"I'm sure he can. And I'm sure he knows that's what you want. Do you think you've been good this year?"

"Yes, I've been very good. I listened to you and Daddy. I help around the house. I haven't gotten in trouble at school." She thought for a moment. "And I don't fight that much with Davy. I help him tie his shoes. Do you think I'll get it?"

"I'm sure you will. You've definitely been good in my book." I kissed the top of her head.

"I love you, Mandy!"

"I love you too, sweet girl."

Davy came over and gave me a hug. "I love you too, Nandy."

"Aw, thanks, Davy. I love you." It was a big love fest. I had so much to be thankful for this year.

There was a knock at the door, and the kids ran for it, yelling, "Grammy is here!"

Ms. Graham let herself in with a cheerful hello, as she often did. The kids gave her hugs and danced around, telling her about the parade and Santa.

Lunch was nearly ready, so I got everyone settled. Missy had helped me set the table the day before. I had kept them home since it was technically a school holiday, and we made place cards while Davy napped. We didn't really need them, but it was a fun activity.

Now Missy was showing Ms. Graham the place cards.

"And this one is for you." She was grinning proudly.

"Oh, it's beautiful. And this looks like a good seat for me. Right between you and Davy."

I had also gotten some artificial flowers from the craft store and made a centerpiece. Missy had helped with that too. Ms. Graham made a fuss over it while Missy explained how we had made it.

Once lunch was ready, I fixed plates for the kids. As we settled in, Missy announced that we should all say what we were thankful for. She said they had done it at school.

"I'll start so you know how it's done." Ms. Graham and I exchanged a smile as Missy continued. "I'm thankful for Mandy, Daddy, Davy, and Grammy. Oh, and Olive and all my toys! Now Grammy, your turn."

"Well, dear, I'm thankful for wonderful neighbors like you, Mandy, and Davy..."

"And Mr. Dailey and Mrs. Dailey, right?" Missy interrupted.

"Of course. My best friends."

Missy smiled, proud of herself for the reminder. "Now Davy, your turn."

"I thankful for Daddy, Nandy, Missy, and Grammy. And tigers. And parades!" He grinned.

"That was nice, Davy," I said. "I guess it's my turn. I'm thankful for both of you, and of course Ms. Graham. I'm thankful for my new friendship with Kate. And for all of our wonderful neighbors."

After dinner, Missy got us all playing her new board game. It was a mix of different games, and I don't think it made sense to anyone but her.

About halfway through, Davy gave up and fell asleep on the couch. The rest of us carried on.

"Oh, look at that! Grammy, you're the winner," Missy declared after several confusing rounds.

"Wow, I'm so excited." Ms. Graham laughed.

"You are really good at this game," Missy said seriously.

"I enjoyed it very much. Thank you for including me." Grammy smiled at her. "I should get home. I loved spending Thanksgiving with you all."

"Thank you for coming. We enjoyed having you." I hugged her.

"We need to do this every year. Our new tradition."

"Yes!" Missy jumped up and down.

That night, after the dishes were washed and put away, the food was stored, and the kids were in bed, I sat and reflected on the past few months.

I didn't have to fight tooth and nail for everything anymore. I didn't have to hide in fear. I had food, friends, and family. I had a growing business, a car, and Jimmy.

For the second time that day, I gave thanks for how much I had going well in my life. For the first time I could remember, the future actually looked bright.

Chapter Nineteen

It was finally the day Jimmy would be home, and soon after, we would have our long-awaited court date.

The kids were beyond excited. They instructed me to have Jimmy pick them up from school. I assured them he would if he got back in time.

That was clearly the wrong answer. Missy got overly dramatic and started crying.

I had to explain for the millionth time that sometimes there were travel delays. It wasn't any different from any other time he had come back, but I guess today I said it wrong, or she was in a mood. Either way, I finally got her calm and into the car to head to daycare.

I had four houses to do. Right after Thanksgiving was even busier than usual because everyone had family over for the holiday, and now they wanted their homes back to normal. They were also gearing up for Christmas. Trees were going up, along with other decorations.

Mr. Dixon had a large extended family, and he loved and hated having all the kids in his yard. His younger grandchildren and great nieces and nephews always ran through his landscaping, stepping on his flowers and plants. He couldn't wait for me to come clean it up.

Unfortunately, I was booked solid, so it was several days before I could get to his house. He was my second stop of the day. He must have been watching from the window because I hadn't even turned off the car before he was heading toward me.

"Mandy girl, thank goodness you're here. Look at my garden." He gestured toward the front of the house.

"Don't worry. I'll get everything back to normal. You'll be the pride of Ridgeway Street once again."

"Thank you. As always, you're a lifesaver." He smiled. "I would love to do it myself, but those days are mostly behind me."

"I understand."

I headed to his garage to grab supplies. I would need a rake and trash bags mostly. They had gotten mulch and leaves everywhere. About an hour later, I put a bag and a half of debris into his garage and hung the tools back in their places.

"It looks beautiful. Even better than before those brats tore it up." He paused. "You know I love my grandchildren, but those parents have no control over them. Back in my day, we knew how to discipline children."

I tried not to smile because I knew he was serious. He did love his grandchildren, but he was obsessed with his yard. He won Yard of the Month more than anyone else. The months he didn't win, he told me it was only because the committee didn't want to show favoritism. I didn't know if that was true, but I always agreed with him because it made him happy.

It was time for lunch, so I headed home. I noticed Jimmy's truck the moment the house came into view.

My heart stuttered. Instant butterflies filled my stomach. A warm blush crept up my neck and spread across my cheeks. I gripped the steering wheel a little tighter and took a breath.

Inhale. Exhale. Inhale. Exhale.

I parked and made my way to the front door, trying to act normal. Whatever normal was supposed to feel like.

"Hey, Mandy!" He met me at the door before I could even reach for the handle, wrapping his arms around me in a big hug.

I melted into it before I could stop myself. He smelled like soap and something warm, like coffee and cedar. I felt so safe in his arms. So completely at ease. When he let go, I had to resist the urge to lean back in.

"Hey, Jimmy. Welcome back." I hoped my voice sounded steadier than I felt. "The kids will be so happy to see you."

"I saw the new pictures on the fridge. Looks like y'all have been busy." He pointed to the box of Christmas ornaments the kids and I had been working on.

"Yeah, getting ready for Christmas. The kids will be excited that we can finally put the tree up. That's all they've been talking about." I set my bag down and followed him into the kitchen. "Oh, and I was given strict instructions that you have to pick them up from school today. Not me."

He chuckled. "Of course I'll pick them up. Right after Davy's naptime is over." He leaned against the counter. "Lunch break?"

"Yeah. Then I need to finish two houses. New clients. This will be my first time cleaning for both."

"That's great. Business has been good?"

"Very good. The more families move in on the west side, the more work I seem to get. I've actually had to turn a few people away." I pulled sandwich supplies from the fridge. "I might need to hire someone to help me."

"Wow. That's really something, Mandy. You've built something real."

The pride in his voice made my cheeks warm again. I busied myself with the bread so he wouldn't notice.

"Did you eat yet? I was going to make myself a sandwich. Want one?"

"I haven't eaten. Yeah, a sandwich sounds good. Need help?"

"Sure. Can you grab some chips?" I pointed toward the pantry.

We worked together in the small kitchen, moving around each other with an ease that surprised me. It felt natural. Comfortable. Like we had been doing this for years instead of months.

While we ate, we caught up on the kids and the latest neighborhood gossip. Mrs. Maxwell had gotten a new car. The Wilsons' triplets had started soccer. Mr. Dailey was responding well to his latest round of treatment.

"That's good news about Mr. Dailey," Jimmy said.

"It really is. Mrs. Dailey has been so worried. I think she's finally letting herself breathe a little."

We talked until I had to head back out to work. The whole drive to my next client's house, my mind kept drifting back to that hug. Such a simple gesture. A normal thing people did when they hadn't seen each other in a while.

So why did it feel like so much more? Why could I still feel the warmth of his arms? Why did my heart keep skipping when I thought about the way he had looked at me?

I shook my head and focused on the road. I had houses to clean. I couldn't afford to be distracted.

But all afternoon, no matter how hard I scrubbed counters or folded laundry, my thoughts kept circling back to him.

When I finally got home, the sun was getting low in the sky. I could hear the kids laughing in the backyard before I even got out of the car. Jimmy was chasing them around, arms raised, growling like a monster. Missy shrieked with delight as she dodged behind the oak tree. Davy toddled after her, giggling so hard he could barely run.

I stood by the back door for a moment, just watching. Just soaking it in.

This was what a family was supposed to look like. This was what home was supposed to feel like.

I had spent so many years dreading coming home. Standing outside the door, counting to ten, bracing myself for whatever disaster waited inside. The smell of stale beer. The sound of Mama yelling. The fear that never quite went away.

But now I stood here with a smile on my face, watching the people I loved most in the world play in the golden evening light. My heart felt so full it almost hurt.

Jimmy spotted me and grinned. He jogged past with a quick wink, still chasing the kids. I laughed and went inside.

He had prepped dinner while I was gone. Grilled chicken, baked potatoes, and salad. The kitchen smelled wonderful. I smiled at the neat row of ingredients on the counter, everything ready to go.

Things were feeling normal again. Our little family, strange as it might be, was back together.

I headed to the back door and stepped onto the porch.

"Mandy!" "Nandy!" Both kids spotted me at once.

They ran over for quick hugs, then immediately fled from Monster Jimmy. He chased past me again, and I sat down on the porch swing he had installed the last time he was home. It had been one of many surprises. A new light fixture in the hallway. Weather stripping on the doors. The squeaky step finally fixed.

What had I done to deserve so much?

After a few minutes, Ms. Graham appeared at the back gate and came to sit beside me. The kids gave her a similar greeting. A quick hello and hug, then gone, back to their game.

"He's good with them," Ms. Graham said, watching Jimmy pretend to be defeated by the two tiny warriors.

"He really is."

"And good for you too, I think."

I glanced at her, but she just smiled and patted my hand.

I offered her iced tea and told her about my new clients on the west side and how busy things had gotten.

"I might need to hire someone to work with me," I said. "So I can take on more clients. I'm not sure how it would work though. Would I pay them a set fee, or let them keep what they make?"

"I would say you pay them a set amount. If you normally charge eighty dollars for a house, they make sixty and you keep twenty. Or you could do a percentage split."

"Maybe eighty twenty? I don't want to be greedy, but I did start the business."

"Sounds fair to me," she said.

"Me too," Jimmy called from across the yard.

The kids piped in with their approval, even though I was sure they had no idea what we were talking about.

"Okay, then it's settled. I'll place an ad after the holidays." I turned to Ms. Graham. "Would you help me interview people? I've never done that."

"Certainly, dear. I'd be happy to."

"Well, I better get dinner going. Want to join us?"

"Oh, I wouldn't want to impose."

"Not at all. We have plenty, and you're family." I squeezed her hand.

She agreed. The kids cheered.

I set the table for five. The kids played until we called them in. Missy led Davy to the bathroom to wash his hands. She knew the routine.

We had a pleasant dinner with good company. Lots of stories and conversation and laughter. Ms. Graham told us about the church potluck and how Mrs. Henderson had brought the same green bean casserole she'd been making for forty years. The kids interrupted constantly with their own observations and questions. Jimmy caught my eye across the table more than once, smiling.

After dinner, we walked Ms. Graham home. The kids ran ahead, then back, then ahead again, burning off their energy before bedtime.

"Thank you for including me," Ms. Graham said at her door. "This was lovely."

"Thank you for being here. For everything."

She hugged me tight. "You deserve every bit of happiness, Mandy. Don't forget that."

I thought about her words as we walked back home. As we went through the bedtime routine. Bath, pajamas, teeth brushing, story time. Jimmy read to them tonight while I tidied up the kitchen.

When the house was quiet and the kids were asleep, I found myself standing in the living room, looking at the box of handmade ornaments. Soon we would put up a tree. Our first real Christmas tree.

Jimmy came down the hall and stopped beside me.

"Big day tomorrow," he said.

Court. The custody hearing. The thing we had been working toward for months.

"Yeah." I felt the familiar knot of anxiety tighten in my stomach. "What if something goes wrong?"

"It won't."

"But what if it does? What if they found Mama? What if she shows up and contests everything? What if the judge decides—"

"Hey." He put a hand on my shoulder, and I stopped. "Laura said we have a strong case. Mama isn't contesting. We have documentation, witnesses, everything we need. It's going to be okay."

I wanted to believe him. I really did.

"I just keep waiting for something bad to happen," I admitted. "Things have been going so well. That's not how my life works."

"Maybe it is now." His voice was gentle. "Maybe things are different."

I looked up at him. In the soft lamplight, his gray eyes were warm. Steady. He believed what he was saying. He believed in this. In us.

"Get some sleep," he said. "Tomorrow is going to be a good day."

I nodded and headed to my room. But sleep was a long time coming. I lay in the dark, thinking about court, about Mama, about the life we were building here.

And about the way my heart had raced when Jimmy put his hand on my shoulder. The way it still hadn't quite slowed down.

Tomorrow was going to be a big day. I just hoped he was right about it being a good one.

Chapter Twenty

I barely slept the night before court. Every time I started to drift off, my mind would spin up another worry. What if they had found Mama? What if she showed up? What if the judge didn't believe us?

By the time my alarm went off, I had been awake for an hour, staring at the ceiling.

I showered and took extra care getting ready. Knowing we had court, I had splurged and bought myself an outfit. I could have borrowed from Mama's things again, but I wanted something of my own. Something that was mine.

I had found a cute peach colored blouse and a navy skirt at the department store in the next town over. The brown pumps came from the clearance rack. I had never owned nice clothes like this before. Standing in front of the mirror, I hardly recognized myself.

I looked like someone who had her life together. Someone who belonged in a courtroom, fighting for her family. The thought made me stand a little straighter.

Jimmy was already up when I came out, dressed in khakis and a button-down shirt. He looked handsome. Professional. Like a father who deserved custody of his children.

"You look nice," he said.

"So do you."

We got the kids ready and dropped them off at daycare. Missy wanted to know why we were dressed up, so I told her we had an important meeting. She accepted that without question and ran off to find Olive.

The drive to the courthouse was quiet. My stomach was in knots. I kept my hands folded in my lap so Jimmy wouldn't see them shaking.

"It's going to be okay," he said, glancing over at me.

"I know." I didn't sound convincing, even to myself.

"Laura said we have a strong case. Everything is documented. Mama isn't contesting."

"I know," I said again.

But knowing and believing were two different things. My whole life, good things had been followed by bad. Every time I started to feel safe, something would come along and rip it away. I kept waiting for the other shoe to drop.

We parked and walked into the building. The courthouse was old and imposing, all marble floors and high ceilings. Our footsteps echoed as we made our way to the family court wing.

Laura was waiting near the courtroom doors. She looked polished and confident in a dark gray pantsuit with pinstripes. The shell under her jacket had a red and blue geometric pattern. I always noticed her clothes because I was a little envious. She always looked so put together.

"Good morning," she said with a warm smile. "How are you both feeling?"

"Nervous," I admitted.

"That's completely normal. But I want you to know, I feel very good about today." She guided us to a bench along the wall. "The judge assigned to our case is fair and thorough. She cares about what's best for children. That works in our favor."

"And Mama?" I asked. "She's not here?"

"She's not. We did our due diligence in attempting to notify her, but she hasn't responded or appeared. That actually helps us. It shows the court that she's not interested in being part of these children's lives."

I nodded, relief and something like grief mixing in my chest. Part of me had wanted Mama to show up. To fight for us, even though I knew she wouldn't. Even though I knew it was better this way.

"When we go in," Laura continued, "I'll present our case. The judge may ask you both some questions. Just answer honestly. You don't need to overthink it. Just tell the truth about what life has been like and what you want for these children."

We sat outside the courtroom for nearly an hour while other families had their hearings. I watched them come and go. Some looked relieved. Others looked devastated. I tried not to think about which group we would fall into.

Finally, we were called.

The courtroom was smaller than I expected. Wood paneled walls, fluorescent lights, an American flag in the corner. The judge sat behind an elevated bench, a middle aged woman with reading glasses and a no nonsense expression.

Laura presented our case. She walked through the timeline. Mama's abandonment. The note she left. CPS involvement. Jimmy's immediate response. The stable home we had created. The children thriving in school and daycare.

The judge listened, making notes. Then she turned to Jimmy.

"Mr. Holloway, can you tell me in your own words why you're seeking full custody?"

Jimmy sat up straighter. "Your Honor, I love my children. I should have been more involved from the start, and I take responsibility for that. But when I learned what was happening, I came immediately. Mandy had been taking care of them on her own, doing an incredible job, but she shouldn't have had to. They're my responsibility. I want to give them a stable home. A real family."

The judge nodded and turned to me. "Miss Holloway, you're not the biological parent of these children, yet you've been their primary caregiver. Can you explain your role?"

I swallowed hard. "They're my brother and sister, Your Honor. Half siblings. I've been taking care of them since they were born. When Mama left, I just kept doing what I'd always done." I paused, trying to find the right words. "I love them. They're my family. I would do anything for them."

"And you're comfortable with Mr. Holloway having full custody, with you serving as guardian in his absence?"

"Yes, ma'am. Jimmy is a good father. The kids adore him. And this arrangement means they'll always have one of us. They'll never be alone."

The judge made a few more notes, asked a few more questions about our living situation and finances, then sat back.

"I've reviewed all the documentation submitted by counsel. The home study was favorable. There's no evidence of the mother's current whereabouts or any interest on her part in maintaining custody." She looked at us over her glasses. "It's clear to me that these children are loved and well cared for. That's what matters most."

She began reading the orders. Full custody to Jimmy. Guardianship to me in his absence. Power of attorney approved. Restraining order against Mama, preventing her from coming near the children without court approval. Child support payments to Mama terminated. Permission to remain in the family home.

Ten minutes after entering the courtroom, we were walking out.

I felt dizzy. Like I might float away.

"Congratulations," Laura said, shaking our hands. "I'm glad this worked out. I enjoyed working with you both. Good luck with the children."

"Thank you," Jimmy said. "For everything."

"I hope you never need me again, but if you do, I'd be happy to help."

We thanked her again and walked out of the courthouse into the bright December sunshine. I stopped on the steps, blinking.

"We did it," Jimmy said.

"We did it." I still couldn't quite believe it.

He pulled me into a hug, right there on the courthouse steps. I let myself sink into it for just a moment.

We had won. The kids were safe. We were a family, legally and officially.

So why was I still waiting for something to go wrong?

An hour later, I got my answer.

I was at Mr. Dixon's house, working on his yard again, when my phone rang. Jimmy's name flashed on the screen.

"Hey, what's up?"

"Davy's sick. The daycare called. They think it might be strep."

My heart sank. "Oh no. Poor little guy."

"I already called the doctor. They can see him in an hour. I'm picking him up now."

"I'll meet you there."

I packed up quickly and explained the situation to Mr. Dixon and Claire, who was visiting again. I promised to update them later.

When I got to the doctor's office, Jimmy and the kids were still in the waiting room. Davy was curled up in Jimmy's lap, looking miserable. His cheeks were flushed, and his eyes were glassy.

"Nandy, my froat hurts," he whimpered when he saw me. He reached out his arms.

I took him from Jimmy and held him close. He was warm. Too warm.

"They said it would be just a few more minutes," Jimmy said.

Almost immediately, a nurse called Davy's name. Jimmy stayed with Missy while I carried Davy back to the exam room.

They took his weight and temperature. One hundred and two. They checked his vitals and swabbed his throat. He cried during the swab, and I held his hand, murmuring that it was almost over.

Fifteen minutes later, the doctor came in.

"It's strep," she confirmed. "We're seeing a lot of it this week. I'll prescribe an antibiotic for him, and I'd recommend prescriptions for everyone in the household. It's highly contagious. If we get ahead of it, we might prevent the rest of you from getting the full-blown version."

"That would be great. Thank you."

She gave me care instructions. Tylenol for fever. Plenty of fluids. Soft foods if his throat hurt too much to eat. Keep him home until he'd been fever free for twenty-four hours.

"What about work?" I asked. "I clean houses. Some of my clients are elderly, and one is going through chemotherapy."

The doctor nodded seriously. "I would avoid contact with anyone outside your household for at least two to three days. Longer for anyone immunocompromised."

Two to three days. That meant canceling clients. Right before Christmas, when everyone wanted their houses clean.

But Davy was more important. Everything else could wait.

We picked up the prescriptions and headed home. Jimmy ran to the store for supplies while I got Davy settled. Tylenol, watered down juice, fresh pajamas. Missy insisted on helping, so she gathered pillows and blankets and Davy's stuffed tiger from the zoo.

They settled on the couch together, Missy at one end and Davy at the other, their feet almost touching in the middle. I put on a Disney movie and watched them for a moment.

This. This was what mattered. Not clean houses or clients or money. This.

I went to start laundry, then sat down to call my clients.

Mr. Dixon's house was first. Claire answered.

"How's Davy?" she asked immediately.

"Strep throat. The doctor says we need to quarantine for a few days. I'm so sorry, but I'll have to cancel my appointments."

"Don't apologize. Family comes first." She paused. "Actually, I wanted to talk to you about something. Could I help cover your clients while you're out?"

I blinked. "You would do that?"

"Of course. I didn't get a chance to tell you earlier, but I'm moving back in with Grandpa. I'm taking some time off from school." Her voice got quieter. "I'm going through some things. I need to figure out my next steps."

I didn't push. Whatever she was dealing with, she would share when she was ready.

"I'm sorry to hear that," I said. "But actually, this gives me an idea. I've been thinking about hiring someone. My business has grown faster than I can handle on my own. Would you be interested? We could do a trial run while I'm stuck at home and see how it goes."

"Really?" She sounded surprised. Hopeful. "Yes. I would love that. It sounds a lot better than going back to Mr. Burger."

We talked for a few more minutes, working out the details. I would put together a simple agreement for us to review once the quarantine was over. In the meantime, I gave her the list of clients I had scheduled for the next two days and as much information as I could about each one.

"I'll call them all to let them know you're coming," I said. "Most of them know you already."

"Thank you, Mandy. Really. This means a lot."

After we hung up, I called each client on my list. Everyone was understanding. Most of them knew Claire and were happy to have her fill in. A few even said they hoped Davy felt better soon.

I couldn't believe how smoothly it had all come together. I had been worrying about hiring someone for weeks, and now it had just fallen into place.

I thought about the day. Court in the morning. Victory. Then Davy getting sick. And somehow, out of that, finding an employee.

Maybe this was how life worked now. Maybe good things could come from bad. Maybe I didn't always have to brace for disaster.

Or maybe I was just tired and emotional and not thinking clearly.

Jimmy came home with groceries, and we fell into the quiet rhythm of caring for a sick child. Soup and crackers for dinner. More Tylenol. A warm bath. Stories and snuggles.

By the time the kids were asleep, I was exhausted. But it was a good kind of exhausted. The kind that came from taking care of people I loved.

Tomorrow we would still be quarantined. Davy would still be sick. There would be challenges ahead.

But today, we had won something important. Today, we were officially a family.

I held onto that thought as I got ready for bed. Whatever came next, we would face it together.

Chapter Twenty-One

The next two days blurred together in a haze of Tylenol, juice boxes, and Disney movies.

Davy was miserable the first day. He barely ate, cried whenever I put him down, and woke up twice in the night burning with fever. By the second day, the antibiotics started kicking in, and he perked up a little. He still wasn't himself, but he managed some soup and even laughed at a cartoon.

Missy started complaining about her throat on day two. I had been expecting it. They shared everything, and strep was contagious. Thankfully, we had all started antibiotics early, so her case was mild. She was tired and a little cranky, but nothing like Davy had been.

Jimmy and I took turns caring for them. He handled mornings while I caught up on sleep, and I took over in the afternoons so he could get things done around the house. We worked together seamlessly, passing off responsibilities without needing to discuss it. Like we had been doing this for years.

By the second evening, both kids were feeling better but still not well enough for their normal routine. No running around outside. No burning off energy before bed.

We played Go Fish at the kitchen table. Davy won twice, though I suspected Jimmy let him. Missy accused us both of cheating, which made Davy giggle so hard he nearly fell off his chair.

These were the moments I lived for. The ordinary, unremarkable moments that somehow felt like everything.

After cards, we tried to start the bedtime routine. Bath went fine. Pajamas went fine. But when it came time to actually go to bed, Davy fell apart.

He threw a tantrum like I had never seen from him. Screaming, crying, kicking his feet. He clung to me and refused to let go, sobbing that he didn't want to sleep, that his throat hurt, that he wanted Nandy.

"I know, baby. I know." I held him against my chest, rubbing his back. "It's okay. I've got you."

Jimmy took Missy to her room for a story while I carried Davy back to the living room. I settled into the old brown recliner and started rocking. Back and forth, back and forth. Slow and steady.

Davy's sobs gradually quieted to sniffles, then to hiccups, then to silence. His small body relaxed against mine, heavy with exhaustion. I kept rocking, kept rubbing his back, kept murmuring soft nonsense words.

The house was quiet. Through the window, I could see the last light fading from the sky. The Christmas lights on the neighbor's house blinked red and green.

Jimmy appeared in the doorway. He had changed into sweatpants and a T-shirt, his hair slightly rumpled. He looked tired, but he was smiling.

"Missy's asleep," he said softly. "She was worried about Davy, but she went down pretty quick. I think she's still fighting it off."

"She probably is. At least we caught it early."

He nodded and leaned against the door frame, watching us.

"Do you need anything?" he asked.

"No. I'm good. Hopefully he'll fall asleep soon."

"He looks close."

He was right. Davy's breathing had evened out, slow and deep. His thumb had found its way to his mouth, something he only did when he was truly exhausted.

Jimmy didn't leave. He stood there watching us, a strange expression on his face. Soft. Almost tender.

"What?" I asked, suddenly self-conscious.

"Nothing. Just..." He shook his head slightly. "You're a natural with them, Mandy. After everything you went through, how you were raised, I'm amazed by you." He held up his hands quickly. "Sorry. That came out wrong. What I mean is, you have this incredible maternal instinct. You always know what they need."

I felt heat rise to my cheeks. "I just do what needs to be done. I love them. They deserve to be taken care of."

"Don't you?"

The question hung in the air between us.

"Don't I what?"

"Deserve to be taken care of."

I didn't know how to answer that. No one had ever asked me that before. No one had ever suggested that I might deserve anything at all.

"I... yes. I think so. And they do take care of me, in their way. Mama did too, I suppose. In her own way. She just didn't know how to show it."

Jimmy pushed off from the door frame and walked into the room. He sat on the edge of the couch, close to the recliner. Close to me.

"I'm here now," he said quietly. "I can take care of you. I want to."

Something shifted in the air. The room felt smaller. Warmer.

"Thanks." My voice came out barely above a whisper. "I've never really had that. A dad, I mean. Or any good male role model. Unless you count Mr. Dixon or Mr. Dailey."

Jimmy laughed softly, but there was something uncomfortable in it. Like I had missed the point entirely.

"I wasn't thinking of it like that, Mandy. Not like a father."

He slid off the couch and crouched in front of the recliner, bringing himself to my eye level. He placed one hand gently on my knee.

My heart stuttered.

"There's only eight years between us," he said. "That's not that much. Not really."

I stared at him, trying to process what he was saying.

"Oh," I managed. "Yeah."

And then, suddenly, I understood.

"Oh."

He smiled, but it was nervous. Uncertain. I had never seen him look uncertain before.

"I'm sorry. I know this must seem strange. But over the past few months, I've found myself thinking about you differently." He took a breath. "You're the first person I think of in the morning. The last one I think of at night. When I'm away on the rig, I catch myself smiling at random moments, remembering something you said. Something you did."

I couldn't breathe. Couldn't move. Couldn't do anything but stare at him.

He stood and moved to sit on the arm of the couch, putting a little distance between us. Like he needed room to say what he was going to say.

"When I'm here, with you and the kids, I'm amazed by you. Your strength. Your kindness. The way you take care of everyone around you without ever asking for anything in return." He ran a hand through his hair. "You've been through so much, Mandy. Things that would have broken most people. But you just keep going. You keep finding reasons to smile. You keep taking care of everyone else."

The only sound in the room was Davy's soft breathing and my own heart pounding in my ears.

"I didn't plan to say any of this," Jimmy continued. "I know the timing is strange. I know the situation is complicated. I was your mother's boyfriend. I'm the father of your siblings." He shook his head. "Believe me, I've thought about all of that. I've told myself a hundred times that I shouldn't feel this way."

He looked at me then. Really looked at me. His gray eyes were open and vulnerable in a way I had never seen before.

"But I do. I can't help it. You're remarkable, Mandy. And I just... I wanted you to know."

I opened my mouth, but no words came out.

I had imagined this moment. Late at night, alone in my room, I had let myself wonder what it would be like if he felt the same way I did. But I had never actually believed it would happen. I had never let myself believe.

"I'm not asking for anything to change," he said quickly. "Not right now. Maybe with time, if you... or maybe nothing will come of it. I don't know." He stood up, suddenly restless. "I just needed you to know how I felt. That's all. I didn't want to keep pretending."

He crossed to where I sat and, gently, so gently, lifted Davy from my arms. The little boy didn't stir.

"I'll put him to bed," Jimmy said. "Get some rest, Mandy."

And then he was gone. Down the hallway. Leaving me alone in the quiet living room with my racing heart and my spinning thoughts.

I sat there for a long time.

How did I feel about him? That was the question, wasn't it?

I thought about the way my heart jumped when I saw his truck in the driveway. The way I counted the days until he came home. The way his hugs made me feel safe and warm and like maybe, just maybe, I wasn't alone anymore.

I thought about his smile. His laugh. The way he looked at me like I was something precious.

Could I fall in love with my mother's ex-boyfriend? The father of my half siblings?

It was strange. I couldn't deny that. My life was not normal. Our situation was not normal.

But what was normal, anyway? Normal was Mama passing out drunk on the couch. Normal was hiding in cabinets and going hungry. Normal was being afraid to come home.

This, whatever this was, felt more real than anything I had ever known.

I got up slowly and walked down the hallway to my room. The house was silent. Everyone asleep except me.

I lay in bed and stared at the ceiling.

I thought about all the reasons this was complicated. All the reasons it might not work. All the ways it could go wrong.

And then I thought about the way he looked at me tonight. The way his voice softened when he said my name. The way he had admitted his feelings even though it terrified him.

He was brave. Braver than I had ever been.

Maybe it was time for me to be brave too.

I didn't know what would happen next. I didn't know if I was ready for any of this. I had never had a boyfriend. I didn't know how relationships were supposed to work. Everything I knew about love, I had learned from Mama, and those lessons were all wrong.

But lying there in the dark, I let myself admit the truth.

I had feelings for him too. Real feelings. The kind that made my stomach flip and my heart race. The kind that made me want things I had never let myself want before.

I didn't know what to do about it. I didn't know if I should tell him or wait or pretend this conversation never happened.

But I knew one thing for certain.

I wasn't going to run away from this. Not this time.

Whatever came next, I was going to face it. I was going to be brave.

I fell asleep with that thought in my mind, and for the first time in days, I didn't dream about all the things that could go wrong.

I dreamed about all the things that could go right.

Chapter Twenty-Two

I slept later than usual the following morning after a restless night. I had gotten up twice to check on Davy, and each time, I lay awake replaying my conversation with Jimmy.

Despite sleeping in, I was still the first one up, showered, and dressed for the day. Not sure why I got dressed as if it were a typical day. It wasn't like I had anywhere to go.

I headed to the kitchen, started the coffee, and checked the news to see what the weather would be like. It was supposed to be nice out, so I might let the kids play in the backyard for a little while, depending on how they were feeling. A little fresh air would probably do them some good. More than likely, though, we would be watching television, playing games, and coloring all day.

Before the coffee was finished, Missy came bouncing in. I gave her a dose of antibiotics, then fixed her a bowl of cereal.

She chatted away about school, cartoons, and her new doll. She was such a cute little chatterbox, and it took my mind off things for a moment. She did say her throat was a little sore, but not bad.

As I was clearing her cereal bowl, Jimmy came in carrying a sleepy Davy.

"Good morning, ladies." He dropped a kiss on the top of Missy's head.

Davy reached for me, so I took him, only making brief eye contact with Jimmy during the exchange. I could feel my face getting hot, so I turned away, hoping he wouldn't notice.

"How are you feeling, little guy?"

"My froat still hurtsed."

"Let me get you some juice and your medicine. Those will make you feel better soon."

Jimmy poured himself some coffee as Missy told him word for word everything she had already told me. He smiled at me while listening to her talk, then popped some bread in the toaster for himself and Davy.

I caught myself watching the way his hands moved. The easy way he navigated our kitchen like he belonged here. Which he did, I reminded myself. This was his house too.

"Since we're stuck at home, what do y'all want to do today?" he asked.

"Cartoons!" they both yelled, not quite at the same time but close.

I usually only let them watch a little TV each day, and sometimes we didn't watch any at all.

"But we can't do that all day," he said with a tease.

"Yes, Daddy, we can. Right, Mandy?" Missy looked to me for confirmation.

"I think we should clean the house." I was teasing them a little.

"You always say that!" She waved her arms around as if showing me the house. "The house is clean. It's always clean."

She was right. The house was always clean now, but it never felt clean enough to me for some reason. Would it ever? Full of all the bad memories that made it feel dirty. Years of smoke, trash, alcohol, and Mama's bad decisions haunted every corner.

The changes and improvements Jimmy had made, along with some of my decorating, had transformed it into something that felt less like the place with all those awful memories. Perhaps someday I could move and get a fresh start, making my own good memories, but this was home for now. The good, the bad, and the ugly of it.

"We can watch some cartoons, maybe do a craft or color, and maybe play Go Fish again. What do you all think? And I won't mention cleaning. I almost promise."

They all laughed but agreed to my plan.

"Annnddd we get to stay in pajamas, except that Mandy already got dressed!" Missy rolled her eyes and sighed in exasperation.

I laughed at her dramatic reaction. Of course, she had the luxury of being a kid without the need to think about routines and organization because I made sure we had them both.

"I will go change into pajamas right after I clea... whoops, after breakfast," I joked.

"You almost said it!" She giggled.

Davy giggled for the first time in more than twenty-four hours. The sound loosened something tight in my chest.

After everyone finished eating, I cleaned up breakfast without mentioning it while the others settled on the couch with a cartoon. I changed back into pajamas and joined them on the sofa. We spent the entire day watching TV or gathered at the kitchen table, coloring and playing various games.

I tried not to notice every time Jimmy's arm brushed mine on the couch. Tried not to analyze the way he looked at me when he thought I wasn't paying attention. But I noticed. I analyzed. And I had no idea what any of it meant.

I took a break from games and cartoons to start a pot of homemade chicken noodle soup. I made enough so we could eat it for both lunch and dinner. Everyone loved it, and I liked to think it made Davy feel better and kept the rest of us from getting sick. My throat had gotten a little itchy and sore, though I never got full-on sick. Jimmy said he felt fine and never got sick.

Claire called in the evening to fill me in on the day. She had done four clients for me.

"I don't know how you do so many houses in one day. Are you superwoman or what?" We shared a laugh, but she added, "Seriously, you have my respect for that. Maybe I will get the hang of it, but I'm worried you'll lose clients with me doing them."

"I'm sure you did fine. You did have a couple of tough ones today. You have Ms. Graham and the Daileys tomorrow. They're both easy to please. I don't know Mrs. Patel very well yet, but she seems nice. Her house is already spotless, so it shouldn't be too difficult."

"Yeah, I'm not as worried about tomorrow. This might seem silly, but I thought it might be good for me to shadow you, almost like training. I really want to see how you work. I mean, I've seen a little bit when you've been at Grandpa's, but it isn't like I was really watching you either."

"That's a good idea. I'll include training, and just in case I have to hire any other employees in the future, it will be nice to have a solid plan for how we all work and what's expected."

We talked for a few more minutes before getting off the phone. She promised to give me a call tomorrow after she was done with day two. Then we had to figure out a time to talk and review the employment agreement. Technically we were quarantining ourselves for three days, but we agreed Sunday might be okay.

I worked on the policy over the next two days since I had some downtime. I had no idea what I was doing, but Jimmy gave me some pointers, and I found information online. There didn't seem to be a right or wrong way. It mostly seemed to be whatever worked best for me. I liked that.

Kate texted to see how we were feeling.

"Getting better," I replied.

"Olive is complaining about her throat," Kate messaged back.

"Oh no."

"Yeah, I'll take her to the doc in the morning."

"Good luck with that. Let me know."

Saturday went about the same as Friday with cartoons, crafts, coloring, and games. By the afternoon, Davy had improved and was back to acting more like my sweet little guy and not a typical "terrible two." Missy wasn't complaining about her throat any longer either, and mine had improved as well. Jimmy never got sick.

It was also obvious the kids needed outside time. They were practically climbing the walls and driving me a bit crazy. So Jimmy went out with them, and they played one of Missy's made-up games.

I stayed in and worked on the employment agreement a bit more while they played. It took me a while to get going, but soon I was on a roll.

Kate texted in the afternoon to give me an update.

"Drama Queen has strep. Lord help me now."

"Oh boy, good luck," I messaged back.

"She is acting like her life is over, but I assured her it's not."

"Ha! We're on the mend over here, so thankfully, it doesn't last long."

"Thank goodness!"

If I ever needed proof that routine was the right thing, the past few days proved it. The kids kept getting bored and whiny and were starting to fight with each other. I was also used to being more active, so by Sunday, we all had cabin fever and were itching to be back to normal.

Missy tried to get me to promise not to clean, but I had to disinfect before having company over and lifting our self-imposed quarantine. Plus, Monday we would go back to work and school, so it was my only day.

"Okay, Mandy, but when will you get another break from cleaning and work?" Missy said smartly.

She had a point, but I enjoyed it too. It was my therapy. Jimmy tried to hide his laughter at her comment, or was he laughing at me? I wasn't sure. Maybe it was both of us he was laughing at. I was still smiling about it hours later.

He hadn't said anything more about his feelings for me, and I wasn't sure if that made things better or worse. I noticed I was watching him constantly, paying attention to what he was doing or saying. Analyzing everything. Probably over-analyzing.

Did he do that because he likes me? Had he said that because he likes me? Am I overthinking this or that because I know he likes me?

At this rate, I would drive myself crazy, and then it wouldn't matter anyway.

Like I always did when things were on my mind, I threw myself into cleaning. First, all the dishes went through the sink in the hottest water I could handle, then ran through the dishwasher. I washed all the blankets and sheets in hot water.

I could almost hear the germs screaming as I disinfected the counters and table. Yes, I had an addiction to cleaning. It was both my therapy and my obsession.

Either way, the house was company ready. Claire had called Saturday evening to tell me about her second day. We had planned to meet Sunday afternoon. She said she would take her chances being around us a bit earlier than our three-day self-imposed rule. We needed to discuss the employment agreement and work out the details before Monday.

Her second day had gone a lot better. I knew it would because the clients she had on Saturday were easy to please. I was excited that this might work out for us. I let her know I had everything written up for our agreement, and we could review it and the week's schedule together.

When she arrived, Jimmy and the kids were outside playing, so we had quiet to talk. I had printed us each a copy of the agreement and handed her one along with a red pen, just in case she had corrections.

"I'm glad y'all are feeling better," Claire said as we settled at the kitchen table.

"Me too. Thanks. That's the first real sickness we've had with the kids."

"Well, it's bound to happen now with them both in daycare."

"Yeah, I guess I had heard that, but I'd hoped they would dodge getting sick. Wishful thinking, right?"

We went through each line of the agreement, making notes as she asked questions or wanted to clarify something. We only decided to make a few changes.

There was only one item I was worried she wouldn't agree to, and that was the salary. You always hear how money is the root of all evil. I was hoping she would be okay with it, and so far, she hadn't said anything either way about it. I wasn't sure if that was good or bad.

I had put in the suggestion from Ms. Graham about my employee making a percentage of the rate per house. I settled on the 80/20 rate. I didn't want to seem greedy, and that seemed fair to me when Ms. Graham had suggested the amount. I had done all the work to get these clients and build a positive reputation for my cleaning and yard work services.

"So, what do you think about the salary?" I held my breath waiting.

"I think that's fair. I mean, you started this. Why shouldn't you get a portion of each house?" She smiled at me. "I know how hard you've worked."

She sounded sincere. I relaxed with what I felt was the biggest hurdle in the agreement behind us. As an eighteen-year-old kid creating my own business, this felt huge. Negotiating employment terms, salary, and hiring were all new to me. I had gotten clients, retained clients, and worked with clients, but having an employee was new.

I mentally high-fived myself and thought what a huge success this was turning into.

We finished reviewing it, discussing the changes once more before heading over to the computer to fix it. Once corrected, I printed us each a fresh copy to sign, and it was done. She would start officially tomorrow, and we would do a two-week training period.

It wasn't exactly training, just shadowing me, before she started on her own. We agreed that longer might be too much, but two weeks gave her time to see various clients and how I managed each. Not that any of this was hard, but I had read online about brand standards and thought I should have some to be legitimate.

I fixed drinks for the five of us, then took them to the back porch. The kids and Jimmy took a break from their game to have a drink before continuing to save the backyard from the evil dragon. I appreciated them keeping us safe.

We chatted a little before Claire excused herself. She had to get dinner going for her and Mr. Dixon. It was on the tip of my tongue to ask why she was living there and why she had dropped out of school, but I didn't want to pry. I wholeheartedly believed in the mind-my-own-business theory.

I joined the game for a bit. Though I liked to clean, I enjoyed these little moments with my family much more. The game changed when I joined. They decided I was the princess that had to be saved, so I had to go sit in the shed. It was the castle of the evil warlord and was being guarded by the dragon. A patio chair was playing the role of the dragon.

"See, Mandy, isn't this better than cleaning?" Jimmy said with a wink.

I smiled, because it definitely was, even if I was currently locked in a castle being guarded by a chair. I mean, dragon.

That night, after the kids were in bed and the house was quiet, I found myself standing at my bedroom window, looking out at nothing in particular. Jimmy was in his room down the hall. Close enough that I could hear him if he moved around. Far enough that we might as well have been on different planets.

He had said he wasn't asking for anything to change. Not now. Maybe with time.

But everything had already changed, hadn't it? I couldn't unheard his words. Couldn't unfeel the way my heart had raced when he said them. Couldn't pretend I didn't spend every moment now hyper-aware of where he was and what he was doing.

I pressed my forehead against the cool glass and let out a long breath.

Tomorrow we would go back to normal. Work, school, routines. Maybe that would help. Maybe keeping busy would give me the space I needed to figure out what I wanted.

Or maybe I already knew what I wanted and was just too scared to admit it.

Chapter Twenty-Three

Monday was a hectic day. I had several clients, including a new one. Plus, this week, I had Claire shadowing me, which was both good and bad. I didn't know yet if she would slow me down or speed things up.

The Martins' house was first, then my new client the Knights, and last the Daileys. Mr. Dailey had recently gotten out of the hospital. He had been fighting prostate cancer for a year. The kids had drawn him a few pictures that they wanted me to deliver to him. They hoped it would cheer him up.

I was a little nervous having them on the schedule right after the strep outbreak in the house, but Dr. Benson had assured me it would be okay now to be around Mr. Dailey. He said no contact or sharing drinks, which would not be a problem.

The start of the workweek made me both glad and sad. I had enjoyed our family time. At least, what I had always imagined a family would be like.

However, I was glad for the distraction and to be away from Jimmy for the day. Things were so confusing, and I needed time to think. Work had always been a pleasant distraction, plus I did my best thinking while cleaning.

Since the weather was beautiful and after days of being stuck in the house, I thought I would walk to the Martins. Claire was pulling up in front of their house when I arrived.

"You walked?" she said as she exited the car.

"Yeah, it's less than a mile."

"You are superwoman."

We got right to work on the yard. I showed her where everything was kept and went through my process. It was winter, so for the most part, it was just keeping the yard neat. No need to mow.

We then headed into their house. The Martins were one of my easier clients because it was only the two of them, and Mrs. Martin always kept things neat, so we were done in no time.

We had the Knights scheduled after the Martins. They lived in the newer west side of town, so I would need my car now. Thankfully, I had Claire today, so I didn't have to walk back to get it, which I typically would have done. I liked the exercise.

When I got to their house, Mrs. Knight answered the door with a faint smile and a crying baby. "Hi, Mandy and Claire, I assume. Come in, come in."

"Thank you, Mrs. Knight," I said.

"Sorry for Grant. He's teething and not a happy baby." She rubbed his back lightly and bounced him on her hip.

"No problem. I used to give Missy and Davy frozen washcloths. I read somewhere that it helped with teething."

"That's a good idea. I will have to try it." She smiled. "And, Mandy, it's okay if you call me Rachel. I'm barely older than you."

"Oh, I... yes. Thanks, Rachel."

I was raised addressing adults this way. It was a habit, but I guess being eighteen now, I was an adult. Weird.

"I really appreciate you taking me as a client. I thought I could multitask better than this. I used to supervise twenty-five employees over multiple projects, but once he starts crying, I can't get anything done." She sighed and then laughed slightly. "I shouldn't complain. I must sound horrible. I love that I can stay home with him, but it's harder than I thought."

"No, you don't sound horrible. I'm glad I can help you, and I promise it does get easier." I tried to offer support and hope. Who would have thought that childless me would be giving advice to a new mother? "Do you want me to start on the laundry? With a little one, I know that's the first thing to pile up."

"You've got that right. Let me give you a quick tour." She walked us around, showing us where the cleaning supplies were, where the laundry room was, and finishing the tour in Grant's room.

"Well, that's it. It's time for Mr. Fussy here to eat. I'll be here for the next fifteen to twenty minutes if you need me."

We walked back to the laundry room and got a load started. Then we headed to the kitchen.

"With a baby, I just think about what she might need to have done and in what order. Laundry and dishes are always the two things that pile up quickly. Then I just go through a list in my head. If I were busy, what would I neglect?"

"Easy," Claire said.

"Yeah, it's silly, but it works." I shrugged.

Together we went through my mental checklist: wipe counters, sweep, and mop.

After talking through it, we decided on a divide and conquer method. Claire vacuumed the living room and dining room while I checked the laundry and folded a load of clothes fresh from the dryer. Then we moved to bathrooms, each taking one and so on.

After an hour, we were done. Rachel thanked me for probably the hundredth time since I arrived. I got her scheduled for her next cleaning, but this time with Claire as her main rep.

We headed over to the Daileys next. Unfortunately, Mr. Dailey had been extremely sick with his cancer treatments, so I hadn't seen them in a while, maybe not since my birthday two months ago.

Since the last time I saw her, Mrs. Dailey looked like she had aged ten years. She was under a lot of stress with Mr. Dailey's cancer and caring for him. Their children lived out of state and tried to come when they could, but with children and jobs, it wasn't easy.

She had mentioned her daughter was coming soon for a few weeks, so I hoped that would be enough to give her a break. Claire and I gave her a hug, and then I handed her the drawings the kids made.

"These are for Mr. Dailey from Missy and Davy."

"Thank you. I know he'll love them. He's sleeping now." She sighed softly as she glanced over her shoulder towards his room.

"We'll be quiet. I'll make some meals while I'm here," I offered.

"That sounds wonderful. Thank you so much. You've been a lifesaver."

"Why don't you go rest for a bit while we get to work?" I smiled. "I'll wake you if I hear Mr. Dailey."

"Yes, go rest," Claire echoed my suggestion.

"I think I will, dear. Thank you so much."

Meal prepping was one of my favorite things to do. I loved cooking. I got lucky with Claire because she liked to cook as well, and having eaten her food before at potlucks, I knew she could handle this part of the job. This could really work out well.

I had planned to make several of my favorite dishes, including a soup that I knew Mr. Dailey shouldn't have any trouble eating. I wanted them to be heartier, healthy meals.

While I finished cooking, I asked Claire how we should divide up the work. I thought it would be a good chance to test her a little. Not that any of this was rocket science, but I wanted to ensure that the reputation I'd built would continue when I started sending Claire to houses without me.

"Thinking of what we did at Rachel's, what do you think we should start with here?"

"I'm thinking laundry. Like babies, sick people can make a lot of laundry too, right?" I nodded. She continued, "Then we work in the kitchen and out from there. Avoiding the bedrooms since they're probably both sleeping in one each."

I nodded, and she started the laundry while I worked in the kitchen. She joined me as I finished sweeping the floor, so she got the mop out and started that. Once we had done most of the cleaning, avoiding running the vacuum or getting too close to either bedroom, we wrote Mrs. Dailey a note and let ourselves out.

I suggested we drop in on Mrs. Wills on our way home. She had been in the hospital recently, and I wanted to check on her and ask if she needed anything. She was happy to see us and seemed to be feeling better.

"I'm so glad you stopped by. With my children and grandchildren so far away, it's nice to have someone come check in on me. I don't really need any help today, but would you like to join me for a cup of tea?"

I drank a lot of tea in my job and heard a lot about living in the 1950s, raising children in the 1970s, and where they were when JFK was shot. I heard about the Civil Rights movement and who they lost during the Vietnam War.

Some of my neighbors were in their eighties, but most were in their late sixties and seventies. Depending on who I was talking to depended on which stories I got to hear. I loved it. Better than any history class. They seemed to enjoy having someone to talk to.

Claire seemed to enjoy it as well. She smiled and chatted right along, sharing bits and pieces she had gotten from her grandfather.

"That was fun," she commented when we got back in the car. "It seemed like we just made her day."

"Yeah, that's my favorite part. I like to make little stops like that occasionally when I have time because it makes them happy, plus I really enjoy their stories and friendship."

We reviewed the schedule for the next day and agreed to meet again at the client's house.

"I'm enjoying this work so far and glad you asked me to join you." She smiled. "I can see why you do this."

"All the free tea!"

"Exactly!" We both laughed.

By then, we were pulling in front of my house. We said goodbye as I hopped out.

Jimmy waved as I walked up the driveway. It looked like he and the kids had just gotten home as well.

The kids ran to me and seemed happy to see me. Missy had some fun stories to share about school. But today, Davy also wanted to tell me all about his day. He was learning from Missy. He never used to be like that. It was cute.

"And, and Wyan said his froat was hurtin' and that he was going to have step froat too. I tolded him it was not fun. No, no, not fun." He looked so serious that I had to stifle a laugh.

"I hope he wasn't really getting sick," I said, bending forward to pick him up.

"His mommy came to getted him early."

"Uh oh, that doesn't sound good."

Jimmy was watching us with a smile. Our eyes caught and held for a second. My stomach fluttered as I returned the smile, then quickly looked away.

"So, how'd your day go? You had a new client, if I remember correctly. And how did Claire like it?" Jimmy finally asked as we all made our way into the house.

"Yeah, one new client. She was nice. She has the cutest little baby boy, Grant. Claire seemed to enjoy it and did great. Oh, and we stopped in to check on Mrs. Wills after the Daileys, our last house for the day."

"Oh yeah? How is she feeling? I heard from Mr. Mulroney that she'd been in the hospital."

"Better. We had a cup of tea and chatted a bit. I enjoy talking with her. Claire said that was her favorite part. Honestly, mine too."

Inside the house, I excused myself to change out of work clothes and check my emails to see if I had any scheduling requests or inquiries. Of course, I couldn't take new business until after Claire was comfortable enough to work alone, but it was exciting to know the company could grow.

Tonight, there was a Christmas special on television. I had promised the kids we would watch it. They were so excited. I swear they asked every five minutes if it was time yet. Missy was learning how to tell time, so I kept reminding her to check the clock and testing to see if she could tell me the time.

They sat in awe once it was on. I admit I was a little too, as I'd only seen bits of the shows in the past. Mama's friends constantly changed the channel when I tried to watch. Sometimes they made fun of me for wanting to watch the shows.

After the show was over, I worked on the computer, writing up my customer agreement and policies that I would put in place in the New Year while Jimmy did the nightly routine with the kids. He came in as I was saving. I had really wanted to escape to my room before he was finished, but I wasn't fast enough. I guess he figured out what I had been doing.

"I wanted to talk to you now that the kids are in bed."

"Oh, okay. What's up?" I was worried but tried to keep it out of my voice.

"Don't worry, it isn't bad." I guess I didn't do a good job of keeping my tone calm. "I applied for a new position a month or so ago." He paused. "I was offered the position last Friday. I didn't want to say anything to you until I talked to my supervisor today."

"Oh, Jimmy, that's wonderful news. Congrats!" I jumped up and gave him a hug before I thought it all the way through. I ended the embrace as quickly as I started it, stepping back and tucking my hair behind my ear.

"Thanks. I'll have to make one final trip offshore to transition my duties, and then I'll be working downtown. I can be here for the kids more and to help you out."

"Wow, the kids will be so excited to hear that."

"I know. I can't wait to tell them. This... this with you and the kids is what I imagined life with a family would be, and when it wasn't like that, I was miserable."

I smiled and nodded my head. "We love having you here. The kids especially love it. They'll be so glad that you'll get to be here with them more."

He ran a hand through his hair, and I recognized the gesture. He did that when he was working up to something difficult. My heart rate picked up.

"I hope that things between us won't be awkward. I don't want that. But I don't exactly know what our relationship will be yet. I'm not your father, and I'm not a brother. Maybe a friend?"

The word landed like a stone in my chest. Friend. After everything he had said just days ago, after I had spent every moment since analyzing what it might mean, after I had finally started to let myself imagine what could be possible between us.

Friend.

"Hm, yes, friends." I found myself feeling a sharp stab of disappointment, but I kept my voice steady. This was probably better anyway. Now, if someone would just tell my heart.

We said good night. I climbed into bed a little conflicted and a lot confused. I lay there, unable to decide if I was angry, disappointed, or thrilled that we had defined our relationship. I knew this was probably the least confusing outcome for us all. The kids wouldn't understand if we dated, would they?

It was probably better that we were just friends. Then, we wouldn't have to explain to people who I was or how we had met or why the children called me Mandy, and that we all had the same mom.

I decided it was a good thing to settle on just friends, and I thought if I really tried hard enough, I would believe this decision was for the best.

But as I stared at the ceiling in the dark, I couldn't shake the feeling that something important had slipped through my fingers. He had told me he cared for me. He had said maybe with time. And now, just days later, he was pulling back.

Had I taken too long to respond? Had my silence made him think I wasn't interested?

Or maybe he had come to his senses and realized how complicated this would be. How many questions people would ask. How strange it would look from the outside.

I turned onto my side and pulled the blanket up to my chin.

Friends. I could do that. I had been doing that for months before his confession.

But tonight, I wasn't trying hard enough to believe it. Perhaps tomorrow.

Chapter Twenty-Four

That weekend we planned to put up a Christmas tree. We toyed with the idea of a real tree but, in the end, decided on an artificial one. We found a pre-lit one with various settings that would change from white to multi-colored and at different speeds. Missy suggested we add additional strings of lights.

"We need more lights, so Santa doesn't get lost. See how many that tree has?" She was looking at one of the displays. I had to admit it was beautiful.

This was technically a first for the three of us, and I wanted it to be perfect for the kids. I had tried to put up a tree once before. I'd found a tabletop one at the thrift shop in town. It was a little beat up, but I tried to decorate it with yarn and paper ornaments I'd made. Mama and her friends laughed at it, so I threw it out and never tried again. I admit it was ugly, but I was only ten at the time. I just wanted a typical childhood experience like my classmates.

Missy looked so darn cute and made a good point, so Jimmy and I gave in. We bought some larger ones, the kind most people line their house with. The tree already had smaller ones, and for some reason, I thought the two different sizes would look beautiful on the tree.

Even though the kids and I had made some, Jimmy suggested buying more ornaments for the tree. Considering how large the tree was, I agreed we would need more. We let each kid pick out three decorations. Davy picked quickly. His picks were a soccer ball, a Superman, and a dog with a Christmas hat.

"Dhis is the cutest doggie I have ever seened."

Missy took longer, making sure she looked at each one and thought about them. Her first and fastest pick was a kitten.

"Olive and I both love kitties the best. Can you take a picture of me holding it and send it to Ms. Kate, so Olive can see it? Please, oh please, Mandy!" Of course, I did.

Next, she picked a snowman. She explained that she thought snowmen were the best because they came to life and played games with the children. We had recently watched the movie, so I could see where she got that. It did look fun to play with Frosty, even if the thought of that really happening creeped me out.

Her last one was a pink, glittery snowflake that was as big as her hand.

"Pink is my favoritest color ever. And wouldn't it be fun if we got snow! I never saw it before. Have I, Mandy?"

"Nope, I don't think we've gotten any snow in this area since... well, I actually can't remember. A few years anyway. I wouldn't mind a little snow either."

"What about you, Mandy? You should pick out a few too." Missy said, grinning but looking at her ornaments. "And Daddy, you too." She waved her hand towards us as if she were a queen giving commands.

Jimmy and I looked at each other as we shared this moment. He winked and studied the ornaments.

"Well, hmm, let's see." He started studying the various choices. "What should I pick?"

The kids helped him, and soon Jimmy had made his selections of a glass Santa, a cowboy boot with holly on it, and a blue snowflake that matched Missy's. So now it was down to me.

I stood there a little embarrassed and unsure of myself. Why? I don't know. Maybe because I always thought of the kids, rarely myself, and wasn't used to picking things out for myself. Not since they were born, and it was clear Mama wasn't going to actually care for them past the bare minimum and only if I wasn't home.

Even that little care stopped once Missy could open the refrigerator to get her own food. I think she might have changed her own diaper a few times while I wasn't home. I know she changed Davy's. The thought always made me sad.

After some encouragement from the kids and Jimmy, I chose my first. A clear glass angel. I secretly thought of my grandmother that I never got a chance to really know. She had provided me a nice nest egg that I didn't even know about for years.

Then I picked a snowman that was a little different than Missy's and a penguin in a Santa hat to match Davy's dog. Davy loved that one and started giggling when he saw it.

"Dhat penguin is funny." His giggle was contagious.

We picked out two dozen multi-colored glass bulbs, some garland, and Missy suggested some red bows with gold glitter on them. Last, we found a light-up star that twinkled and blinked in multi-colors to go on top.

"Santa will love it!" Missy declared, and as he always did, Davy nodded his agreement.

"Well, with the tree decorations picked, we need stockings, right?" Jimmy looked at the kids.

"Oh, yes, yes! Can we get some? We must or where will Santa put... well, whatever he puts in stockings!" Missy skipped off to the section with stockings without waiting for an answer.

Davy bounced after her. The kids' excitement was infectious, and I was feeling the Christmas spirit for the first time. It was all new and exhilarating.

She had no trouble finding one she wanted. They happened to have a kitten on a glittery pink stocking. All her favorite things in one. Whoever made stockings knew what little girls liked. Of course, she asked me to take another picture to send to Olive. Kate's reply was instant.

Olive is loving all the pictures and is insisting we go shopping immediately

Davy found one with a train on it that he liked. Jimmy got one with a cowboy Santa on it. Again, I was the last to pick and decided on a snowman riding a sled. Davy clapped at my selection.

"That's the bestest one, Nandy! But not as bestest as mine." He gave his stocking a hug and a soft little kiss.

At Jimmy's suggestion, we selected outdoor lights and a dozen plastic candy canes to line the landscaping in the front of the house. As we were heading to the checkout, Missy spotted three-foot-tall wood cutouts. They weren't too big and not too pricy, so we got three: two snowmen and Santa. At the last minute, Jimmy grabbed a sign that said, "Santa stop here," and the kids thought that was the best idea ever in the world. Missy's words, and Davy repeated it.

Once home, we took everything inside and sorted it out. I'm not sure who was the most excited, me or the children.

They wanted to do the tree first because they were so excited, but Jimmy convinced them it might be best to do the outside first before it got dark, so we could see what we were doing and enjoy it as soon as the sun set. So, we all headed outside with the outdoor decorations.

When we came back outside, Ms. Graham was on her porch, so the kids ran over to tell her all about the new Christmas stuff. She oohed and aahed at all the right parts as they told her about the decorations. The excitement of the kids was spreading. Every one of us was smiling and laughing. A joy I'd never had before.

Once the outside was done, the kids were a little disappointed because we couldn't see the lights until night. We still had several hours before the sun would go down.

"While we wait on dark, let's go decorate the tree," Jimmy suggested.

"Yay!" The kids cheered.

"You should join us," Missy turned to Ms. Graham.

"Oh, yes, I'd love to. Let me just run into my house and grab something, then I'll be right over."

We got to work setting the tree up. It was easy peasy with just a few pieces to put together. First, Jimmy put on the additional lights. He then pushed the tree into the corner, so we could get the full effect of it. The mix of larger and smaller bulbs made it look enchanting, and the kids' faces lit up with the magic of it.

Ms. Graham walked in at that moment, carrying a box that was slightly larger than a shoebox.

"I got here right at the perfect moment. Look at that beautiful tree. Santa will love it." The little kids giggled, grinned, and danced around as only little kids could. "I brought over some things I would like to pass to you." She directed the last part to me.

She opened the box to reveal glass ornaments. There were no words to adequately describe them. Stunning, gorgeous, and beautiful all missed the mark.

"I got these in the early eighties when I was over in Germany. They are hand-painted by an artist there. I'm sure he is long gone. He was nearly eighty years old when I was there. Anyway, I wanted to give them to you because I don't put up a tree anymore, and they're too beautiful to sit in a box." She handed me the box.

"Oh my, Ms. Graham, are you sure? They look so fragile, and I would hate if any got broken."

"Yes, dear, they'll be fine. I've dropped them so many times. I mean, I wouldn't recommend it, but they're fairly sturdy." She handed me the box.

There were eight of them, and each one was different. I gently touched one that had a beautiful Christmas wreath painted on it.

"These are... beautiful. Thank you. I'll cherish them." I gave her a hug.

"I'm glad you like them."

I took the first one out and put it on the tree. The kids clapped loudly while Jimmy and Ms. Graham smiled and watched.

"That looks so perfect. I'm so glad I saved them." She said, tears of joy in her eyes.

I had the kids start putting ornaments on the tree. I had to remind Davy to spread them out. He kept putting them all on the same two branches. In all fairness, he wasn't tall enough to put them in many other places, so I picked him up so he could put them higher up.

"Come on, Daddy, you have to help." Missy instructed and handed him an ornament. "And Grammy, you too."

"Oh well, of course, dear." Ms. Graham said, taking the offered ornament from Missy.

Once it was completely decorated and the star was on top, we all stepped back to admire it. Little Davy danced and hopped around, cheering. Missy moved all around, admiring this ornament or that one, commenting on each.

"This is the best Christmas tree ever!" she declared.

"I think it just might be," Ms. Graham said with a grin. "I'm glad you let me lend a hand."

Jimmy and I cleaned up the various wrappings and ornament boxes while the kids told Ms. Graham all about other things we saw at the store.

"They had these giant, like the biggest ever..." Missy said.

"Bigger than Daddy," Little Davy added.

"Yeah, bigger than Daddy. Blow up things. They had Santa and a snowman and Snoopy in an airplane. And like everything you can imagine!"

Little Davy moved his hands way up like he was trying to show how big they were. "Like bigger and bigger!"

We invited Ms. Graham to stay for dinner, but she declined. She was having dinner with the Daileys again.

"Norm is feeling better, so I'm glad to spend some time with them," she let me know.

"Oh, I'm glad to hear. Well, tell them we send our love."

After dinner, we loaded the kids into Jimmy's truck and drove around the different neighborhoods to see Christmas lights. So many people had put them out.

Jimmy put it on the local station that was playing Christmas music. We all sang along as we drove. It was one of those heart-melting, will never forget moments. Something I figured families did together, but I had never gotten to, so I just soaked it all in. Jimmy and the kids laughing and singing made me smile.

Something loosened in my chest as I watched Missy conduct an imaginary orchestra from her car seat, belting out the words to "Jingle Bells." Davy clapped along, slightly off rhythm but utterly delighted. This was what childhood was supposed to look like. This was what I had always wanted for them.

The holiday lights were on when we got home. The kids cheered at the sight. We sat and watched them twinkle for a moment.

I took another moment to soak it all in. The happiness, the cheers, and the holiday spirit. I knew how fleeting moments could be, and we all had to enjoy the good ones when they came.

Jimmy seemed to be thinking the same thing because he looked over at me and smiled. He reached for my hand and gave it a slight squeeze. The warmth of his fingers wrapped around mine sent a jolt through me.

Friends. He had said we should just be friends.

But I don't think friends look at their friends like that or cause their hearts to nearly beat out of their chest with a single touch. It was at that moment that I knew I couldn't just be friends with him.

As fast as that moment happened, it was over. The kids were yawning from the back seat, so we unloaded them. Then, walking in the house, the tree was lit. The magic reflecting in the kids' sleepy eyes made my heart swell with love.

I never understood the Christmas spirit or what the big deal about Christmas was until today. It was about the magic that children believe in, the happiness of being together and loved. I never had any of that, which is why I never understood it.

Jimmy took the kids to get them dressed and ready for bed. I could hear them going through the routine of getting changed, teeth brushed and tucked in. I listened for a few moments before slipping into my room.

I didn't want to discuss feelings or feel the awkward way I felt around him lately. There would be enough of it tomorrow. Today had been perfect, and I wanted to hold on to that moment as long as possible.

But as I changed into my pajamas, I couldn't stop thinking about the way his hand had felt in mine. The way he had looked at me in the glow of the Christmas lights.

He had said friends. But everything about today had felt like something more.

Maybe he was as confused as I was. Maybe he didn't know what he wanted either.

Or maybe he knew exactly what he wanted but was giving me space to figure out what I wanted.

The question was: did I know?

I crawled into bed and pulled the covers up to my chin, listening to the distant sounds of Jimmy saying goodnight to the kids, his footsteps in the hallway, his door closing.

Today had been magic. Real, actual magic.

And I wasn't ready to let it go.

Chapter Twenty-Five

In a flash, it was Christmas Eve. The kids couldn't contain their excitement. Jimmy's mother, Virginia, and sister, Emma, had come to visit. This was only my fourth time meeting them. They had come twice when Missy was a baby and once when Davy was. They lived in Florida. His sister was a year older than me and went to a local college while living at home.

They had moved there a few years ago for his mom's job. She worked for a NASA contractor. The company had transferred a couple hundred jobs from the Johnson Space Center in the Houston area to the Kennedy Space Center in Florida.

Virginia took the job rather than being laid off. She had lived in Houston her entire life and thought a change would be good. She loved living in Florida but did miss her friends and family in Houston.

His dad had died when he was around eleven years old, and his sister was about five. He'd been a police officer and was killed during a traffic stop. The car he had stopped was full of stolen guns, including the one that killed him. Jimmy didn't talk about it much, but I had heard the story from his mom that first time they came to visit.

I couldn't remember why she brought it up. I think it must have been around the anniversary of his death because, looking back, it seemed like an odd topic.

They were staying in a hotel that Jimmy reserved for them in Pearland. It was a larger city than Glenn Lake and was located just north of us, also a suburb of Houston.

Glenn Lake didn't have any hotels, but we were close enough to Houston and Galveston. Between them and the other cities nearby, there were plenty of places to stay.

"Emma, Emma... look at this, look at this." Missy loved having her Aunt Emma here.

They were all playing in the living room with Davy's blocks.

"Oh, that's a beautiful house, Missy. Great job." She leaned over and gave her a hug.

"Em, Em. Looky at mine!" He had stacked up some blocks into a crooked pyramid.

He'd recently learned how to stack them this way. Until recently, he would only stack a few straight up.

"Wow, Little Davy, I love it." She gave him a hug too.

He smiled up at her with the sweetest grin. I smiled as I watched because it made me happy to see the kids have family that loved them.

Jimmy had made us a lovely dinner of baked chicken, salad, and roasted veggies. It was delicious as his food always was.

It was drizzly and cold out, which limited anything outside. Nonetheless, they had kept both aunt and grandmother busy all day chatting and showing them everything in the house. They also played several of the kids' board games and some of Missy's made up games. So now we were enjoying time visiting in the living room, watching the kids play.

"I can't believe how big they've gotten. I just keep looking at them." Virginia paused. "I'm sorry we haven't been around more. It's just... well, I'm sorry, Mandy, you understand, right?"

She meant Mama, and yes, I did. When Davy was a month old was the last time Virginia and Emma came, and Mama was a complete nightmare. She had thrown things and insults like they were beads during a Mardi Gras parade. I liked Virginia and Emma a lot, but Mama was... well, typical Mama.

"I know. I understand." I looked at her with a smile.

She was sitting near enough to me that she patted my hand then gave it a little squeeze. People were always apologizing to me for how they felt about Mama. They all looked at me with that same look of pity too. It made me sad and ashamed. Why couldn't I have been part of a regular family?

"I don't want to let as much time go by this time between visits. I really want to be in y'all's lives."

"Yes, me too," Emma added from the floor. "I have always wanted a sister, so I hope we can be like that, Mandy."

"That would be nice. I'd like that too."

"I want to be your sister too!" Missy protested with a slight pout and cross of her arms.

"You get to be something better because you are my niece! That's even more special than a sister." Then seeing Davy look up in surprise, she added, "And you are my favorite nephew, Little Davy."

He flashed his sweet baby grin and went back to his animals. He had run off at some point to grab the little plastic animals I had bought him after our last trip to the zoo. I saw them at the dollar store and thought they would be perfect. He was currently putting them all over his pyramid.

I kept checking the time to make sure I got them to bed close to their usual time.

"I know you want to stay on schedule, Mandy, but it is Christmas Eve," Jimmy whispered close to my ear. His breath warm against my skin sent a shiver down my spine. "It's okay to get out of routine once in a while."

I didn't miss the slight tease in his tone.

"Okay, okay... I will relax a bit." I chuckled softly.

I think I craved the routine, the normal, and the predictable more than the kids. Though I had read or heard somewhere that it was good for kids to have structure and not have surprises in their day. I was the one with the emotional scars that needed that routine.

I zoned back into the conversation in the room. Jimmy was telling his mom about his new job and how he was excited to be moving back to an office job and have the ability to be home more.

"I love being here with the kids. They're good kids." Then he nodded and looked towards me. "Thanks completely to Mandy."

I blushed and smiled, brushing a stray hair from my face.

"I wanted them to have a good childhood. They deserve that," I said.

Virginia looked at me when I said it and squeezed my hand again. I think I knew what she was thinking. I imagined it was the same thing Jimmy asked me every time I said that. Don't you deserve that too? It was true. I squeezed her hand a little in reply.

"We are here for you now. All I can say is I'm sorry for walking out. I just couldn't handle things before. I didn't think... well, I thought of only myself and Emma back then. We're here now and won't do that again," Virginia said.

It was nice to have a family. But each day, my family got larger. I didn't feel so alone, yet I still didn't have my own family, only Missy and Davy. I was okay with it most of the time, but sometimes I missed Mama or at least the idea of what things could have been.

Over the past few months, I had gained two friends, so I had them to talk to now, and that was something new and positive for me.

Kate and I spoke several times a week and got together a few times a month with the kids.

I worked with Claire, and we were starting to get closer. But we still weren't telling each other our darkest secrets, not that I really had any, but we were beginning to talk more than just about work and the people we knew.

"Should we put out the cookies and milk for Santa?" Missy asked, stifling a yawn. She was tired but didn't want to admit it, as she was over the moon excited about Santa. "I hope I have been a good girl this year, so Santa brings the dollhouse I want. I hope, hope, hope!"

We all laughed and reassured her that she had been a good girl and that we were sure she would get the dollhouse. Though I had a sad thought at her statement. She probably thought in the past he didn't come because she hadn't been good, which wasn't at all true.

"I want animals! I a good boy, right, Nandy?"

"Yes, you've been a good boy."

We all went to the kitchen to get Santa's cookies and milk ready. We had made cookies that afternoon. With a lot of practice, Missy was getting good at measuring the ingredients. Virginia and Emma were impressed with how smart she was.

Once each kid had selected a cookie for Santa, we poured some milk and placed them both on an end table near the tree. Then Emma said she would get the kids dressed for bed. We could hear them giggling with her. After they were dressed, they came running into the room to say good night, hugs and kisses all around, and then Aunt Emma put them to bed.

When she came back into the room, she and Virginia got their things together to leave.

"We'll be back bright and early in the morning for Christmas."

"Well, early. It might not be bright yet," Emma added with a groan.

"I'll be sure to have plenty of coffee," I assured her.

"You better! I know I will need it by the gallon full. I'm not a morning person."

Jimmy agreed. She playfully punched his arm. Ah, the sibling relationship. I hoped Missy and Little Davy were like this as adults.

Once they were gone, I went to peek in on the kids, and Jimmy started getting their gifts out.

The attic access was right outside of their room, and no matter how much we oiled the hinges, they always protested with a loud squeal when opened. We thought that would be better than going into the attic while the kids were trying to sleep. So, we had moved them from the attic to his closet a few days ago while the kids were still at daycare.

"They're asleep," I whispered as I came back into the room.

We started grabbing everything and moving it into the living room.

"I'm glad we had pulled it all out of the attic before tonight," Jimmy whispered as we were setting everything out.

"Me too," I said. "If we had put all those stickers on the dollhouse and on the furniture on Christmas Eve, it would have taken us forever."

We wrapped a few things and kept the larger things open. That way, they had a mix of surprises and instant gifts. Davy's big gift was a zoo playset and additional animals to go with it. In addition, they both got some books, puzzles, and a few little toys that weren't on their lists.

We also got them both some new clothes. I couldn't wait to see their surprised faces in the morning.

I laid out the wrapped gifts I had gotten for Jimmy, Ms. Graham, Virginia, and Emma. I had already given Kate and Olive gifts from us. We had lunch last weekend with them and exchanged gifts. I also gave Claire and Mr. Dixon gifts. Everyone else got homemade banana bread and Christmas cards.

While I had been making the banana bread, I couldn't help but think of Mama. I wondered where she was and if she was making some too. The moments didn't come around often, but I missed her sometimes. After all, she was my Mama.

Jimmy got some wrapped packages from a bag and placed them under the tree. I didn't see the names on them, but I assumed they were for his mom and sister.

"Do you want one of the cookies?" He was eyeing the cookies with interest.

"Oh, wow, I almost forgot about those. We should probably eat them." I giggled.

"I'll grab another glass, and we can split the milk, yeah?"

"Sure."

He came back and poured half the milk into the second glass.

"Merry Christmas, Mandy."

"Merry Christmas."

We clinked our glasses together and smiled. Then we sipped the milk and ate the cookies. The perfect sugar cookies. Not too soft, not too hard.

"I'm glad we got to do this together." He nodded towards the tree and gifts.

"Me too."

We were quiet for a few minutes as we watched the lights blink on the tree, just soaking in the moment together. The soft sound of the radio playing Christmas music added to the moment. It was peaceful. It was comfortable. It was the perfect Christmas Eve.

"Well... I guess we better get some sleep. I'm sure the kids will be up early," he said, standing, but he didn't move towards his room.

Instead, he got closer to me and then wrapped his arms around me. My heart stuttered in my chest. After a few heartbeats, he leaned back and looked at me.

He kissed my forehead and held it a moment longer than a just friends kiss would warrant.

"Good night," he whispered, then turned and walked to his room.

I was left standing there, staring after him until my heart started beating again and my legs stopped feeling like jello.

I floated to my room with butterflies in my stomach and a smile the size of Texas.

Did that really happen? It was a wonderful moment of intimacy. It was perfect, I thought as I climbed into bed.

I lay there in the dark, touching my forehead where his lips had been. Friends. He had said we should be friends. But friends didn't kiss each other like that. Friends didn't look at each other the way he had looked at me.

So what were we?

I didn't have an answer. But for the first time, I wasn't afraid of the question.

Chapter Twenty-Six

We knew the kids would be up early with all the excitement, but no matter how much you try to mentally prepare, it felt much earlier. I rolled over to check the clock as two cherub faces stared down at me. I groaned when I saw it was only 5:30 a.m. and far too early for me.

After playing Santa with Jimmy the night before and our sweet moment in the kitchen, I had gotten to bed late and then tossed and turned, overthinking the moment. The ghost of his lips on my forehead had kept me awake for hours.

I had them climb into bed with me to try and sleep a little longer. Then, I told them we needed to wait on Grandma Virginia and Aunt Emma. I would try to stall as long as I could.

An hour later, Missy announced she might explode with excitement if we didn't get up and see if Santa came. Since we'd never had a real Christmas before, I was kind of feeling the excitement building too.

With a stretch and a yawn, I agreed to get up. I said they should wake up Jimmy as I headed straight to the coffee pot. I had promised to have it ready for Emma. I pushed the on button and then headed for the living room, so I didn't miss the little kids' faces as they saw their gifts for the first time.

The expressions on their little faces will be ingrained in my mind forever. It was one of those priceless moments. Virginia and Emma knocked on the door at that moment. I guess they saw the lights come on. They were loaded down with boxes and bags of gifts.

"Perfect timing! We just got up."

"Coffee?" Emma said through a yawn.

"Coming up." I came back with four steaming mugs, handing one to each of the yawning grownups.

The kids were bouncing around, looking for their gifts.

"I got my dollhouse! I got it. I just knew Santa would bring it. I just knew it!" She ran to me for a hug. "You were right. I was a good girl! Santa knew."

Again, I had that same sad thought that she did think she'd been bad the other years. I would try to ensure she never felt that way again. At least as much as I could.

"A zoo. I gotted a zoo! Looky, looky." He started moving animals around the zoo and making all the animal sounds.

We let them start opening their other gifts. They took their time, exclaiming over everything. I had expected chaos and shredded paper flying through the air, but this was a new experience for them. They might not realize they were doing it, but to me, it felt almost like they were trying to savor the moment.

"Here, Mandy. For you." Jimmy handed me a little square shaped package wrapped in snowflake paper.

I felt my face start to blush. I hoped the room was still dark enough to hide it.

"Oh, thank you." Our hands touched slightly, and we shared a moment of eye contact. The memory of last night flickered between us. I broke the eye contact first by picking up and handing him one with his name on it. "From me."

"Thank you." He opened it quickly with a smile. It was a shirt I had found that said World's Best Dad. Missy and Davy both cheered when Jimmy read it.

"You are the best Daddy in the world." Missy ran and gave him a hug. Of course, Little Davy had to follow suit.

I opened the little gift. Inside the box was a delicate chain with two heart-shaped charms on it. One had Missy's birthstone in it, and the other was Davy's. I nearly cried. It was the most thoughtful, perfect gift. I suddenly felt a little embarrassed about the cheesy t-shirt he just opened.

"It's a mother's necklace, and I know, I know you aren't technically theirs, but... ya know, you kind of are." He took it from me and put it around my neck. His fingers brushed against my skin as he fastened the clasp, and I held my breath. "There, it looks perfect on you."

"It's so beautiful. Thank you." I stood and gave him a hug. "I love it."

The necklace felt warm against my chest. A mother's necklace. He saw me as their mother. He saw what I had been doing all these years, the sacrifices I had made, the childhood I had given up for them. And he had found a way to honor that.

Virginia and Emma commented how perfect it was for me, and Missy came over to examine it.

"Oh Mandy, this is sooo you! Good job, Daddy." She gave him a thumbs up and went back to her gifts.

I wasn't sure what she meant by the "so me" part, but I agreed. He had gotten this perfect.

The rest of the gifts got opened without much ceremony but lots of thank yous. Then came the fun of pulling all the kids' toys out of the plastic wrappings and twist ties. We had several trash bags full by the time it was all said and done.

I took a break to get a ham in the oven, so it would be ready for lunch. It needed a few hours to cook.

Ms. Graham was going to join us for lunch. Everyone else would be with family. She was kind of like me in that she didn't have much family. One brother was still alive, and she had nieces and nephews, but she wasn't close to any of them.

I refilled mugs with fresh coffee, oohed and ahhed over gifts, and joined in the cleanup. Everyone was enjoying themselves.

Later I excused myself again to prep the side dishes and check on the ham. We were having mashed potatoes, corn casserole, and green bean casserole plus rolls. There was also an apple pie and cookies for dessert.

Emma joined me in the kitchen while I was starting to put casseroles together.

"Can I help with anything?" she asked.

"Sure, do you mind helping me peel potatoes? I have two peelers."

"No problem." She grabbed one of the peelers and a potato. "So, what's the deal with you and my brother? I mean, you like each other, right?"

"Oh, wow, you got right to it, didn't you?"

"Yeah, I'm like that, especially when it comes to my brother, and you, my dear, are stalling... spill, spill." She said with a twinkle in her eye.

"Well, I think... I mean, I know he likes me. He told me, but I'm..." I shrugged, a bit flustered by her question. I took a deep breath then blurted out, "This is new to me. I was never that girl with a boyfriend or even a crush."

"Yeah, okay, I get that. But you like him, right?"

I nodded slowly. Happy to be talking about this with someone. It would be nice to hear someone else's view on what I was thinking.

"But you have to understand how I grew up. I saw men as... well, mean and evil. Aside from a few older neighbors, Jimmy is the first man to treat me well. I'm having a hard time separating true feelings from the knight in shining armor coming to my rescue. Does that make sense?"

"I think I understand, but why can't it be both? Does it have to be so hard?"

My brain filled in what I knew she was thinking. Well, does it? I didn't know the answer.

"I don't know. All I know is that right now, I am letting it all sink in. Ya know? My mother didn't set the best example for me, and my ideas on relationships might be skewed a bit." I thought for a moment. "This is a little deep for Christmas morning, don't you think?"

We both laughed.

"Okay, but one more thing before I let you change the subject." She winked. "I think my brother would be lucky to be with you and you with him. Y'all are so cute together. It would show the kids what love and a relationship can be, so try keeping your heart and mind open. Okay, sooo, not another word about that, changing the subject."

We talked about the kids' gifts and how much fun it was watching them open presents. She talked about what it was like at college, her classes, and what she hoped to do in the future. She asked me questions about my business. Before long, we had everything ready and right on time because I heard Missy open the door for Ms. Graham.

As I wiped my hands on a dish towel and headed toward the living room, I caught a glimpse of myself in the hallway mirror. The mother's necklace glinted at my throat. Two little hearts. Two little lives that I had poured everything into.

Emma was right. Why did it have to be so hard?

Maybe it didn't. Maybe I was the one making it complicated. Maybe all I had to do was let myself feel what I was already feeling.

The thought was terrifying. And exhilarating.

I touched the necklace once, took a deep breath, and went to greet Ms. Graham.

Chapter Twenty-Seven

The time flew by, as it does. Christmas came and went in a blur. Virginia and Emma went back home. We all missed them almost immediately.

They briefly talked about maybe moving back to the area, but I'm sure it was just talk. We'd all gotten caught up in the holiday spirit and family togetherness, but it was a nice daydream.

A few days later, Jimmy would have to head back for his last offshore rotation. He wanted to soak up every minute with the kids.

For New Year's Eve, Glenn Lake always hosted a festival in the town square, complete with a huge firework display at Glenn Lake Park. I wasn't sure if the kids would make it through to the fireworks, but we were at least going to the festival. Another first for us.

Usually, for New Year's Eve, the kids and I would hide out behind the shed, and we'd sleep there all night because Mama would have a huge, drunken party. It wasn't safe for any of us to be around her and her friends on New Year's Eve.

We drove over with Ms. Graham, who was meeting Mrs. Dailey, and we'd be meeting Kate and Olive there. Parking was at the school, and the various activities would be scattered around the town square, side streets, and into the park. As we got close to the school, we had to wait in a line of traffic before pulling into the parking lot.

"Maybe we should have walked," I said, looking at all the traffic.

"Maybe, but I was worried if the kids got tired. We'd have to carry them and our chairs home." Jimmy expertly maneuvered into a parking spot.

There had never been a lot of traffic in town until the last year or so with the new neighborhoods on the west side, not to mention Glenn Lake being featured in a few magazines as a destination for antiques and small-town shopping. It was good for business, but some of the quaintness was fading with the growth. The city council was trying to keep it as controlled as possible to keep that small town feel that people liked but still ensure the town survived.

I texted Kate when we got parked. They were caught in the traffic coming from the west side. I told her we would head over to the festival area. The kids were chatty, bouncy, and eager to see everything. Since this was our first time attending, I must admit I was excited too.

We walked over to the town square area and were met by delightful smells of all the different foods. Hot dogs, burgers, fries, funnel cakes, and fresh baked cookies, just to name a few.

The cookies were from Mary's Bakery booth. She had a couple of portable ovens set up under her booth. I knew I was going to buy some of those before the end of the day. I hoped she had her famous, and only available at this time of year, snickerdoodles.

The kids were pointing at everything. They saw classmates and greeted them with smiles, hellos, and some with hugs. We found Mrs. Dailey, so Ms. Graham headed off with her.

I watched as they hooked their arms, chatting and laughing together as they melted into the crowd. They had a sweet friendship.

My phone chimed with a text. "Okay, she said they just parked. They'll be here in a few minutes."

"Finally! Olive is missing everything!" Missy said with a stomp of her foot.

We turned and walked back towards the parking area to meet up with them. As soon as Missy and Olive saw each other, they hugged and then held hands. Oh, to have a friendship that sweet and innocent.

"Can we rided the rides now!?" Little Davy asked as he bounced from foot to foot.

They had pony rides, a train, bumper cars, a merry go round, and many other fun rides.

"I wanna rided that one and that one and that one," Davy said.

"I got you covered, little guy," Jimmy said, then headed over to the ticket booth.

He bought each kid a wrist bracelet. This would give them an all-day pass to ride the rides as many times as they wanted.

"You're such a sweetheart to buy one for Olive. Thanks, Jimmy!" Kate gushed.

"No problem at all."

We strapped the bracelets on and sent them to the first ride, the ponies. They waited their turn and were chatting happily about which pony they wanted to ride. Little Davy couldn't stop smiling and giggling.

Several rides later, they were getting hungry and thirsty, so we headed to Big Ron's booth to get them each a hot dog, chips, and lemonade. While Kate and I grabbed that, Jimmy ran over to Abuelita Carmen's booth for tacos for the adults.

We got the kids settled at an empty picnic table and waited for Jimmy. When he arrived, he had tacos and a couple of white paper bags with Mary's Bakery logo stamped on them.

"Your favorite, snickerdoodles." He winked at me and then turned to the kids. "And chocolate chip for the kiddos." They cheered.

"Oh, you remembered! I wasn't sure if she would have these available. Thank you." I think I could have kissed him right then and there but thought better of it.

The thought caught me off guard. A few weeks ago, I wouldn't have let myself think something like that. But now, after his confession, after the forehead kiss, after the way he'd held my hand at Christmas, the thought didn't feel so impossible anymore.

The tacos were terrific. I'd never eaten at Abuelita Carmen's. Mama always said it wasn't good, the workers were rude, and the place was dirty. We rarely went out to eat, so I wasn't going to waste money on a place that wasn't worth it. But based on these tacos, we might have to try it sometime.

The rest of the day was primarily spent chasing the kids from ride to ride or activity to activity. There were clowns, face painters, and a few local bands that took turns on stage. The kids wanted to see and do everything. They were having a blast, and I was having fun watching them.

Soon it started to get dark and close to fireworks time. The kids were hanging in great, so we decided to stay for fireworks. Jimmy ran back to our truck to grab our chairs, and we all followed the crowds out of the town square, down the street, and into Glenn Lake Park. Ms. Graham found us, so we could all sit together, plus we had her chair. Mrs. Dailey had gone home to care for Mr. Dailey.

Everyone was seated in clusters and chatting all around us. We found a nice spot, set up our chairs, and got the kids settled in with blankets as the evening had gotten chilly.

The crowd cheered when the first fireworks started. The kids were in awe of the different colors and patterns.

"Look, a red one!" Missy pointed.

"That one is two colors," Olive said.

"Oh, look a heart." Missy chimed in again.

It was amazing.

"I'm glad I get to enjoy this with you," Jimmy whispered to me.

He reached over and held my hand. It was only a few moments, but those were the best moments as we looked at each other while the sky lit up above us. The colors reflected in his eyes, and I forgot to breathe. He smiled and then let go, turning back to the show. I sat in stunned silence with a silly grin. I looked around to see if anyone else noticed, but everyone's heads were facing up.

The show was reaching the end as they sent several colorful bursts into the air all at once. The crowd clapped and cheered at the sight. When it ended, the crowd stood as one, grabbing their chairs and blankets to head home.

We headed back to our car, loaded up, and sat in the line of cars. Little Davy was out before we even made it out of the parking lot. Missy chatted about this and that, but when the back seat fell silent a block from the school, I knew she was asleep too.

Once home, Ms. Graham thanked us, wished us a Happy New Year, and headed to her house. Jimmy got Missy out, and I got Little Davy.

I could hear her mumbling something to Jimmy as he tucked her in. Little Davy was out like a light, even as I got his shoes and jacket off then tucked him in bed.

"So, do you want to stay up until midnight, or are you going to bed?" Jimmy asked once we were back in the hallway.

"I hadn't thought about it yet. Are you staying up?"

"I was thinking of at least watching the ball drop in New York, so not technically midnight here but close."

"Okay, I'll stay up too." I had never even seen the ball drop in New York City and had no idea what it meant exactly, so I was excited to find out.

We grabbed drinks and snacks and settled in on the couch. He smiled over at me, and I melted on the inside.

As we waited for midnight on the East Coast, I reflected on the past several months. Things had been so bleak, and then like a flash, everything turned around. It was amazing.

That man with the gorgeous smile was the reason for it. He gave me hope, made me feel safe, and saved us all from being lost forever. With him, I felt like the best version of myself. I felt like I could do anything, though I had already proven I could do almost anything without him, so with him, the sky was the limit. Or at least that's how he made me feel.

My heart did flip flops, thinking about it. Then, as if sensing my thoughts, he pulled me to his side and put his arm around me. He didn't try kissing me, but it was more intimate than anything else I could imagine at that moment.

I let my head rest against his shoulder. It felt natural. It felt right. For the first time, I wasn't analyzing or overthinking. I was just being.

The ball dropped in New York. We cheered quietly from our place on the couch and then switched over to a local channel to finish the last hour for our time zone.

"Happy New Year, Mandy," he said softly, his arm still around me.

"Happy New Year, Jimmy."

We sat there in comfortable silence, watching the celebrations on the screen but not really seeing them. I was too aware of the warmth of him beside me, the steady rise and fall of his breathing, the way his thumb traced small circles on my shoulder.

This was what I wanted. This quiet intimacy. This feeling of belonging to someone and having someone belong to me.

Emma's words echoed in my mind. Why can't it be both? Why does it have to be so hard?

Maybe it didn't. Maybe I just had to let it happen.

The year had ended perfectly. And as the clock struck midnight in our time zone and the new year officially began, I made myself a silent promise.

This year, I would stop being afraid. This year, I would let myself have this.

Whatever this was becoming.

Chapter Twenty-Eight

The day came for Jimmy to leave again. At least this was his last trip, and we wouldn't have to do this any longer. It always felt like just when things were getting good, he had to leave.

The kids cried a little but tried to be grown up about it.

"I know you'll come back, but it just feels like almost forever when you're gone," Missy said with a stomp of her foot for emphasis.

I didn't verbalize it but felt the same way.

"I know it feels that way, but I promise I'll be home as quickly as I can, and with my new job, I won't have to leave like that again." He hugged them both and kissed their heads.

Then he turned to me. For a moment, neither of us moved. The air between us felt charged with everything we hadn't said.

"I'll miss you," I said quietly. It was the most honest thing I'd said to him in weeks.

His eyes softened. "I'll miss you too." He pulled me into a hug, and I let myself sink into it. Let myself memorize the feel of his arms around me, the smell of his soap, the steady beat of his heart against my cheek.

"We'll talk when I get back," he said against my hair. It wasn't a question.

I nodded, my throat too tight to speak.

We went from a full house for the holidays with lots of love and family back to just the three of us in a blink. We should be used to it, but it's easy to get wrapped up in love.

We did our everyday thing. Work for me, daycare for the kids, and then home to enjoy our time together. They were growing so fast. Missy was already starting to talk about her fifth birthday, which would be in May. Being January, I figured I had plenty of time to plan. But, of course, Little Davy didn't want to be left out and asked about his birthday.

"Yours is after July Fourth. Do you know what that is?" I asked him.

"America? Fireworks?"

"Yes, that's it. But we still have almost six months to go. Do you remember Ms. Cindi at school talking about the months?"

It was still something new he was learning at daycare. I loved how they started the little ones learning so early.

"Jan-u-ary, Feb-u-ary, March... October... August... July!" He jumped up as he said July.

"Well, kinda, but you missed a few." I chuckled. "But don't worry, buddy, I won't forget your birthday. We'll have the biggest party you have ever had."

Satisfied with my answer, he grinned and ran off to play.

Claire had learned quickly how I handled things with each client. Again, not rocket science. We had started doing jobs separately, so we could schedule more clients. We could each do three to four a day, and we worked six days a week. That was a lot of houses.

I had already doubled clients from just a month ago. I was becoming the most popular household service in Glenn Lake. But, of course, I was the only one that was truly in the area.

The big question on my mind now was, should I hire another person or two to help us? There were plenty of new people moving to Glenn Lake, so there was a steady stream of potential new clients.

Then as there weren't exactly many jobs immediately in Glenn Lake, it gave us the opportunity to find someone locally to work with us.

It was also good to have a break from Jimmy, so I could think. We had a few special moments that I would remember forever, but I needed this time apart to sort out my feelings a bit, especially after my conversation with Emma. She'd made a lot of sense, and I realized maybe I was making it more difficult than it needed to be.

Plus, he had given me that beautiful necklace, and that had to mean something. It sure meant something to me. He knew that those kids were the most important thing to me, so not only was the necklace gorgeous, but the sentiment it held for me was beyond words. He must have put a lot of thought into it. I touched it now, thinking of him.

I think my main concern and why I was so hesitant wasn't that I didn't have feelings for him, because clearly I did, but more what people might think of us. Dating my Mama's ex-boyfriend and the father of my half siblings. Wasn't this something you saw on a midday talk show?

I seemed to be the only one having issues with it. Everyone else seemed to think nothing of these facts. Even his sister thought it was perfectly fine and questioned why we hadn't already admitted to our feelings. Well, I guess he had, but I hadn't yet.

When he comes back at the end of the month, I'll talk to him about it. I think I was finally ready to admit I wanted to move forward with a relationship. I'm just not sure how.

We already live together, so where do we go from here? On a first date? Do we say okay, we are dating now? How do all the logistics of this work?

We would have a lot of things to discuss before moving forward, or I was overthinking it. But, like Emma said, why does it have to be so hard?

The house felt emptier without him. Not just quieter, but somehow less alive. I found myself looking up every time I heard a car in the driveway, my heart doing a little leap before reality set in and reminded me he wasn't due back for weeks.

At night, after the kids were in bed, I would sit on the couch where we had watched the ball drop together. I could still feel the ghost of his arm around my shoulders. Could still remember the way his thumb had traced circles on my skin.

I had made myself a promise on New Year's Eve. This year, I would stop being afraid. This year, I would let myself have this.

Now I just had to figure out how to keep that promise.

The days stretched out, long and ordinary, but underneath the routine, something was shifting inside me. Every time I touched the necklace at my throat, every time I thought about the way he looked at me, every time I remembered his whispered "we'll talk when I get back," I felt a little more certain.

I was done being scared. I was done making excuses. I was done pretending I didn't know exactly what I wanted.

When Jimmy came home, I would tell him. I would finally say the words I'd been too afraid to say.

I just hoped I was brave enough when the moment came.

Chapter Twenty-Nine

January came and went without much notice. Jimmy would be back from his last offshore rotation today. Knowing he always came in on a Thursday, I decided to break out of our routine and let us all skip the day. I blocked my schedule so I could take the day off. I also pulled the kids out of school for the day.

Finally, not following the rules, not following my routine. I felt like a rebel.

The kids and I couldn't wait for him to be home. Davy asked every five minutes if it was time for Daddy's surprise yet. Of course, I was excited too and kept checking the clock myself, so I couldn't blame him for asking.

"Not yet, but soon, buddy. I think he normally gets in around lunchtime."

We hung up a banner that said, "Welcome Home." We bought some streamers and balloons too, so we got those hung up.

"What do you think? Will Daddy like it?" As I said that, the front door opened, and in walked the man himself.

"Daddy!!!" Missy squealed.

"Su'pise Daddy!" Davy jumped up and down.

"Oh, Jimmy, hi. Surprise!" I waved my arms towards the banner.

Then we rushed him for welcome home hugs.

"Wow, that's a welcome home for sure." He hugged us. "Not what I was expecting at all. What are y'all doing here? What about daycare? And work?"

"We su'pise you, Daddy," Davy said.

"Yeah, we missed you, Daddy," Missy added.

I smiled and let the kids do all the talking. All the courage I had built up over the past month seemed to evaporate the moment I saw him. I was suddenly not sure I was ready to talk to him about us. Maybe tomorrow or Saturday or perhaps next week.

"We made this banner for you! Welcome home, Daddy." Missy was proud.

"Yes, yes," Davy was bouncing around, so animated.

"I had a special dinner planned, but we weren't expecting you until after lunch, so I didn't really have anything planned for lunch. I was planning to give them sandwiches and fruit."

"Well, why don't we go out for lunch? My treat, since y'all did all this for me."

"Oh, yes, yes! Can we, Mandy? Please?" Missy begged.

"Peas, Nandy!"

"Um, oh yeah, sure. I mean, it isn't really my decision, is it?" I half laughed. "But yes! That sounds fun."

As the kids were putting on their shoes, Jimmy leaned over, putting a hand on my hip to pull me closer to him as he whispered, "You rebel, you broke out of your routine."

His hand on my hip sent electricity through me. I giggled and smiled at him. "Yes, I did."

We decided to go to FunStuff Pizza. We hadn't been since the day we got them back from CPS. They had been asking to go ever since, so today was as good a day as any.

We ordered two pizzas and let the kids go play before the food arrived.

"So, how have things been?" Jimmy asked as we settled into a booth.

"Good, very good. The kids have been doing well at daycare, of course, and work has been going well. Claire is working out amazingly. I'm almost starting to think I should hire a second person."

"Really? That's good news. I'm glad it's going well."

"How was saying goodbye to your old job and crew?" I asked him.

"It was a little bittersweet, actually. I had a good group of guys, and I did enjoy that job, but it was time to move into the office. I want to be here for you and the kids."

For you and the kids. Not just the kids. For you. I tried not to read too much into it, but my heart fluttered anyway.

We continued with the small talk until the pizza arrived. Jimmy rounded up the kids from the play equipment while I plated everyone a hot slice.

"Oh, this place is so much more fun than I remembered. We need to come like all the time." Missy declared as she climbed into the seat next to Jimmy. Davy sat next to me.

"So fun. So fun." He repeated.

We ate our pizza and listened to the kids, mostly Missy, talk about their favorite parts and what they wanted to do first after they ate. Missy continued by filling Jimmy in on everything that happened while he was gone, and I mean everything. Even more amazingly, she managed to eat two and a half slices of pizza while giving a month's worth of daycare news.

"And Robert told Olive that he thought she was a dumb girl. Well, Ms. Christy told him that was a mean thing to say, so he had to apologize and sit out of free time for five minutes. It isn't Olive's fault she doesn't like reading. I have been trying to help her like it, but she just doesn't. She said the words get all mixed up... And then we have this new girl named Bailey..." She kept talking, but something she said was a light bulb moment for me, so I sent a text to Kate.

"I know she's still young, but has Olive ever been tested for dyslexia?"

"No, why?" Kate messaged back.

"Missy said that Olive said the words get mixed up when she reads. I don't know if it is because the words are new or if it could be dyslexia. Worth a check, yes?"

"OMG, yes. Thanks for telling me. Will investigate!"

I hoped that helped Olive and Kate at least a little bit. I knew it really bothered Kate that Olive didn't enjoy reading, and if this were the reason, it could help. On the other hand, she was still young, and most four-year-olds were just learning to read, so maybe they could get on top of it quickly.

The kids were finished eating, so I took them to the restroom to wash their hands and faces. Then I let them go back to play for a little bit. Jimmy joined them while I watched. Laughing, smiling, and waving when the kids would catch my eye. Unlike last time, Davy's motor skills had improved, and he could move through the ball pit much easier. He was also a bit taller, which helped too.

After about an hour of playing, we headed home. Davy needed to nap, and even though Missy didn't nap anymore, I could tell she was tired from all the excitement. She would probably sleep.

Once we were home, Jimmy got himself settled. Washed his laundry and unpacked all his things.

I went over my schedule for the next week and paid some bills online. Basically, we avoided each other. There was an energy between us, but it wasn't exactly negative. More of an electric spark. The kind that made you hyperaware of where the other person was in the room at all times.

Once the kids got up from their naps, things were back to mostly normal. The only difference was when Jimmy and I would make eye contact, he would flash me a knee weakening smile, and I would smile, blush, and look away.

I kept berating myself for being a chicken. I needed to talk to him, but this was so new that I didn't know how to start the conversation. Maybe tomorrow.

Maybe tomorrow became my theme for each day. We didn't talk about our relationship but would move about our day, sharing little moments here and there.

A brush of hands when we both reached for the same dish. A lingering glance across the dinner table. The way he always seemed to find reasons to be in whatever room I was in.

One evening, the kids were playing in their room because it was too cold and a little icy outside. I was working on the computer, figuring out my taxes for the business. Jimmy was watching TV. I could hear him hysterically laughing, so I gave in to the sound and joined him.

"What are you watching?"

"Some show with dumbest criminal videos. I can't believe some of these."

We sat there laughing together for nearly an hour. It felt good to do something together that was so simple. So normal. Like we were already a couple, even though we hadn't said the words.

When I went to bed that night, I was so wrapped up in happy thoughts and feelings. I couldn't stop smiling.

But underneath the happiness was a growing frustration with myself. I had promised myself I would be brave. I had told myself I would stop being afraid.

And yet here I was, still dancing around the truth.

Tomorrow, I told myself as I drifted off to sleep. Tomorrow I'll tell him.

But even as I thought it, I wondered if tomorrow would ever actually come.

Chapter Thirty

The phone rang a little after two a.m. Being sound asleep, I didn't fully register the sound, but my subconscious knew, and I answered the phone before I was completely awake.

"Hello?"

"Hi, is this Mandy Walker?" The unfamiliar female voice on the other end of the phone asked.

It caused me to wake up quickly.

"Yes, it is."

"I'm calling from Methodist Hospital. Your mother, Becca Walker, was brought in about an hour ago. Unfortunately, she was in a car accident and is in ICU, and we need you to come down to the hospital."

"Is... is she...?" My brain wouldn't let me ask.

"She's in critical condition, but we have her at least stable right now. I can't give much more detail at this time. When you arrive, a doctor will be able to fill you in completely."

I got the address and what floor to come to. I threw on some jeans and a T-shirt then went down the hall to let Jimmy know.

I knocked lightly on the door. I heard a mumble and him stirring behind the door. Then he opened the door. Bedhead and shirtless, he looked so good, but with worry over my mother in my head, I couldn't think that way right now.

"Mandy, oh gosh, is everything okay? What's wrong?" He said as he rubbed his eyes.

Tears sprang to my eyes, but I managed to say, "I just got a call. Mama is at Methodist in ICU. She was in a car accident, but they didn't give me much information. Just that I needed to come to the hospital to talk to a doctor."

"Do you need me to go with you?"

"No, no, if you could stay with the kids, and I'll call when I know more."

"Are you sure? You're upset, and I can drive you."

"I promise. I'll be fine. I'll call in a few hours or so. As soon as I know something and can, I'll call."

He nodded his head and gave me a quick hug. Even in my panic, I noticed how his arms felt around me. How I didn't want to let go.

I turned, grabbed my jacket, purse, and keys, then nearly ran out of the house to my car. I felt I had to get there quickly. The hospital was roughly twenty miles away in the Medical Center. I had a lot of time on the way to think and worry, crying most of the way there. No matter how she treated me growing up, she was my mother, and I knew in her own way, she loved me.

Besides my sister and brother, I had no other family, so all the worry fell on me as the oldest. They were too little to be a support system and comfort at this moment. They depended on me as if I was their mother.

I was so glad I had Kate now. We had become good friends, the kind you could call on in an emergency. Well, maybe not at two a.m. We weren't that close yet. But maybe at 8 a.m. when you needed someone to bring over coffee and vent to, or the "can you pick up the kids for me because I am stuck at work" kind of friends. We had done both those things. I knew we would probably get to the two a.m. emergency friends, but we weren't there yet.

I also had Claire in my corner now, but we weren't even the bring over coffee and vent kind of friends yet. Or were we? Though she didn't hesitate to help me out when Davy got sick, so who knew what type of friendship we would have in the future.

As always, I had Ms. Graham too, and while I knew I could call her day or night, I didn't want to wake her up. At least, not until I had more news anyway. I'd call her in the morning.

Jimmy was enough for tonight, and I only woke him because of Missy and Little Davy. I might not have a large family, but I had good friends, and thinking about that made me smile a little and take my mind off of whatever was waiting for me at the hospital, if only for a minute.

My mind drifted to thinking about how Mama's father was killed in a car accident when I was young, and her mother had such severe injuries she was left with disabilities and never really recovered. The irony of this weighed heavily on my mind as I drove towards the hospital.

"Relax. Relax. There's nothing you can do until you get there." I repeated out loud as I drove.

I didn't know what I would be walking into and had to get there as soon as possible. There were things I needed to say, and if given a chance, I would say them.

Arriving at the parking garage, I parked and walked as normally as I could manage in my near panicked state. Fighting the urge to run to her crying the whole way, but instead, I walked fast and kept my head down.

I found the desk for ICU. One nurse was sitting behind it.

"Hi, may I help you?"

"Yes, my mother was brought in earlier, Becca Walker. Someone called..."

"Oh yes, Mandy, right? I'm Tasha, the nurse that called you. Let me get you signed in, and then I'll see if the on-call doctor is ready and able to meet with you."

"Okay." That was all I could manage to say.

She asked for my license, so I gave it to her and then signed the sign-in sheet while she printed a visitor pass for me. Then, she handed back my license while she called the doctor. She smiled at me as the phone rang.

"Yes, Dr. Stevens, Becca Walker's daughter is here... Okay. Yes... I'll tell her. Thanks." She hung up and turned to me. "She said she'll be out shortly and will take you back. If you could have a seat anywhere."

"Thank you."

I turned around to face the room behind me. I hadn't noticed when I first came in how crowded it was. It was full of people in various states of sitting or lying around, crying, or angry. Some looked shell shocked, while others seemed oddly calm.

Sitting there alone drove home the emptiness I sometimes felt at not having siblings close to my age or family that I was close to, like a cousin or a trusted aunt or uncle. I didn't have any of those things. I had only those few friends, again, none I would call at now 3 a.m.

My mind and eyes wandered. I took in the various people in the waiting area but didn't actually see them. All I could think of was

Mama. What was her condition? Was she going to live? Was she going to be disabled like grandmother? I had to hope for the best.

My eyes caught a man across the room looking at me, and when I realized he was, in fact, watching me, my mind focused on him. The way he looked at me was almost like he knew me, but I didn't know him. So, I tried to look at him without looking directly at him.

His hair was greasy and matted, and he was covered in cuts that looked fresh. Most were bandaged, but some were too small for that. He looked like he hadn't showered in a week. What was wrong with him?

After a few seconds of staring, he stood and stumbled towards me. I shifted in the chair and tried to look casual and relaxed.

"You're Becca's daughter, aren't you?" He slurred.

"Hmm, yes, I am, and you are?"

"I knew it. You look just like her. I'm Butch, your mother's boyfriend. I told them to call you." He was the first to ever say I looked like her.

I imagined I must look more like my father, whoever that was. Mama had a fair complexion and a petite frame, while I was darker with a larger frame. Not fat, just taller and larger build.

His appearance made more sense, though. It didn't look like he showered regularly.

"Oh, umm, hi. You don't happen to know how she's doing, do you? I assume you were with her at the time of the accident. Are you okay?"

"I just want to be near Becca." He ran his hands through his nasty hair. I fought the urge to gag. "They won't tell me nuthin' and won't let me see her neither."

He was slurring his words so badly that I could hardly understand him. He seemed either drunk, or that bump on his head was causing him to appear that way. I couldn't decide which. Either way, I wasn't comfortable with him and hoped the doctor or a nurse would hurry.

We didn't get to talk more because a tall brunette doctor approached us. She kept her eyes on him the whole time, right up until she got to us, then she turned her attention to me.

"Mandy Walker, I assume." I barely had time to nod before she continued. "I'm Dr. Stevens. I'm the doctor currently caring for your mother. Let's go to the back, and I will fill you in. Excuse us." She said curtly to Butch.

Was that a bit of disgust in her voice? Glad I wasn't the only one that thought so poorly of him.

Butch looked sad and lost but shuffled back to his seat without a word. I don't think he liked being excluded from the conversation. I would have almost felt bad for him, but there was just something about him that made my skin crawl, like most of Mama's boyfriends throughout my life.

"Sorry about that. The police are on their way to arrest him." She paused. "They were both drinking at the time of the accident. The car they hit had a family in it. Only the baby survived, but he's in bad shape. They have him over at Texas Children's right now."

"Oh, my goodness..." I put my hand over my mouth, and tears sprang to my eyes. That poor family.

"Sorry to put this so bluntly, but I find that honesty is best. I find it does me no good to beat around the bush."

I nodded but didn't reply, so she continued.

"I'll be honest with you, I'm not sure your mother will make it. That's why I didn't send a nurse out to get you." That made sense, and I had thought it odd the doctor came to get me instead of a nurse. "I wanted to give you the information before you see her, plus the nurses are short-handed tonight."

She paused in the hallway and turned towards me.

"She has numerous internal injuries and broken bones. We do have her stable at the moment, but the next 24 to 48 hours will be critical to know if she can pull through this, and even then, I just don't know. She's on a ventilator, and with that comes risks, mostly ventilator-associated pneumonia. We know to watch for it, so we'll be ready. I want to prepare you. She looks bad."

We had stopped outside of a room, and the doctor gestured for me to go in. I took a deep breath and then pushed the door open.

The room was dimly lit, and at first, it was difficult to see clearly. I could hear the hum of machines, the inhaling and exhaling sound of the ventilator, and the beeps and chirps of various monitors.

As my eyes got used to the dim light, I could see her clearly. Tubes and wires were running all over her, connecting her to the various machines. Her face was severely bruised and covered with various sized cuts. Her hair was missing in places, and she had large scrapes where her hair once was. What hair was there was caked with dried blood. For thirty-three years old, she looked so frail.

"Oh, Mama..."

As tears streamed down my face, I stared at her, and a thousand memories flooded my mind. Her laugh, her smile, her hugs. Though all those had been rare.

My mind decided only happy memories were the ones I should remember now. Like the time she taught me to ride a bike or the time we made a cake that didn't quite turn out. We both laughed at the mess and nicknamed it ugly cake. We often referred to it anytime we had a cake.

"Mama, I don't know if you can hear me, but I'm here." I took her hand gently in mine. "I'll stay as long as I need to. As long as you need me."

All the things I had wanted to say were forgotten. Instead, I started talking about anything and everything, telling her about our lives, about things around town, the weather, and any other random thing that popped in my head. I probably sounded a lot like Missy now, but I heard it was good to talk to coma patients, and I wanted her to know she wasn't alone.

Nurses would come and go, checking monitors or turning off alarms. Sometimes making notes on her chart or adding medicine to her IV. I watched but didn't question them on her condition, knowing the doctor had to be the one to tell me.

Several hours later, a nurse suggested I go for a walk. She said they would be taking her for a CT scan anyway. I thanked her. Stretching my legs, getting some fresh air, and getting away from here for a few minutes sounded like an excellent idea. It would give me a chance to call Jimmy to fill him in, and I really wanted a cup of coffee.

Jimmy answered quickly. "Hey, Mandy. Oh, I'm glad you called. I've been worried. How is she? How are you?"

"She's in bad shape. Her boyfriend was driving and is in custody now." I took a deep breath. "They were both drinking. The accident killed a family, except for the baby."

"Oh wow, I saw it on the news and was wondering if it might be her. Fortunately, they didn't release her name, just his. Neither car was recognizable."

"Seeing how she looks, I can only imagine. What makes me mad or frustrated is Butch, her boyfriend, didn't really have any serious injuries. He looked a little beat up, but nothing was broken, and my mother is barely clinging to life, a family is dead, and their youngest member is next door at Texas Children's. It just isn't fair. Well, I mean, I guess she had a choice, but that family didn't."

"You're right. It's not fair at all." He said. "Do you want me to come up there after I drop the kids at school?"

I hesitated because I wasn't sure what to say. The comfort would be nice, but with the odd energy between us, would it be a comfort? Plus, I knew he had plans before starting his new job on Monday. He was going to do a few final projects around the house. But in the end, I really needed a friend here with me.

"Actually, yes, it would be nice to have someone to sit with for a bit. I know you had some things to work on today, but if you don't mind... I think we can have two people in the room. I'll check when I go back upstairs."

"That's okay if I can't. I'll sit in the waiting area or somewhere nearby in case you need me. Do you want me to bring you anything? Books, magazines, anything?"

"My toothbrush?" I said with a little laugh. My teeth felt gross this morning. "And you know that book I'm reading, that would be good too."

I gave a brief list of other things I needed before disconnecting. Jimmy was going to let Ms. Graham know so she could spread the word for me.

I called Claire, so maybe she could help cover my clients today. We each only had two today, so she could probably handle all four in my place. Of course, we might have to rearrange going forward, depending on how long Mama was in the hospital or, well, I didn't want to think about that part.

I sent a quick text message to Kate. She replied quickly, letting me know to call with any news and that she could help with anything.

Having taken care of all the calls or texts I needed to, I walked around the block to get some air and stretch my legs as the nurse suggested. I was used to being active with my job, so sitting for hours had felt odd to me. Plus, I could feel the stress throughout my whole body. It was tense and achy.

As I was walking, I noticed a news crew set up near Texas Children's Hospital. With Jimmy saying the accident had been on the news, I assumed they must be reporting on it and maybe the baby's condition. I really hoped he'd be okay, but I also thought of what his life might be like without his mother, father, and siblings, knowing only he survived. I hoped he had grandparents or aunts and uncles that could and would care for him.

With my own lack of a large family, I thought a lot about families and how important they are. But friends could be better than family because they choose to be in your life. The thought put a slight smile on my face.

I turned and walked in the opposite direction of the news crew. I didn't want to hear anything they had to say and didn't want to chance they would stop me for any reason.

With that last thought and change in direction, I headed back to ICU, the most uncomfortable chair in the world, and Mama. I hoped she was back from her CT scan and that the doctor had some news, any news, for me.

There was a new nurse at the reception desk in front of the ICU. I showed her my badge and mentioned I was expecting a visitor. She confirmed there could be two people in the room at a time and would send him back once he arrived.

When I got back to Mama's room, someone had turned on the lights, and she was back in the room. Finally, I could see her more clearly, and even though I'd been sitting with her all night, I gasped. It was heartbreaking to see her like this. I tried to compose myself in case she could hear me.

"Hi, Mama, I'm back. I went for a quick walk outside. It's a beautiful day. Clear and sunny, a touch chilly maybe but warmer than normal. The perfect day." I rambled on for a while, so she knew she wasn't alone.

The doctor didn't really have much news. Her brain activity was normal, and there was no swelling on her brain. Everyone was surprised by that, considering her injuries, but said they were hopeful she could survive this with few long-term effects. He repeated what

Dr. Stevens had said the night before, that the next day or two would be the key to her survival and give more clues to the future.

About an hour later, there was a soft knock on the door, and when it opened, Jimmy walked in. Seeing him, I was instantly on my feet, tears in my eyes. He wrapped me in his arms. I felt safe and protected, like no matter what, this was going to be okay, and I was safe.

"I'm so glad you're here," I whispered into his chest.

"Me too." As the hug ended, he looked at Mama. "Wow, you said she looked bad, but seeing her, just wow."

"Yes, it's bad. She looks so much worse than just a few hours ago, but the doctor said there isn't swelling on her brain, and it's functioning normally."

He wrapped his arms around me again, and we stood there looking down at Mama. Then, after a few minutes of silence, I let him know I had been talking to her.

"It probably seems silly because she can't answer me, but I'd heard it was good for coma patients."

"Yeah, I've heard that too. Not sure if it's true or not, but it couldn't hurt."

I turned to her. "Mama, Jimmy's here to see you."

"Has she responded in any way when you talk?"

"No, but I keep hoping she can hear me. I just want her to know I'm here."

"That is very generous of you considering..." He squeezed my hand. "You're amazing, you know."

I fought back the tears while Jimmy continued holding my hand. We sat in silence off and on for a few hours, talking only briefly. There really wasn't much more to say at this point but wait. The nurses came and went, and time ticked by.

Before long, it was lunchtime, and we decided to take a break from watching Mama. I let the nurses know, and I'd have my cell phone if they needed me or if anything changed with Mama.

We headed downstairs and found a deli. We ordered a couple of sandwiches, chips, and a couple of waters and then walked over to Hermann Park. It was a little crowded for a workday, but I wasn't too surprised with the unseasonably pleasant weather.

It also looked like a few schools might be having a field trip either to the zoo or maybe one of the museums. The park was a favorite for a picnic lunch.

We found a picnic table that was in a shady spot. From here, we could watch children at the playground, joggers and walkers on the walking path, and see the traffic moving around the Medical Center.

"Oh, Jimmy, what am I going to do if I lose her?" I had tears in my eyes. "I know she treated me horribly growing up, but she's still my mother, and I know somewhere in there is a good person."

I wasn't much of a crier, and except for maybe the two weeks the kids were in foster care, this was the most I'd cried in my life.

"I know." He took my hand. "No matter what happens, I'm here for you."

"I love her, and I know she loves me, Missy, and Little Davy. How can I explain to them what's happened? I obviously would have to tell them if she... if she..." I couldn't finish the sentence. "I couldn't let them go on, thinking that she might come back into our lives. But at the same time, they don't ask for her, so I don't know."

"Of course she loves all of you. She just didn't know how to show it. From what you both have said, her parents didn't show her much love." I nodded my agreement. "And as far as telling the kids, we would tell them together, but let's hope she improves. Let's try to think positively now. Okay?"

"Okay," I said it so weakly he may not have heard me.

I wasn't sure I could be optimistic right now, but he was right. I needed to be more positive.

"Plus, the reason those kids don't ask for her is that you are their mother. At least you treat them as a mother should. You fill that role for them, so they aren't missing anything from their lives right now." He rubbed my hand lightly with his thumb.

"That's true."

We sat in silence for a few minutes watching the world go by and enjoying the weather. Then, with the weather so beautiful, we decided to take a walk around the park before heading back to her room. We took the path around McGovern Lake and near the zoo entrance. Some of the trails ran close to the train tracks.

There were a lot of other people out since the weather was so beautiful. We stopped a few times to watch the ducks in the lake or watch a squirrel scurry around and then up a tree. The train passed us once, and the conductor waved, so did a few people on the train. Happy families, moms with small children, and even a few couples. We waved back. It put a smile on my face and helped my brain click back to positive. I repeated it as we headed back to the hospital.

Positive. Gotta think positive.

Nothing had changed while we were gone. Jimmy stayed a bit longer, but soon he had to leave to get the kids and head home. I promised to call if anything changed. He gave me a long hug and kissed my forehead before leaving.

He left my book plus another I had, a few magazines, a change of clothes, and some toiletry items. He said tomorrow he would sit with Mama, so I could go home to change and shower if I wanted to.

The evening nurse brought me a much more comfortable chair. It reclined nearly flat, so I could sleep. She also brought in a pillow and a few blankets. There was a bathroom in the room, and she let me know I could use it, including the shower. With those few comforts, I might not have to leave after all, which was good as I felt like I needed to be right here.

Whether she woke or passed, I didn't want her to go alone. No matter how she treated me growing up, nobody deserved to die without someone with them.

Chapter Thirty-One

Mama had been in a coma for three days now. She had some eye movement, twitching, and responding to pain stimulation, but all normal for a coma patient from what the doctors had told me, at least in her condition.

A huge goose egg had formed on her head, likely from hitting her head on the dashboard. So, they did another CT scan to check for injury and brain activity. Thankfully when the results came back, she still had regular brain activity and no damage. The doctor said it appeared to be superficial bruising.

They finally weaned her off the ventilator, and she appeared to be breathing on her own with no issues. Now we had to watch for pneumonia.

The swelling around her face had gone down, and some of the more minor cuts were healing. Luckily, the bruising hadn't gotten worse. Though over the past few days, they had changed colors the way bruises sometimes do. Most were now a dark black with some yellowing around the edges.

The doctor suggested that some might not have been from the wreck, but maybe abuse at the hands of Butch, or she could have been in a fight. I suspected it was the former.

As part of the drunk driving investigation, the police had interviewed the owner of the bar where they had been. They asked about how much they had to drink and what he might have observed. The owner said he hadn't had any reports of a fight, and Butch wasn't confessing to hitting her. So, either he couldn't remember, or he was hiding it.

Just thinking about him made my skin crawl. I hoped he was given the maximum punishment. But, of course, his lawyers were trying to get him put in a treatment facility without any jail time. I knew they were doing their jobs, but it made me mad, nonetheless.

After finding out I could shower in the patient's bathroom, I didn't have to leave, so Jimmy and Ms. Graham took turns coming to see me, bringing me things I needed.

"Did the bad people take you?" Missy asked when I finally got to speak to her on the phone.

"No, no. I'm fine." I thought for a moment, how much should I say? "Mama was hurt in a car and is sleeping. I need to stay here with her, so when she wakes up, she sees me."

"Oh." Her voice held a note of speculation, but she didn't question me again.

"Nandy, I got my animals. A cow. Dis horse and a hippo." Davy's sweet innocence warmed me.

He didn't ask about Mama. Did he remember what happened that night? Do two-year-olds hold grudges? Did he even remember her?

"Oh Mama, I really hope you come through this. I have so much I want to tell you."

I laid my head on the edge of the bed and was gently holding her hand. Tears burned my eyes. I hadn't cried so much in my life as I had this past year. Suddenly I felt a little squeeze of my hand, so light I wasn't sure if I was imagining it or not. I looked up, and Mama was looking at me. She didn't say anything but tried to squeeze my hand again.

"Mama? Are you awake?" I held her hand tightly.

She blinked a few times and tried to smile. It wasn't quite a smile, but it was something. She squeezed my hand again, this time a little tighter.

"Mama, I'll be right back. I'm going into the hall to get the nurse."

I walked out the door, gesturing for the nurse and whispering, "She's awake."

I immediately went back into the room, not waiting to see if the nurse followed me.

Mama was looking a little more awake now. She blinked a few times and tried to speak but couldn't quite get out whatever she was trying to say.

"Hi Becca, I'm Nancy, your nurse for tonight. If you can hear me, blink twice." She slowly blinked. "Good, now if you can hear me, squeeze my hand." She squeezed Nancy's hand. "Great. You've given us quite the scare, but I'm glad to see you awake. Your daughter has been here the whole time, three days now. I'm going to go call the doctor to come check in on you. I'll be right back."

She checked a few things on the monitors and then stepped out.

"I'm so glad to see you awake. You did give us a scare. How do you feel? Oh, that's a silly question, I'm just happy right now..." She was looking at me and tried to smile again, then tried to speak. "It's okay, Mama, don't try to speak yet. Let's see what the doctor says and maybe get you water or juice or something. You might be thirsty."

She slightly nodded her head and closed her eyes but kept a tight hold of my hand and would give a little squeeze every few seconds to let me know she was awake.

The doctor came in, followed by Nancy, the nurse.

"Hello Becca, I'm Dr. Stevens. You can hear me, yes?"

"Yes." It came out very weakly and almost not audible.

"Okay, good. How're you feeling? Much pain?"

"I... no... pain. Tired... weak... What... what happened?" Mama said. Her voice was gritty and low.

"You were in a bad car accident and were thrown from the car. It appears that you and your boyfriend had been drinking. Do you remember that?"

"No... well, a little... it's fuzzy. Where... is he?"

"Last I heard, he was in jail. There was another car involved, and that family didn't survive, except for the youngest member, who I hear is improving daily at Texas Children's. He's only a year old." Dr. Stevens said bluntly.

She shut her eyes and made a slight moan as if she might cry.

"I'm sorry. I know that must be hard to hear, but it's important that you know the facts. I'm sure once the police hear you're awake, they'll have questions." Dr. Stevens looked at me and then back at Mama. "They'll also be asking you if you have suffered any abuse at the hands of Mr. Stevens. Having examined you, it appears some of your injuries might not have been caused by the accident."

"I... yes... hit me. He hit me and...." She made another sound like she was still trying to fight crying.

I held her hand tightly. I didn't want to let go ever.

"That's what I thought might be the case. We can get you help if you need it, but for now, we need you to get rest and get stronger for your family. If you are up for it, you can have some water, juice.

Basically, liquids for now. Not much, just a little to start with. We will work you up to solid foods as you get stronger." She typed a few things into the computer. She then looked back at Mama. "I'll recheck you in an hour or so. Call Nancy if you have any issues or questions. Nancy, could you bring some water and juice for her?"

"Yes. Becca, apple okay with you?" Nancy asked.

She nodded, and both the doctor and Nancy left.

"I'm so sorry that you had to go through that, Mama."

"Well... yes, but I can't hide from it... I hate that... I hate him." She shut her eyes, but I could tell she was still awake. "I tried to end it." She finally choked out with her eyes still closed.

"I'm here for you now, Mama."

She squeezed my hand but kept her eyes closed and didn't try to talk again.

Nancy brought in water and juice. She got Mama sitting up a little to help her drink. Her first sips dribbled a little out of her mouth, and she choked but soon took a smooth sip.

"Good. How did that feel? Okay? Is your throat sore at all?"

"No, fine. I feel... well like I was thrown from a car." She was joking a little. That was a good sign.

Nancy and I chuckled softly at her joke. However, she still sounded extremely weak, and her voice sounded soft and scratchy. I could tell it was taking a lot of effort for her to talk.

"Good, that's how you should be feeling right about now. So, let's try to get you feeling less like that and get you home to your family where you belong." Nancy looked at me with a smile. "I'll be right out here or close by if you need anything."

After the nurse left, there were a few moments of silence. The only sounds were the hum of the various monitors and machines still in the room. Mama was the first to break the silence.

"Tell me about the little kids, please. Tell me they don't hate me."

"They don't. Missy asked about you yesterday. She was worried. I tried to explain things to her, and I think she got it. Davy is getting big. They're both in school. Missy is in preschool, and she's doing well. Then Little Davy has been thriving in daycare. He is starting to speak more clearly and has been learning so much. He's made a few friends too."

"That is great to hear. And what about you, how are you?" She spoke carefully and with her eyes shut.

"I'm doing well. I've expanded my business. It's an actual company now. I even have an employee. The employee is Claire Dixon, but still, she works for me. And I've been debating hiring another soon. Oh, and Jimmy has been a huge help to me as well. Helping with the kids and encouraging me to grow the business."

"Jimmy? My Jimmy?" Her eyes flew open at his name.

Whoops, I hadn't meant to say anything about Jimmy yet. It just slipped out.

"Well, yeah, kind of. You haven't dated for quite a while, but yeah, that Jimmy. He lives with us now in my old room. I'm in yours." I paused, trying to decide if I should share anything else. "He starts a new position tomorrow. He'll no longer be going offshore."

"Oh, that's great." She had an odd look on her face.

I didn't know what that meant. Was it pain, jealousy, or confusion?

I offered her some water, and she drank it with no issue. Much easier than the last time. We chatted for a few more minutes before she said she would try to sleep and that maybe I should as well.

I guess I fell asleep because the next thing I knew, the doctor and a nurse were examining her, checking her vitals, and asking her some questions. Mama sounded a lot more rested and awake.

"Later today, the nurses are going to try to get you up and walking a little. We'll bring in a walker to help you. Even though you broke your hip, it wasn't serious enough for surgery. It's stabilized, and you should be up and walking a little." Dr. Stevens said. "After that, it will just be short walks to the bathroom and back or into a chair to sit up for a while and then back to bed. Nothing out of the room yet and no marathons for a while."

Mama laughed, which was nice to hear after the last several days of nothing.

"Do you have any questions before I go?"

"Do you know how long I'll be here?"

"Not yet, but if you keep improving like this, maybe a few more days at most. We want to monitor you a little more and ensure your hip is healing well. The oncoming doctor will check on you when he gets in and will decide about solid foods, but my recommendation will be by dinner. Good luck, and I'll see you tonight."

Dr. Stevens waved to me as she left.

"Oh, Mandy, I didn't realize you were awake. Good morning." Mama smiled at me.

"Good morning. Yeah, I'd just woken up." I sat up and stretched. "Sounds promising, yes? And you're feeling a little better?"

"Yes, a little sleep, and I feel a lot better than earlier. I was still very foggy headed. Much clearer now." Mama said. Her voice was still rough, and she spoke softly but better than last night.

"Oh good, everyone will be glad to hear it." I checked the time. "I better go call Jimmy. Do you mind if I step out for a minute? The cell reception is bad in here."

"No, I don't mind. I'll be here." She said, patting the bed.

"Do you want me to bring you some juice or anything when I come back?"

"Yes, actually, juice would be nice. If they have cranberry, I wouldn't mind that for a change, but if not, whatever is available."

"You got it. The kids are going to be happy to hear you are doing better. It will make Missy's day."

She smiled at that. I knew she loved them, but she didn't know how to be a mom.

I walked out and passed the waiting room to find a little quieter place to talk. I had wandered around a little over the past couple of days, and I knew that one floor down and over a bit was a specialist clinic, and at this time of the morning, they wouldn't yet be seeing patients, and the open waiting room would be nearly empty.

I stood close to the windows and as far from the hallway as possible.

"Good morning, Mandy. How's it going up there?" Jimmy asked when he answered the phone.

"Good morning. Guess what? Mama woke up last night."

"Really? That's great news. How's she doing?"

"She seems like she is doing well. The doctor said they may have her out of bed later today, and she may only be here for a few more days. That is as long as she continues like she is and doesn't have any issues, like pneumonia."

"Well, that's great news. Do you need me to come up there?"

"I don't think so. Plus, it's your first day in your new position, and you should go."

"I can come after. Ms. Graham or Kate could pick up the kids for me, and I will get them later. I'd like to see her but for selfish reasons, really, so she knows that I'm back in the kids' lives, and I have no intention of going away." His voice softened as he added, "Plus, I really want to see you. I didn't get to see you yesterday."

My cheeks warmed in response, something that seemed to be happening a lot with him.

"I did miss seeing you yesterday too." That was a little hard for me to admit out loud, but I said it, and it felt good.

"Then it's settled. I'll ask Ms. Graham or Kate to pick up the kids for me this afternoon, and I'll come up there after work."

As I hung up the phone, I realized something had shifted. In the middle of all this worry and fear about Mama, in the chaos of hospital rooms and coma vigils, I had finally said something honest to Jimmy about how I felt.

I missed him. I had said it out loud. And the world hadn't ended.

Maybe that was the first step. Maybe all those "maybe tomorrows" had finally added up to today.

I took a deep breath and headed back upstairs to tell Mama the good news about the kids, about Jimmy coming to visit, about all the things that had changed while she was gone.

And maybe, just maybe, to start figuring out what our family would look like now.

Chapter Thirty-Two

They did get Mama up and walking a little that afternoon as promised. She struggled, and the color drained from her face in the process, but once she was back in bed, she seemed fine. The nurses said she did amazing, and they would try again in a few hours.

They brought her scrambled eggs, a piece of toast, and a banana for dinner. The doctor had said it would be light to start with, and they would work up to more substantial meals as she could tolerate it.

I had told her Jimmy would be stopping by sometime that evening. She didn't say much about it, and I couldn't tell if it bothered her or not.

Shortly after her dinner tray was removed, there was a soft knock on the door. I went to open it as Jimmy walked in. He was dressed in a nice button-down red plaid shirt paired with dark blue slacks and brown leather shoes. He'd gotten a fresh haircut. I missed his slightly longer, messy look, but this was nice too.

Having only seen him dressed nicely like this once before, for court, it stopped me in my tracks for a moment. I made a mental note that I liked the look of this Jimmy as much as the shirtless, sweaty one.

"Hi, Mandy." He wrapped me in a hug and then looked over my shoulder at Mama. "Hi Becca, how are you feeling?" He asked as he released me from his embrace.

I moved back towards the chair I'd been sitting in. Feeling very self-conscious as Mama eyed us both. I sank back into it, hoping it would just swallow me up, so I didn't have to face a potentially uncomfortable confrontation.

"Hi Jimmy, I'm feeling okay, considering." She smiled and smoothed the blanket around her. "I didn't expect to see you again, but Mandy said you've been helping her with the kids. Thank you."

She didn't say it coldly as you might expect but with sincerity. I sat forward a bit, hopeful of a positive outcome.

"No reason to thank me. I love my kids, and I'm happy to be in their lives." He paused. "And I'm glad to hear you are doing better. Were you able to get up and walk today? Mandy had mentioned that was the plan."

"Yes, twice. It was tough, but I think I did better the second time." She looked to me for reassurance. I nodded. Why did I suddenly feel like a little kid next to her? I mean, technically, I was. "I got to eat some solid food this evening too. They're hopeful that I can go home in a few days. It depends on my progress. Though I'm not sure where home is for me now, but I'll figure it out. I always do." She coughed and sounded a bit breathless as she spoke.

"What's happening with your boyfriend? Last I saw, he was still in jail. Something about nobody could post his bail. Or maybe I got the story wrong."

"Yes, something like that. I'm still catching up on the past several days. And he is my ex-boyfriend. No plans of continuing that." She coughed again. "I'd broken up with him just before the accident, but he didn't take it well." She stared off towards the window for a moment. Another cough. She'd been coughing a little here and there this afternoon, but it sounded worse by the minute.

I was really hoping she wasn't getting pneumonia. That was one thing the doctors had said to watch due to the ventilator and lack of activity for several days. It could set back her recovery and push out her coming home. Jimmy noticed too and gave me a puzzled look.

"Mama, you can come home with us. You can share the room with me, or I can sleep on the couch or with the little kids. We'll figure that out once we know more about your recovery and when you will get out." I said, bringing it back to her earlier comment about where she'd live.

"I plan to move out actually, and with Becca home, it makes even more sense. Of course, I'll find a place close by, so I can still be involved with my children." He said that a bit sharply.

His statement caught me a bit off guard. Both because of his tone, but also, we hadn't yet talked about living arrangements for the future.

"Thank you." She said softly and coughed again. This time she tried to hide the cough.

The nurse checked on Mama and let her know that she would be off shift soon. Nancy would be the evening nurse again that night, and Dr. Stevens would be in to check on Mama when she did rounds.

Mama didn't cough when the nurse was in the room and didn't say anything about it. Should I speak up? I tried to make eye contact with her, but she just checked a few things and left.

Without the nurse as a distraction, Mama looked at us for what felt like a minute but was probably a second. I shifted in my chair, but Jimmy stood firm and relaxed.

"Why don't you both go get something to eat? Mandy hasn't left the room in hours and could probably use a walk and some food. I'll probably watch a little TV and maybe take a short nap." She was starting to look a bit pale.

Alarm bells were going off in my head. Why hadn't I noticed sooner? Why hadn't the nurses or a doctor? Now being honest with myself, the signs had been building all day.

This was probably from a combination of all the other activities going on today between her physical therapy, eating, and then, of course, the ventilator and inactivity. I wasn't a medical professional and had no experience in this, so I trusted the speed they were moving with her recovery. Maybe I should have questioned it. Was that my job?

"Are you sure you'll be okay?" I didn't want to leave her now that she was awake. Plus, her color and cough were concerning. But, again, not a medical professional and had no idea if this was normal for her recovery.

"Yes, I'll be fine. Please go and take your time. But if you could bring me maybe a drink back with you? I'm getting a little tired of apple juice and water." She made a face.

"Yes, of course. Anything else?"

"Nay, just something different to drink."

Jimmy said his goodbyes. He wasn't planning to come back after, stating he needed to get back to the kids before bedtime.

We headed to one of the many fast-food places nearby, making small talk along the way. I asked how his first day had gone, and he recounted the weekend I missed with the kids. We ordered a couple of burgers and ate in near silence. About halfway through eating, Jimmy broke the silence.

"I didn't mean to seem rude to her, but I still have some resentment for missing out on my kids' lives for nearly a year and the way she treated all of you. I mean, yes, I had a choice, and I shouldn't have let her push me around, but you, Missy, and Davy didn't have a choice."

"I know."

"I was trying to be as polite as possible considering what she has been through, but... well, I'm going to have to learn to forgive her, huh?"

"I think we all have to find a way to forgive her. But I also think she needs to take responsibility for her actions and apologize to us at some point. At least to you and me. Missy and Davy won't remember as much and may not understand, but she also wasn't as mean to them." I thought for a moment. "Unless she was the one that called CPS, then I don't know if I can forgive her or if I would let her live with us again. But I may never know who called. I hate to think it was someone that I work for that I trust and feel close to."

"You aren't saying Ms. Graham, are you?"

"Oh gosh, no, I was just thinking of any one of the other neighbors. Not her or Mr. Dixon and not the Daileys, but it could be almost anyone else. I guess I almost hope it was Mama, though. She has let me down so many times that it would be less of a surprise."

"What do you think of her cough? Has she been coughing all day?"

"Not all day, but it started late this afternoon, and it's starting to become more frequent. She looked a bit pale before we left. Did you notice?"

"Yes, but I wasn't sure how she had looked earlier, so I didn't know if it was new."

We finished eating. Jimmy cleared our trash, and then we walked over to the hospital store. I selected two drinks for her: lemon lime flavor and a watermelon one. I thought she might like those for a change.

I also grabbed another book for myself. Having nothing but time on my hands the last few days, I had already gone through the two I had. While I was in the gift shop, I picked up a magazine and also one with various word and math puzzles for Mama. I remembered she used to enjoy those as well.

Jimmy walked me back to the ICU area but said he wouldn't go back with me.

"Thank you so much for coming. I really appreciate it." I inhaled for courage. "Also, I didn't say it before, but you look nice all dressed up."

"Well, thank you." He struck a supermodel pose, making us both laugh. "I was happy to come. I had missed seeing you and wanted to make sure you were okay. I probably won't come back up unless you need me. Call me tomorrow night, though, please? We'll need to start talking about living arrangements. I was serious about me moving out. Part of that is again me being selfish. If I move out, it won't be so weird for us to go on a date." He gave a half smile and winked at that last part.

Hadn't I wondered how dating, newly dating that is, and living together would work? I guess he had the same thoughts.

"Okay, I will. Let the kids know I love them and miss them. I'll be home soon."

"We'll have a lot to work out, especially with the restraining order and custody agreement we put into place." He said. "I'll call Laura and see what she says."

"Okay."

"And you want her to live with you all again?"

"Yes. It's probably stupid on my part to just forgive her, but this scared me to death. She's my mother and one of the few blood relatives that I have." I fidgeted with the hem of my shirt as I thought. "I just don't have much family. I'll be cautious around her, and if it seems like things are getting bad again, you take the kids, and I'll leave. I don't have to stay with her anymore."

"As long as you are sure, I support your decision."

We hugged, and he kissed my forehead again, holding his lips there just a touch longer than casual, before turning and walking away. I never understood the word swoon before. I do now.

I stood there for a moment, watching him disappear down the hallway. My forehead tingled where his lips had been. Every time he did that, it felt like a promise. Like he was waiting for me to be ready, and when I was, he would be there.

I decided to call Kate and Claire before heading back to Mama's room. I wanted to check in with Claire on how business was going, and I needed to let Kate know what was going on. I had promised.

The call with Claire shouldn't take too long, so I started with her. She was happy to hear from me and let me know not to worry. She had been able to rearrange clients, and everyone understood. After I finished up business with Claire, I called Kate.

"Mandy! Ohmygosh, I've been waiting to hear. How is your mom doing?"

"Hi, she's doing pretty well. They had her up and walking today. She even ate some solid food this evening."

"That sounds promising. Have they said when she can leave?"

"Maybe in a few days. It depends on how well she does. No relapse and continues to improve, which I'm starting to worry about. She's started to develop a cough and looked pale before I left the room."

"I hope the cough is nothing. When I picked up Olive, Missy was telling me about how worried she is."

"It's weird. We haven't talked about Mama for months, not since she left, but Missy is worried. I mean, I am too, but I didn't think the little kids would be. Little Davy hasn't said a word about her."

"Yeah, kids surprise us," Kate said.

"Yes, that they do." I paused, taking a deep breath for courage. "Jimmy just left, by the way."

"Oh yeah? I'm surprised he came up there. Was it to see you or your mom?"

"Both. He said he wanted to make sure she saw him and understood she wouldn't bully him again. Not his exact words but basically that he planned to stay involved with his children. He also said he wanted to see me. He missed me." I couldn't help but let out a little giggle as I said that.

"Oh, really?" She said with a slight laugh. "Do tell. And don't think I missed the excitement in your voice."

"I know. I know. I have denied it for a while, but I guess I'm finally letting myself feel it. Yes, I have a crush on him, feelings. There I said it out loud." My whole body relaxed. It felt so good to say it.

"Girl, I knew it." She said.

"I told him I missed him too. We talked a little about what happens when Mama comes home. He thinks it might be best for him to move out because it would be easier for us to date." I said with another giggle. I was sure I was blushing.

"Oh my, that is huge. Exciting!" She giggled with me. "Y'all are too cute together."

"Well, you know, with Mama back, it makes things feel... kinda weird again. Just when I admit to myself I have feelings for him, and she's back in the picture. How do you date with the ex-girlfriend around, forgetting for a minute that the ex is my mother?"

"Yeah, I see your point... But who cares? This is you and Jimmy. I don't think many people in town think it's weird. Everyone I know is cheering for you two to end up together. I think they are taking bets down at the courthouse on when you'll be in for the marriage license."

"Oh, shut up, they are not!" I said it with a laugh.

"Well, I wouldn't put it past Ms. Barbara. She's always starting a pool of some sort. When will so and so have her baby? When is so and so getting divorced? She's funny like that. I think she needs a twelve-step program."

More laughs. It felt so good to be happy again and laugh. Then I could hear Olive in the background. It was time for her bath and bedtime, so we got off the phone.

Before I could turn my phone off and head to Mama's room, Jimmy sent me a text message letting me know he'd gotten home. I was glad I hadn't gone back in the room yet, so I got to see it before the morning. I replied and then shut my phone off for the night.

As I walked back toward Mama's room, I felt lighter than I had in days. Maybe longer. I had finally said it out loud. I had feelings for Jimmy. Real feelings. The kind that made me giggle like a schoolgirl and blush when I thought about him.

And he wanted to date me. He was willing to move out just so we could do this right.

For the first time, the future felt less like a tangled mess of complications and more like something I could actually look forward to.

Chapter Thirty-Three

When I got back to Mama, she looked paler, and I could tell she was getting sick.

"I come bearing gifts. I grabbed a magazine and a puzzle book for you, plus a couple of drinks."

"Thank you, sweetie." She kept her voice low.

"Has the doctor been in yet? You look pale. Do you need the nurse?"

"No doctor yet. I hate to say it, but I think I might have pneumonia. I know they were worried about that." She coughed and had trouble catching her breath.

As if on cue, Dr. Stevens walked in. "How are you feeling?" She paused to look at Mama. "You look pale. Have you been coughing?"

"Yes, she's been coughing quite a bit. It started late this afternoon and has gotten progressively worse. I stepped out for a short time and just got back. She looks paler, and I can hear her breathing and wheezing."

"Let me have a listen." She listened to Mama, checked some of the monitors, noting that her blood oxygen was lower than she would like it to be. "I'll order some tests, but I suspect we are dealing with pneumonia. As we had talked previously, this can happen due to the ventilator and lying in bed for so many days, and why it's so important to have you moving."

She typed a few things into the computer before continuing.

"If this gets worse, it could be serious, so we want to get ahead of it as much as we can and hopefully get you on the mend right away. We want to make sure you can go home on time. Shandra will be in shortly with new medicine, and I'll be back after we get the results."

The nurse came in a bit later to add antibiotics to the IV. Then Mama and I settled in for the evening. I put the television on the Game Show Network and started reading my new book. Mama pulled out the puzzle book and started on a math puzzle. She had always been good at math.

An hour later, a couple of orderlies came to get Mama to take her for the chest x-ray. Once that was done, she tried to sleep, but her cough started to get worse. It would wake her up. She seemed like she was getting weaker, or was I being paranoid? I had just gotten her back and now was wondering if she would be taken from me. My worry meter started all over again.

At some point, Dr. Stevens came in and confirmed that Mama did have pneumonia. She said they would continue the antibiotics in the IV and monitor her closely.

"Hopefully, we caught this and started the treatment early enough to get her turned around. But, unfortunately, this can happen."

The nurse came and added another medicine to her IV. I'm not sure what it was, but whatever it was, it helped her sleep a little more peacefully. I was thankful for that. If she slept, maybe she would get her strength back.

After Dr. Stevens and the nurse left, I settled in with my book again, but my mind kept going in a hundred different directions. Jimmy and our situation. What would life be like when and if he moved out? What would the kids think of having her move back in and Jimmy moving out? Would she get better? What about this guy Butch? I hoped she was telling the truth about breaking up with him. He seemed like bad news.

I must have fallen asleep because later, I woke with a start, not knowing why or what woke me.

"Mandy... Mandy?" It sounded far away, but then I realized it was Mama. Her voice was so weak.

"What's wrong, Mama? Do you need the doctor or nurse?"

"Nothing, baby. I'm sorry to wake you... I've been thinking, and maybe it could've waited until morning but..." She coughed a bit and fought for her breath. "Just in case I don't get the chance, I want to tell you some things."

I reached out and gently patted her arm. Then I took her hand. "Shh, Mama, you should rest..."

"No, no... I don't think it should wait. Mandy, I'm so sorry. For all I put you through as a child. I'm just so sorry. I wanted to be a good mother." She had to keep pausing to cough or catch her breath. "I was a kid and didn't know what I was doing. I tried... No excuses. I'm sorry."

"It's okay. I know. I mean, I didn't always understand, but..."
She held out her hand to me as if to say wait a minute, so I stopped.
Her gesture wasn't aggressive or rude. I just waited.

"You deserved better. You deserved to be loved. I should've
shown you that I did and do. My first baby." She squeezed my hand
lightly. "You made me a mother. You showed me what love was. You
won't remember, but I really tried at first. For the first several years...
life just got harder and kept pushing me down. I just flat out got tired
of getting back up." She shook her head a little. "No excuses on my
part, really just telling you. None of it was your fault, for whatever it's
worth, I'm sorry."

She stopped for a moment and closed her eyes. I was about to
speak when she continued. "Seeing you with Jimmy and him with you,
wow baby, I wish I would have found that kind of love. Or, well held
on to the one I did have... Y'all have chemistry that anyone can see."
She smiled at me then. "I'm glad and a little jealous but mostly just
happy for you."

"But we aren't... a couple or dating exactly." I shook my head
slowly. "Don't you think it would be weird? He's your ex-boyfriend."

"No. I mean, yes, to some people, it might seem weird, but if
anyone took a second to see and got to know you both, they would
know that you were meant for each other. So, I guess somehow I got
in the way of fate."

"But..." I just stopped talking.

I knew my heart was going to win out over my brain, and even
though I had already admitted to Kate that I had feelings for him, I still
didn't know how to deal with them or where to go from here with my
emotions.

"Mandy, don't let something phenomenal go because you are
worried about what other people might think." She took some deep
breaths. "Trust me, there are so many times I needed that advice in
my life."

We sat there for a moment, a silence between us, while
Mama caught her breath again. Her body was so damaged and
working so hard to heal. You could see it on her face that it was taking
its toll on her.

"Baby, one more thing before I try to sleep again, please, if
something happens to me..." I tried to interrupt her, but she put her

hand up again. "If I don't make it, please make sure Missy and Little Davy know that even though I wasn't the best mother, I do love them with all my heart... please promise."

"Yes, Mama, I promise."

She closed her eyes and patted my hand, then took it in hers. She fell asleep a moment later, her breathing a bit ragged but steady as if she were asleep. I sat there, holding her hand and listening to her ragged breathing. I thought about all she had said. A few tears spilled from my eyes. I had to have faith she could get through this.

I wanted to have a good, positive relationship with her. I'd lost so much time with her already, and I wanted to have that mother-daughter relationship that I felt we both deserved. I knew we could have that if only we were given another chance.

I also thought of Missy and Little Davy. They were still young enough and needed a mother. Could she be the mother they needed? I knew I could be, but they really needed their mother, our mother. I wanted to be just the big sister.

Her hand relaxed and released mine as she fell into a deep sleep, so I sat back in the chair. I watched her for a few more moments before I drifted off to sleep myself.

Mama slept the rest of the night. She didn't even wake as the nurses did their regular checks. She was still asleep when I left around seven in the morning.

I needed a walk and to check in with Jimmy. When I got to the ground floor, I noticed news crews next door at the Children's hospital. I moved closer to see if I could hear if they were talking about the baby, but not too close as I didn't want to get caught on camera.

"I'm reporting from the Medical Center where we have learned that baby James, whose family was killed in the drunk driving accident late last week, is recovering. He is alert and doesn't seem to have any life-threatening injuries. He could be released from the hospital to his paternal grandparents as early as tomorrow. We have also been told that the passenger of the car has awoken from her coma and has spoken briefly with family members. No further update on her condition. Butch Stevens remains jailed, charged with the deaths of the Jones family. I'm Meaghan Franks reporting from the Texas Medical Center. Back to you in the studio."

I was glad to hear the baby was going to be okay. I was sad that he lost his family. He would never know them, but at least he had extended family to take him in. I hoped they would love him and give him a happy, full life.

I pushed the button to call Jimmy. Instantly butterflies filled my stomach at the thought of hearing his voice.

"Hey, Mandy. How's it going? How's she doing?" His voice instantly calming me.

"Hi, she's doing okay. The doctor confirmed what we had suspected. She does have pneumonia. They started her on antibiotics, and now we wait to see if they caught it in time. How are the kids?"

"They are both good. Missy asked me about her this morning."

"What did you say?"

"I was as honest as I could be that she was still sick, and the doctors are doing the best they can to make her well."

"I hate this for the little kids. Missy shouldn't be worried about this." I said.

We talked for a few minutes more before he had to head to a meeting at work. He asked me to call him that evening so I could talk to the little kids. I missed them so much.

I found a coffee shop and bought myself a coffee and two slices of banana bread, one for me and one for Mama. I wasn't sure if she could have the banana bread, but I wanted to have it for her just in case.

She was awake and sitting up when I got back to the room. Her breakfast had also arrived. It looked like they would allow her to continue eating solids, so I didn't see the harm in the banana bread. She smelled it almost instantly when I walked in too.

"I hope you brought some for me." She said with a smile and hope in her voice.

"Of course. I know it's your favorite."

I pulled out one piece and laid it on her plate next to the scrambled eggs and then pulled the second piece out for myself. We both bit into it at the same time. The bread was fresh. It had a sweet banana flavor with the perfect sized pieces of pecans in it.

"Mmmm..." We said at the same time, then laughed.

She looked a bit better this morning, not as pale and weak, but she still had wheezing in her chest and a nasty cough.

"How are you feeling this morning?" I asked.

"A little better. I think the sleep and these meds are helping."

"Has the doctor been in?"

"Yes, she left right before breakfast arrived. She wants me to sit up as much as I can tolerate today, but they aren't going to try to get me up and walking again. She wants to give my body a little bit of a break. She said sitting up would be good for my hips but also to help the fluid drain. She seemed hopeful that I could get over this."

She took another bite of the bread. "I meant what I said last night. I am sorry. When I recover, I want us to have a better relationship than before. I want to make up for my mistakes in the past. I know for you and me, we will probably be more like friends than mother and daughter, and that's okay. You're already grown and more mature than I was at your age. Heck, more mature than most people at eighteen, but I want us to have something, and hopefully, you can forgive me."

"I can, and I want that too."

"I hope it's not too late for me to be a mother to Missy and Little Davy."

"I don't think it is too late. I called Jimmy while I was out of the room. Missy asked about you again this morning."

"She did?"

I nodded in reply.

She smiled. "Well, I hope that means she forgives me for being a bad mom."

"Missy loves you. We all do."

"I hope so. I know I haven't been a mother to any of you kids, but I'm going to try."

We finished our breakfast, then Mama worked on her puzzle book, and I read. We had the television on for background noise. This is how we spent the rest of the day.

Something had shifted between us. Not a complete transformation, not yet. But a crack in the wall that had stood between us for as long as I could remember. For the first time, I felt like maybe, just maybe, we had a chance to build something new.

I touched the mother's necklace at my throat, the one Jimmy had given me for Christmas. Two little hearts for two little lives.

Maybe there was room for one more heart in this family. Maybe Mama could find her way back to us after all.

Chapter Thirty-Four

Mama's health improved over the next few days, and she began walking with either a cane for support or a walker for longer walks. Her cough had almost cleared, and she was growing stronger. The doctors were confident she would be going home any day now.

With her being out of the woods, I finally went home to sleep. It was so nice to be home with the kids. They were so excited to see me. Missy cried, which made Little Davy cry too. Then because I had been on edge for so long, I started crying with them. Jimmy shook his head at us with a smile, but I could have sworn I saw a few tears in his eyes.

"Y'all are a mess." He laughed.

"I missed you so much, Mandy. I'm so glad you are home." She sniffed. "Is Mama coming home too?"

"Yes, I think she will be. Either tomorrow or the next day. She'll still need our help as she gets better, but I know you are strong and can help. Right?"

"Yes." She nodded.

"I strong. I strong." Davy flexed his arms to try to show off muscles.

"Oh, look at those muscles. Yes, you can help too." I admired his muscles.

"So, I wanted to talk to you both about something very important." Jimmy sat on the floor next to the kids. "When your mom comes back, I'll be moving into my own place."

"Noo, Daddy. Why?" Missy started crying again.

"Mama needs to have a room, and Mandy is going to move back to her old room. So, I'm going to get my own house close by. I already have one picked out. I will pick up the key next week." He smiled. "It's close to Ms. Kate and Olive's house."

"Oh, they don't live far."

"No, and neither will I. That means I'll still be able to take you to school or pick you up. We can go to the park some weekends like we do now. But we must make sure your Mama gets time with you too. You'll see. This is a good thing, I promise."

"Mandy?" Missy said. She was looking at me for a reaction.

"Yes, this is a good thing. Mama, Daddy, and I have all discussed this and feel it's going to be a positive new beginning for our family." I said.

They've had their world turned upside down a few times over the last months with Mama leaving, being taken to foster care, and their Daddy coming back. Then Mama being in the accident and me spending so much time away. They were ready for routine. But to be honest, I was too.

I continued, "You have a lot of people that love you very much. We're all trying to make sure we can come to the best solution for how to care for the two of you."

Missy hugged me. "I love you, Mandy."

"I love you, Nandy," Davy joining in the hug.

"I love you both too."

When I arrived at the hospital the next day, Mama was all smiles and standing by the window. For a second, I panicked, seeing her standing there, but I noticed her walker and cane were both close by in case she needed either.

She turned. "They said I could go home today! I'm just waiting for the discharge papers. Possibly before lunchtime."

"Oh, that's great news. The little kids will be so happy to have you home. I will too."

"I can't wait. On to a new chapter in life."

She was going to start counseling and had already begun working with a social worker at the hospital. This time it seemed that she really wanted this for herself and for us.

I wanted to believe, but I didn't want to let my guard down yet. She'd promised me so many times that she would change, that things would be different. Was this going to be the real deal or more talk? Only time would tell.

The difference for me now was I'd learned I could do this all on my own, and unlike her, I didn't let life kick me and keep me down. I'd pulled up my bootstraps, building a business, had friends and family to lean on. I learned I had inner strength and confidence in myself. If push came to shove again, I'd be able to stand up to her and knew I could easily walk away.

For now, I would focus on the positive and help her get better and support her recovery.

We chatted about the house, the kids, and the weather while we waited for her paperwork. Finally, a nurse came in and let us know she could go.

"Do you need help getting dressed?" The nurse asked.

"No, I can do it. My daughter will help if I get stuck. So, that's it?" Mama clasped her hands together.

"Yes, ma'am. You're free to go. We'll have someone walk out with you once you are ready, but that's it. Just buzz when you're dressed." She smiled and left the room.

An hour later, I settled Mama on the couch and put her bags in her room. We would be sharing for the next week until Jimmy closed on his new house.

"Wow, the house looks great! So, you did all this?" She scanned the room.

"Jimmy and I both did. Mostly him. The little kids helped us with painting. I think Davy got more on himself than the walls, but he had fun." I smiled at the memory.

There was a knock on the door, and then it opened. Ms. Graham came in with a loaf of banana bread, knowing it was Mama's favorite as well.

"Hello, dear. I'm so glad you are home." She gave Mama a hug. "Banana bread for you."

"Oh, you remembered. Thank you so much." Mama said.

"Of course, dear. I watched you grow up." She smiled and headed for the kitchen with the banana bread.

She came back with a few plates of banana bread. She was more than a neighbor. She was our family.

We ate the still warm from the oven treat while we visited.

After our snack was finished and we had gotten caught up, Ms. Graham excused herself.

"I'll let you rest, Becca." She said. On her way out, she gave me a friendly hug, whispering to me, "You have done so well. I'm very proud of you."

Her words settled into my heart. I had done well. Despite everything, despite all the odds stacked against me, I had built something real. A business. A family. A life.

Jimmy said he would pick up the kids that afternoon on his way home from work, so I had all afternoon in the house to take care of Mama and ensure she was settled.

Once she was resting on the couch, I wanted to get our things unpacked, start some laundry, and then prep for dinner. It was nice to get back into a regular routine. I had been at the hospital for close to two weeks.

Claire had been holding down things with the business, and I knew she was ready for me to be back. We would start finding another person to help balance the load, especially if something like this happened again.

Hopefully, not this exact thing, but if one of us needed to be out or would like to take a vacation, it would be nice to have a third person to help.

The kids came running in an hour later. Perfect timing. The casserole needed only five more minutes before it would be ready to eat.

"Mama... Mama..."

I walked into the living room to see Missy hugging her, but Little Davy kind of stood back watching. Did he remember that night so long ago?

"Hi, baby girl," Mama said with tears in her eyes. "Oh, I missed you. Look at you. So grown up."

"I missed you too." Missy said with some hesitation. "But, Mandy and Daddy said, you are going to stay. Is that true?"

"Yes, baby, that's the plan. I'm going to try to be a better mother too. I know I've made mistakes, but I hope this time I can do better." She smiled at her and then looked over to where Davy was standing. "Davy, do you want to give me a hug too?"

She reached a hand towards him but not forcefully. It looked like she was trying to give him space to remember her.

"Mama?" He tilted his head.

He looked in my direction, and I nodded my head at him to reassure him. He walked cautiously and leaned on her.

Jimmy walked in and looked over at me. His expression was hard to read. Maybe a little bit concerned, a little awkward. I'm not sure, but it was nice to see him. This almost felt normal with him coming home at the end of the workday, me with dinner almost ready, and the children happy to be home. Mama was the part that felt odd or different. My brain couldn't process how this all worked together.

"Dinner is almost ready. Missy, do you want to help me set the table?" I asked.

"I want to sit with Mama."

"I can," Jimmy said, putting down his computer bag and walking towards the kitchen.

I followed behind him, so I could pull the casserole out and finish putting the salad together.

"How has it gone this afternoon?" He asked once we were in the kitchen.

"Fine. We got home, and she has mostly been resting on the couch with some limited walking. Doctor's orders."

"Good. You okay too?" His voice was soft as he moved closer towards me.

"Yes, it feels a little odd to be home but wonderful at the same time."

He put his arms around me, and we held each other for a moment.

"It's good to have you home. I missed you very much."

"I missed you too." He looked like he might kiss me and not on the forehead, but the moment passed without a kiss.

Soon, I thought. Soon we would have that moment. But not here, not now, with Mama in the other room and the kids waiting for dinner. We had waited this long. We could wait a little longer.

After that, we worked in silence as Jimmy got the table set, and I started plating food for everyone. Missy helped Mama to the table. Mama and I looked at each other, knowing full well she could have gotten there by herself, but Missy had insisted. I think Mama liked the attention as much as Missy enjoyed helping.

Missy chatted all through dinner, getting Mama caught up on life over the past few months. She told Mama all about school and her friends and Christmas and going to a couple of birthday parties. She then talked about her birthday, which was still a few months away, but she had big plans.

"And I want to invite my whole class. Ms. Laura says it isn't nice to not invite everyone because it could hurt feelings if someone didn't get invited, and I agree, even if some of the boys are mean. I want to have it at Glenn Lake Park like Olive did, and I want a bounce house and a clown that does face painting and balloon animals and a piñata and... and... all the decorations should be pink and green, not like green grass but like a different green. I'll show you, Mama, those are my favorite colors. Like most favorite ever."

Mama watched her as if she were seeing her youngest daughter for the first time, and maybe in some way, she was. Davy mainly was quiet, but occasionally, he would add something.

"I go to the zoo. I like animals. Tigers, elephants, lions...."

"Maybe when Mama feels better, we can take her."

After dinner, Missy told Mama it was time to play outside. Mama insisted that they help me clean up after dinner, so dinner was cleared and the kitchen back in order in minutes. We all headed outside. Jimmy and the kids ran around playing one of Missy's made up games.

"They have grown so much. I feel like I have been gone years, not just months." Mama said, watching them play.

I nodded in response.

After playtime, Missy walked Mama through our whole nighttime routine. Mama helped with baths, read them their story, and tucked them in. At the end of the night, she looked a little pale and in pain, so I got her pain meds and helped her to bed.

"I'll sleep on the couch tonight, so you can rest."

"No, no... it's a big enough bed for both of us, plus I was looking forward to it. Kinda like a sleepover." She rubbed my forearm. "I know it sounds silly but just humor me."

"Okay, Mama. I'll be right back."

Jimmy was in his room, soon to be my room again. He'd started packing his things to move. I would miss seeing him every day, but I knew he wouldn't be far away. We agreed Mama or I would get the kids to school each day, and he would bring them home, so really, I would see him daily.

I got Mama settled in bed with the promise I would be right back. I knocked softly on his door. He opened it. When he saw me, he smiled that knee-weakening smile.

"I just wanted to say good night," I said, brushing my hair back behind my ear and looking up at him.

"I'm glad you did." He pulled me into his arms.

I wanted to remember this moment forever. The smell of his soap, the warmth of his arms around me, and the strength and safety I felt there. Then, far too soon, the embrace ended.

"Good night, Mandy."

"Good night, Jimmy."

I walked back to Mama's room with my heart full. Everything was changing. Everything was new. But for the first time in my life, I wasn't afraid of change.

I was ready for it.

Chapter Thirty-Five

It had been three weeks since Mama had come home and two since Jimmy moved out. Things at home had both stayed the same and changed. I moved back to my old room, and Mama got settled back in hers. We took turns cooking in the evening, and the other would do the kids' nighttime routine of bath, reading, and tucking in.

I was starting to move from the mother role to the big sister role. While Mama was, for the first time, embracing her role as the mother. It was a process and still new to all of us, but I had faith we'd get there.

Our days were pretty routine too. I took the kids to school, I went to work, and Jimmy brought the kids home. Mama couldn't drive yet, so twice weekly, I took her to counseling sessions. She really seemed to be doing better and seemed happier, like genuinely happy for the first time that I could remember. I still wasn't entirely letting my guard down, but I could actually see a change in her.

Claire and I had hired another employee. She was going to start shadowing me on Monday. The business was growing quickly, and we had yet to spend a dime on advertising. It was nice to be back at work and back in our routine.

However, tonight was different. It was the first time I would go on a date of any kind. I was nervous. I'd bought a new dress. I never wore dresses, so this was strange and new.

I was in the bathroom with Mama and Missy, both fussing over me.

"Mandy, you should wear this necklace," Missy said, holding up the one Jimmy had given me at Christmas.

The mother's necklace. Two little hearts. The gift that had told me everything I needed to know about how he saw me, how he saw us.

"Let me curl this last part. Stop fidgeting." Mama teased me.

Davy was sitting on the edge of the bathtub giggling and smiling. He'd taken a few days to warm up to Mama. After that, I think he was more like me in the cautious way he approached things. At times he trusted Missy's judgment, and at other times he went with what he thought. But for now, he was back to happy Little Davy with a big heart.

"So, he is taking you to that new place up in Houston that you were talking about?" Mama asked.

"Yeah, I have never been somewhere so fancy. I'm nervous."

"You'll love it!"

I heard my phone notify me of a text, so I picked it up, which resulted in a bit of groan from Mama.

"Whoops, sorry," I said. She had a flat iron in my hair at the moment and needed me to be still. "It's Kate wishing me luck and asking for a full report after."

"We all want that," Mama said with a wink in the mirror.

Then there was a knock on the door, and we heard Ms. Graham's voice call out, "Hello?"

"In the bathroom, Grammy!" Missy called to her.

"Oh, look at you, Mandy. You look beautiful." Ms. Graham said as she stepped into the bathroom.

"Thank you. I hope I don't fall over in these heels. I've never really worn heels."

"You'll be fine. I just wanted to stop by and wish you the best. You deserve this. Oh, and I left some cookies for some good little kids in the kitchen."

"Yay! Cookies!" Davy took off towards the kitchen.

Ms. Graham took a seat on the edge of the tub where Davy had been sitting. She and Mama made small talk, with Missy joining in here and there.

I stood there looking in the mirror and not quite recognizing myself. I couldn't believe this was happening. I was the girl that never thought this would be my life, but it was.

The girl who had hidden in a shed on New Year's Eve while her mother partied. The girl who had raised her siblings because no one else would. The girl who had built a business from nothing, who had faced down social workers and court dates and her own mother's failures.

That girl was standing here now, in a new dress, with people who loved her fussing over her hair, about to go on her first date with a man who had seen her at her worst and her best and had chosen to stay.

At that moment, I heard a knock, and Davy yelled, "Daddy!"

There he was.

"Hiya, sport! How is my big guy?"

Mama whispered, "Are you ready?"

I nodded and turned towards the door of the bathroom but didn't move for a moment. Once I walked out, I couldn't have this moment back. I wanted to savor the anticipation of it. The hope, the fears, the joy of that first date. Deep breath.

I walked into the living room. Jimmy was sitting on the couch with Davy standing in front of him, chatting away. He turned his head and then stood when he saw me. "Wow. Hi."

"Hi." I smiled.

"You look beautiful, Mandy."

"Thank you. You look very handsome yourself."

"Thank you. Are you ready?"

"Yes," I said.

He held his arm out, and I hooked mine through it.

As I headed out for my first ever first date, I didn't know what my future held, but what I did know was that I had friends, family, and a growing business. I had this man who had been by my side through so much, and while I didn't know if there would be a second date, I didn't care. At that moment, I knew I was ready for whatever the future had in store for me.

I was going to live in the moment and enjoy my new normal.

I had spent so long being afraid. Afraid of what people would think. Afraid of letting myself feel something. Afraid of wanting something for myself.

But I wasn't that girl anymore.

I was Mandy Walker. I was a big sister, a business owner, a friend, a daughter finding her way back to her mother. And tonight, I was a woman walking out the door on the arm of a man who had waited patiently for her to be ready.

Jimmy opened the truck door for me, and I climbed in. As he walked around to the driver's side, I looked back at the house. Missy and Davy were waving from the window. Mama stood behind them, her hand on Missy's shoulder.

My family. Imperfect and complicated and mine.

Jimmy got in and started the truck. He reached over and took my hand.

"Ready?" he asked again.

I looked at him. At those kind eyes that had seen me through the hardest year of my life. At that smile that still made my knees weak.

"I've been ready," I said. "I just didn't know it yet."

He squeezed my hand, and we pulled out of the driveway together.

Into whatever came next.

THE END

Before you go: If you loved Mandy's Story, be sure to visit my website to sign up for my newsletter (if you haven't already) and to stay up to date on new releases and other bookish things.

When signing up, you will receive **Chef Jessica's Alphabet Soup Recipe** as a free gift. I have "had" it; it is yummy. (Okay, so obviously, it is my recipe, but still, I recommend it!)

Continue to the next section for this book's recipe!

Also, check out my other books! You can find links on my website.

www.ejwheltonwrites.com

Author note:

Thank you for reading. I hope you enjoyed this story as much as I enjoy writing it. These characters were the first to speak to me, to help me develop their stories, and to finish the book.

As with all my books, I have many people to thank, but there are just too many. I'm afraid if I start naming, I will leave someone out and hurt feelings. That's never my intention.

Everyone knows who they are, so I will say a general thank you so much to those who have helped in the big ways (my BETA Readers and editors). Thank you to those who have listened to my countless hours of talking about writing (but not writing). To those that have answered my numerous questions about everything from phrases to grammar, thank you. If you have given me any feedback, just know I appreciate it all.

For this Finding Herself Series, I have roughly 20 more stories planned. You won't have to wonder what happened to your favorite characters as they will be making cameos in future books and share what they have been up to. It just may take me some time to get to every wonderful story.

Next up is Becca's Story. She will tell you what happens after her car accident and talk to us through her recovery as well as finally finding a purpose for her life. We will also meet Mandy's father, and he, in turn, finally learns about her.

Thank you, and happy reading!

For more information about this and my other work, please visit my website:

www.ejwheltonwrites.com